THE INCIDENT

THE INCIDENT
Andrew Neiderman

Severn House Large Print
London & New York

This first large print edition published 2017
in Great Britain and the USA by
SEVERN HOUSE PUBLISHERS LTD of
19 Cedar Road, Sutton, Surrey, England, SM2 5DA.
First world regular print edition published 2016 by
Severn House Publishers Ltd.

British Library Cataloguing in Publication Data
A CIP catalogue record for this title is available from the British Library.

ISBN-13: 9780727895080

Severn House Publishers support the Forest Stewardship Council™
[FSC™], the leading international forest certification organisation. All
our titles that are printed on FSC certified paper carry the FSC logo.

MIX
Paper from
responsible sources
FSC® C013056

Typeset by Palimpsest Book Production Ltd.,
Falkirk, Stirlingshire, Scotland.
Printed and bound in Great Britain by
T J International, Padstow, Cornwall.

For Diane, without whom I could do nothing important.

Prologue

She heard him call out to her, and, for a moment, all the days, months and years from the Incident until now evaporated. She was back in high school and, like most of the girls in her sophomore class, smitten with Bart Stonefield, a senior who, at six feet one, with broad shoulders and rich ebony hair complementing his striking blue-gray eyes, looked ready at a moment's notice to step on to the cover of a teen magazine. His glance and smile toward her set her heart pacing.

Halfway to the customers' lobby to wait for her car to be serviced, she turned to see him emerge from his service manager's office and head toward her. Time, which could be so wicked to so many, seemed to have become his servant. If anything, he was even more handsome, the maturity in his face enhancing his stature. Unlike so many high school boys she had known, he hadn't lost his youthful, athletic figure. Bart was always a better dresser than most of his friends, so seeing him now in a white shirt, black tie and black slacks seemed appropriate.

Her parents had bought her Chevy Impala at Stonefield's as a graduation present. It was waiting for her in the driveway when her father brought her home from the bus stop. She had graduated Columbia summa cum laude with a major in English. There had been a time when

1

getting through any four-year college program would have equated to reaching the moon.

After a week of driving her new car, she had trouble with the ignition. It was her car, but assuming responsibility for herself had so much more significance than for most girls her age. When would the asterisk beside her name be erased? Sometimes she imagined it was visible above or beside her head. Time hadn't erased or even dimmed it. It was always the first reason that she believed local residents looked at her.

She was afraid to look back at anyone, even to acknowledge her parents' friends, but especially young men. The shadows followed her and could slip into the body of that man eyeing her. That evil could turn his smile into a lustful glare. How do you walk alone in the evening ever again or simply cross the street to your car without feeling followed and terrified?

She knew that Bart had gone to work for his father after he had toyed with some community college attendance and had become the service manager, so she thought he was doing what he was trained to do for any of their customers: be pleasant and accommodating. But there was something more in his smile, and it wasn't that soft pitiful look she got from former local high school graduates.

'Sorry about the car trouble,' he began. 'We'll get it solved quickly.'

Her heart seemed to dip a little with the disappointment. He did sound as if he was placating just another customer.

2

'Congratulations. Summa cum laude! Wow,' he said.

She smiled, not surprised her father had been bragging while he was buying her the car.

'Thank you.'

'What are your plans now?' he asked.

He suddenly looked very nervous, moving his hands from his hips to behind his back, averting his gaze.

'I'm not sure. I'm taking some time off. I'm not sure.'

Damn, how dumb that sounded, repeating *I'm not sure*.

'So, you're back for a while?'

'For a while,' she said. She felt her whole life was *for a while*.

She looked around. A secretary was watching them, her hand resting on a phone as if planning at any moment to call someone and report this chat between Victoria Myers and Bart Stonefield.

'I took a course with your mother at the community college, but I didn't complete it. Dad talked me into coming into the business. He had expanded the dealership. We employ almost forty people now.'

'How exciting for you.'

'So, did you enjoy college in New York?'

'I didn't take enough advantage of what it has to offer,' she confessed.

'More than here, I'm sure.'

'Sandburg still has its charm,' she said, surprised that she had said it. She wanted so much to love it again.

Was that weird?

3

She and her parents lived in Sandburg, New York, a hamlet in the Catskill Mountains, spawned by the railroad that feathered the failed farms converted in desperation into boarding houses and small hotels. For ten weeks, it turned the community into a New York City satellite, servicing tourists who fled the oppressive summer heat cooking their shoe soles on the pavements. The fresh, cool country air was even believed to be a remedy for tuberculosis. Here, there was spring water, fresh produce and bakeries that rivaled anything in the five boroughs. A continuous flow of traffic snaked up the New York Thruway and Route 17, some cars so loaded down with luggage that they looked more like families fleeing an invasion.

For the remainder of the year, though, there was a semi-rural life here that should have always been thought of as idyllic.

'There have been quite a few changes,' Bart said. 'They developed that ski hill and lodge in Centerville, and there are some new restaurants and housing developments.'

'You sound like you work for the chamber of commerce.'

He blushed, a delightful ruby shade that only made his eyes more striking.

'Training to be sales manager,' he said, laughing at himself.

Her one close girlfriend here, Jena Daniels, occasionally peppered her gossip with headlines about Bart Stonefield – how he had come close to an engagement with a girl from Monticello, but broke up, and how, in fact, despite his good looks and bright financial future, he hadn't developed any serious relationships.

'My father fills me in from time to time,' she said.

'I tried to get my father to steal him away from the high school and become our business manager,' Bart said. 'Your dad's a great guy. He always reminded me of Randolph Scott, the Southern gentleman cowboy.'

'My mother claims that was why she fell in love with him.'

'Yeah, well, he's just as good-looking as Scott. I can see it in you, too.'

Now she was blushing. It felt good to blush because of a compliment.

'Not that your mother couldn't be a beauty queen.'

'Oh, she'd hate to hear that,' Victoria said. 'You know that famous question, if you had one wish, what would it be?'

'World peace,' he recited with her, and they both laughed, followed by a moment of silence – the kind her world literature teacher called *a pregnant silence*. What it would give birth to was unclear. She looked at the lobby sofa.

'Nice to see you, Bart,' she said and turned.

Before she took two steps, she felt his hand on her arm and turned back to him, surprised.

'I was wondering if you had any commitments tonight. I'd like to take you to dinner at Dante's.'

'Dinner? No, I'm not doing anything,' she said.

'Great. I'll come by about six thirty.'

'OK.'

'Let me get on my mechanic,' he said quickly.

He looked stunned about what he had just proposed and what had happened as a result. Was he sorry she had said she was free? Was he simply being polite?

She nodded and he hurried away.

Did this just happen? she asked herself. She hadn't been out on a real date for years, and the first offer she gets is from her old high school's heart-throb, a young man who is even better-looking now and more of a catch.

Social life had always seemed out of reach. She had never joined a sorority or attended college parties. She had never gone out on a date in New York City with a college boy, or any boy for that matter. She had gone into therapy, but that hadn't brought her back to where she had been. She didn't really go out much afterward and had accepted an invitation to the high school prom more to satisfy her father and mother than herself.

Who would have blamed her for her self-imposed celibacy? While many of Victoria's friends drifted away after the Incident, as her mother liked to refer to it euphemistically, Jena Daniels had drawn closer. She was the only girl-friend to visit at the hospital. Victoria told her far more than she had told her mother or her father – even the police, for that matter.

Sometimes Jena's probing questions were downright pornographic, but Victoria tolerated it simply because of Jena's willingness to listen without overt pity. Over time, she became a sort of filter, a way for Victoria to test her own feelings.

6

The local police department had no female officer then and still didn't. She couldn't imagine saying much to anyone during those first twenty-four hours or so anyway. She was under sedation. Eventually, the state police sent in a female officer, but with her cropped hair, manly shoulders and clipped, military-style speech, she wasn't much different from any of the male detectives and police.

It was 1962, not exactly the Dark Ages, but the emphasis was mainly on her physical injuries even though psychotherapy was desperately needed. In the emergency room, she had been prescribed a tranquillizer, and Dr Bloom, their family doctor, continued the prescription after she had left the hospital. He was thinking of giving her mood enhancers to fight depression, but her psychologist, Dr Thornton, wanted her drug-free, if possible.

Dr Thornton's practice was located in Middletown, New York, a small city about thirty-five miles away. Her mother took her there because Thornton was female, more likely to sympathize, and she was someone with clients who had suffered similar 'incidents'. Victoria's mother didn't want anyone in the community knowing what went on in these sessions. No matter what local therapists claimed, private information would surely slip out. Just mentioning Victoria's name at a social event would result in some facial expression that would inevitably lead to a revelation. Better to be with someone who didn't know people familiar with Victoria or the Myers family.

Despite that, whenever they had guests for dinner or relatives visited, she could practically feel their eyes moving over her, looking for scars. She had gotten so that she rarely looked directly at anyone who knew what had happened to her, and really, in this small community, who didn't? She was terrified of their inquiring, intrusive eyes. They were waiting for her to burst into tears or uncontrollable screams. Her gaze was always to the side or down when she spoke. Her mother often blurted, 'Victoria, look at people when you speak to them.'

No one in her class was more excited about getting away from home than she was, but something had caused her to postpone taking the next step in her life; something had brought her back. Did she want to confront the old demons and destroy them before moving off?

Neither of her parents was home when she arrived. They had the better part of two acres on one of the newer residential roads leading out of the hamlet to the New York Thruway. They were just under a mile from the center of the town where the only traffic light was turned on in early July and turned off in mid-September. During the late fall and winter, it hung like a dead crow and moaned in the wind.

Ever since she was twelve, Victoria was permitted to walk to the drugstore or the candy store and soda fountain. She would go to town to pick up some small grocery items as well, and never was there a sense of danger, even during the summer months.

Like most everyone in Sandburg, her father enjoyed looking after the property himself, doing his maintenance on weekends and some gardening when spring came. It was something he had done on his family's farm in Richmond, Virginia. Her parents gave up on a vegetable garden because deer and rabbits and other animals got through any fencing. They toyed with the idea of putting in a small pool, but never did it. There were six other homes on their particular street, only two of which – theirs and the Weiners' – were ranch-style. The other four were variations of Queen Anne, with attics and wood siding that required painting often.

Despite the distance between the homes, everyone knew everyone else. According to the old-timers, many of whom had come to America after the Second World War, Sandburg hamlet and the surrounding community were reminiscent of European communities, save for the resorts that were on almost every side road. Their road, Wildwood Drive, catty-cornered into Oak Tree, on which there was Okun's bungalow colony. On summer nights, the vacationers took long walks after dinner, and she could hear their voices and laughter. Beside the peepers and distant car horns, the music flowing from a convertible, that laughter was the music of a summer night. Everything conspired to make her world serene and blissful, but wasn't that why Satan entered paradise? He wanted to ruin it, and ruin it he did for her.

She hurried to her room and threw open her closet. What would she wear? What about her hair? She regretted now not going to the beauty salon when her mother offered to make her an appointment at the same time as her own. But who expected this? It was like a streak of lightning. She glanced at herself in the Chinese Chippendale mirror. She thought she wore the look of someone caught in a frenzy. Had she been too eager to say yes? The invitation was practically still on his lips when she agreed. Had Bart gone back into his office and laughed?

Did he expect her to tell him she had a college boyfriend? She had been so nervous. She had surely made a fool of herself. Her mother might even be disappointed. 'You – someone who graduated from a prestigious university with honors – leaps to go out with a car service manager? What are you going to talk about – carburetors?'

How would she feel if her mother said that?

All these complications and worries were attacking her like wasps while she pondered what to wear. She fiddled with some loose strands of her amber-brown hair, the color of the patches of freckles on the crests of both her cheeks. She had almost had it styled in a bouffant with curled flicked-up ends, a hairdo popularized by Jackie Kennedy, as well as actresses and singers such as Dusty Springfield, but she anticipated her mother criticizing her and telling her, 'Like all girls your age, you behave like lemmings.' Then there would be that speech about how young people don't think for themselves anymore.

As she stood before her full-length mirror and turned to look at herself from different angles, she recalled how her mother would prepare for an event, how she would scrutinize herself, her clothes, her makeup and jewelry. Everything coordinated. She looked perfected but not sensuous, and she could easily if she wanted to, Victoria thought. Her mother could be quite stunning, in fact.

When she was Victoria's age, her mother did have her figure, but she kept it more subdued. She had a very good figure for a woman her age now. There just wasn't an early picture of her in which she didn't seem to be hiding her sexuality. She was almost without a waist, and V-necks were avoided. Only her father knew she had a cleavage. And she grew up in the roaring twenties! Only she wasn't one who roared. She was too studious. Sometimes, from the way her mother described her youth and her early social life, it seemed as if finding a husband and having a child was like checking off items on a grocery list. She often began a description with the words, 'It was time for it, you see.'

Even so, there was so much about her mother she admired. She wanted to have her mother's self-confidence and attract the same respect and admiration. But did she have to be a carbon copy? Was it terribly wrong to think you were sexy and good-looking? Somewhere in the back of her mind, buried deep under layers and layers of therapy, was the idea that maybe what had happened was her fault.

Dr Thornton had told her that wasn't unusual. 'It helps us rationalize the "Why me?"'

Yes, but had she been too proud of her maturing figure, too eager to display it?

She lunged defiantly for her black dress with

mesh shoulders atop a sweetheart neckline and a dipped V-back. She had yet to wear it since she had bought it almost on a dare with herself. Quickly undressing, she slipped it on and admired how the body-hugging sheath of flexible fabric accentuated her hourglass figure. Yes, it was sexy, but elegantly so.

'What are you doing? Where are you going?' her mother asked from her bedroom doorway.

Victoria had been so self-absorbed that she hadn't heard her enter the house.

'Oh. Thinking about what to wear. Bart Stonefield asked me to dinner tonight.'

She tried to sound casual about it, but she was sure her mother could hear the slight trembling in her voice.

'Bart Stonefield?'

Victoria held her breath, waiting for the negativity.

'When did this happen?'

'Just today. I brought my car in for that repair.'

'Oh, right. He's their something-or-other at the dealership,' she said.

'Service manager. He told me that he had taken a class with you at Sullivan County Community College.'

'And quit midway.'

'He said he had, yes.'

'He was doing well, too. Good insights. He should have gone to a four-year school. He had very decent high school grades.'

Victoria wasn't surprised her mother knew that much about him. She was meticulous when it came to scrutinizing her students.

12

'But I suspect there were family pressures,' her mother added.

'Pressures?'

'To groom him for the business. John Stonefield is one of those fathers who believes his son should be grateful for what he's created for him, and, contrary to what every other parent would take pride in, he derides any greater ambitions his son might entertain.'

'Why?'

'His son's greater ambitions diminish his own achievements.'

Victoria didn't know whether to laugh or acknowledge another of her mother's brilliant observations about people. She was like an amateur psychologist who would happily drop the word *amateur*. She had, after all, a worldly education at Vassar and had graduated with honors with both her B.A. and M.A.

'Doctor Myers, I presume,' Victoria surprised herself countering.

Her mother lifted her eyebrows. 'Teaching is like working in a mental clinic these days. Thank goodness I have a background in psychology.'

'I'm not sure what to do with my hair,' Victoria said, shifting topics as quickly as she could.

'I think you should brush it and pin it back. You have the face for it. I'll help you,' she offered.

'Really?'

'Let me change and see what I'm making your father for dinner. That dress, by the way . . .'

'Yes?'

'Looks stunning on you,' she said and walked

off, leaving Victoria gazing after her with a new sense of hope.

Later, after her mother had helped her with her hair and her makeup, Victoria made some finishing touches and stepped out of her bedroom, taking a deep breath like someone about to go underwater. She had a thin, soft white silk shawl her grandmother had given her years ago, but it was probably warm enough in early July, even in the Catskills, not to need it. Nevertheless, she felt more comfortable with it.

As soon as she stepped into the dining room, her father looked up from the dinner table where he had just sat. He was still in his dark gray suit and soft blue tie. His reddish brown hair was stroked with a little more gray along his temples. Their dinner was always special on Friday nights, if they didn't go out to eat. It gave them the feeling of reaching the end of the week. Both he and her mother called it the TGIF effect. It wasn't only educational personnel who were thanking God it was Friday. Almost all government workers did, as well as many business people. It was like finishing a marathon. No more need to run.

The teardrop chandelier above the table glittered like diamonds. Mozart's *Magic Flute* streamed in from the stereo in the living room. Victoria's parents believed music was relaxing and that relaxation enhanced digestion. 'How you teenagers can eat with that rock and roll playing is beyond me. Every organ in your body must be twitching,' her mother told her. Victoria didn't come to her generation's defense. Maybe that was what her mother wanted her to do – fight for something.

There was an opened counter between their living room and kitchen, where her mother was preparing dinner. Their house was a step-up from what would be called a modest ranch-style home. It was one of the larger houses in the small community. Their hamlet and six other entities made up the town of Fallsburgh, and the township was one of thirteen other townships in the county. They were still in what would be called the heyday of the Catskill resort world, a world still populated with boarding houses, small and large hotels, and bungalow colonies, some so large they had their own entertainment halls, tennis courts and, of course, swimming pools. Her father told her the population after the Fourth of July went from 7,500 people to close to a half a million. The tourists swept in for most of ten weeks and then, after Labor Day Weekend, were like rats deserting a ship.

'You look very nice, Vick,' her father said. Her mother closed the refrigerator sharply and grimaced. Despite her constant criticism of it, her father never stopped reducing Victoria to Vick.

'Mom helped me with my hair and makeup,' she said.

'Oh?' He didn't have to say anything more. She hadn't done that for years. 'Where ya goin'?'

'Dante's.'

'Oh, right. We haven't been there for quite a spell.'

15

'Whose fault is that?' her mother snapped, and he laughed.

They heard the door buzzer. No one moved. The last time a young man came to the house to take her out was the night of the senior prom. That was Jack Martin who had never been able to throw off the tag *a few bricks short of a load.* He was shy and almost as withdrawn as Victoria was. All night she heard, 'Birds of a feather stick together,' followed by laughter. He danced with her as if she could infect him, but he was polite and sweet, apologizing for almost anything he did, regardless of whether it was right or wrong. After the prom, he nodded at her and said hello in school once in a while, but he never asked her out again. Not that she wanted him to ask or would have said yes if he had.

Bart seemed to glow in the entryway light. His eyes were electric, his smile like the smile of a little boy about to get on to a rollercoaster for the first time. There was that sort of innocence in a face so handsome and manly that he could easily recall a Clark Gable or an Errol Flynn, not that they had his twinkle of innocence. Bart wore a light blue tie with his dark blue sports jacket and light pink shirt. He was wearing cufflinks, too. Somehow, in spite of how much he worked indoors, he already had an even summer tan. She hadn't noticed at the garage. In fact, all that was like a blur now.

'Hi,' he said. She hadn't spoken after she opened the door. She was wondering if she wasn't in some dream.

'Hi.'

'You really look beautiful, Victoria. Now I'm glad I brought this,' he said, bringing his hand out from behind his back to show her a white rose corsage. She stared at it as if she didn't know what it was or what it was for. 'It's OK, right?'

'What? Yes, of course. I was just so surprised.'

He took it out as her parents stepped up beside her.

'Good evening, Mr and Mrs Myers,' he said but concentrated on pinning the corsage on correctly.

'You look very handsome, Bart,' her father said.

'Thank you.'

'Yes, very nice,' her mother said. 'You know you still owe me a term paper on *Huckleberry Finn*,' she added. She sounded serious, but that was her mother's sense of humor.

'Oh, I knew there was something. I'll get right on it, Mrs Myers,' Bart said. He smiled at Victoria.

'You can always come back,' her mother said. 'I promise. It will be like you never left.'

'I might just do that.'

'You guys have a good ole time of it, yer hear?' her father said.

Bart looked relieved. He took Victoria's hand and started them away.

'Night,' he called back.

'Enjoy,' her father said. He closed the door.

Victoria could hear Bart release a trapped breath. She held on to his hand, more tightly than he expected, she was sure. But she couldn't help it.

There were no streetlights here and she couldn't get past that feeling that they were always out there, wearing the shadows, watching her, their lust insatiable.

There was no doubt in her mind. They knew where she lived.

They always knew where she lived.

One

It was an unusually warm summer that year of the Incident. New Yorkers trying to escape the city heat were not happy about the temperatures invading the ordinarily cooler mountains. Usually, everyone dressed a little warmer at night than they did during the daytime, but the high eighties and low nineties hung in until the wee morning hours. It seemed as if the air had amnesia when it came to those characteristic cool breezes.

Victoria was just fifteen then. She seemed to have matured into a young woman overnight. Her first period had come much later than it had for most of her girlfriends, and for a while her breasts appeared to have frozen in their development. It weighed on her mind so much that many times she was tempted to ask her mother whether or not she needed to see a doctor. Her mother didn't pick up on any of her hints, though, except to say, 'Don't be in a rush to get older. It's not what it's cracked up to be.'

An essential part of innocence was an

unawareness of how much and how often you were attracting male interest. It was almost as if she woke up one day, noticed the looks and knew she had crossed a line. At first, it seemed to Victoria that she was drawing the eyes and smiles of men and not the eyes of the boys at school. Perhaps they were too used to seeing her in that in-between state, but that soon began to change. Her mother, despite her apparent disinterest in Victoria's maturing, practically leaped at her one day and said she wanted take her shopping for a more appropriate bra and new jeans, blouses and skirts. She was growing out of everything.

As it was for most of her girlfriends, the filling out of her figure felt like an accomplishment. Her self-confidence was racing to catch up. She was still a little unsure of herself, unsure of how far she should go to highlight her new feminine attributes. Millie Brockton, a girl in her class, suffered no such hesitation. She wore blouses and skirts that were obviously too tight. Her excuse was she had to wear hand-me-downs from her older sister, but anyone could see how much she enjoyed toying with the boys by leaning back in her chair and straining the buttons. She had the breasts boys called *bumpers*.

On the other hand, Victoria's mother pounced whenever she caught so much as one button on her blouse undone, especially the one that enabled the revelation of the top of her deepening cleavage.

'Don't be oblivious, Victoria,' she would say without elaborating. So much of what her mother told her those days was between the lines. 'Figure

19

it out yourself,' she'd reply if Victoria questioned something. 'Don't make me say it.'

Did all mothers hold their daughters to such a high standard?

There were definite class distinctions in Sandburg and the other small villages in the township and county. Perhaps it was because people in small towns knew so much about each other – knew who had money or who had some black sheep relative, or knew who was cheating on her husband or his wife. People in the late fifties and early sixties who had achieved college diplomas and professional status had an air of superiority about them. Her father wasn't as obvious about it as her mother, who had the best posture of any woman Victoria knew. She had told her that Grandmother Annie had her parade about with a book on her head for hours when she was barely five.

She didn't have Victoria walk about with a book on her head, but she was always reminding her not to slouch. Early on, her mother set down a higher level of achievement for her. It was not uncommon for her to hear her mother say, 'We don't do that,' when remarking about something someone else her age had done or their parents permitted. There was a level of expectation that Victoria resented. Children of teachers and school administrators didn't break rules or get sent to the principal for discipline. And daughters? Especially daughters could never be promiscuous. The level of expectation was stifling.

Although she was fifteen and could work, she didn't have a summer job that year. Her mother wouldn't let her work in one of the resort hotels. The parties the busboys and waiters and waitresses had in those were notorious. There was little or no supervision of the younger ones. Some even moved into the helps' quarters and were already like college age kids off on their own, smoking, drinking and having sex. She laughed when she first heard it put that way – *having sex* – as if it was something you could order in a restaurant. 'Are you having the shrimp special or are you having sex?'

Her mother taught a summer semester at the college, and her father's job was not the same as a school teacher's. He was working most of the summer, too. When she was invited, Victoria could go over to Mindy Fein's house to swim. Mindy's parents had put in a pool two years ago. Her father owned the drugstore in town. Most of the time, Mindy worked there, even before she was of legal age, but occasionally she had week-days and weekend days off and there was a pool party. They were one of the only families she knew who had a live-in maid, a black woman who, besides having to clean and cook, was left to supervise. She seemed like part of their family.

Victoria's main activity during the summer was to care for the house, clean and polish furniture, do laundry and, if she had a mind to, cut the grass now that she was old enough to ride the mower. When she did that, mostly out of boredom, she wore her two-piece and often heard car horns when boys drove by. She pretended to be deaf, but smiled to herself and commanded herself not to slouch.

Even back then, the question haunted her. Was she beautiful or just sexy now? Could you be one without the other?

On Friday and Saturday nights, the teenagers in Sandburg gathered unofficially in front of George's soda fountain store, a small confectionary store where toys and cigarettes, pipe tobacco and cigars were sold as well. The volume on the jukebox was turned up so that the music spilled out of the opened doorway. To older people, it was as if a dam had been breached. They quickened their pace to walk by, shaking their heads with disapproval as if similar memories of their own youth had been stolen. Sometimes kids would literally dance in the street, annoying passing drivers whose horns blared, only encouraging them more. Those teenagers who had their driver's licenses and cars would go from village to village, looking for action, but always returned before the night ended, just in case they missed something.

Teenagers from New York whose parents had rented bungalows nearby mingled with the locals. Occasionally, the firehouse, where there was a big room for community events, was opened for a Saturday-night dance. It broke reasonably early and the kids would pour out still high on excitement to hang in front of George's and continue this mating process that generated summer romances, peppered with rides in convertibles, necking and petting under bridges or on lightly traveled side roads, going to the drive-ins, for pizza, or night swimming in the nearby Sandburg Lake – and all of it always with a track of rock and roll to stamp a memory over a kiss or a vow of love.

Will you still love me tomorrow?

Virginity was in far more danger during the summer. The boys of summer with soft large dice hanging off their car's rearview mirrors, swooped in like birds picking off baby turtles that struggled over beaches to reach the safety of the sea. They homed in with their eyes and smiles full of challenges and daring. You started to smoke, if you didn't already. You started to drink alcohol seriously, and you recognized the sound of a condom being unwrapped. You even knew the scent.

Victoria intended only to skirt the edges of this world. She thought of herself as an interested observer, not yet ready to become part of anything. After all, she had just gotten her wings. She left for the village that Friday night intending to meet up with Jena and Mindy. There was talk of a party at Sandburg Lake that particular evening. Her parents would never approve of her going, but she was intrigued by the idea of doing something forbidden. Toby Weintraub, a senior, had her driver's license and her mother's car. She was closest to Mindy and said she would take the three of them, but only bring them back to the village afterward.

'I'm not going to be anyone's taxi home.'

Nevertheless, it seemed perfect.

Victoria's parents were going to dinner just down the road at the Levys' that night. They left with the usual warning about her eleven o'clock curfew. She was, in their minds and hers, one year away from a midnight curfew. One year and she'd become another Cinderella. Her mother didn't notice that she was wearing her bathing suit under her school T-shirt and bright madras plaid Bermuda shorts. She thought she would say something about her wearing shorts at night, but only her father made a comment, telling her that, contrary to popular belief, Bermuda shorts did not originate in Bermuda. 'They were created by the Brits servin' in tropical climates,' he explained.

'Trivia to die for,' her mother said with a histrionic sweep of her right hand and then told him to move along or they'd be rudely late for the Levys' dinner. Was there any other kind of late?

'Lock up,' her mother called back.

Victoria went to check on her hair and add some makeup her mother would have disapproved of.

She set out for the village full of anticipation. Despite everything, even years later, she could vividly recall the tingling all over her body as she hurried to the village that night. There was no doubt that what made it more exciting was the forbidden nature of what she was doing – going to a lake party at night, where surely there would be alcoholic drinks and all sorts of wild activity. There would be boys she didn't know, and the boys she did know would be very surprised to see her there. Would one or more of her girlfriends drift off with someone? Would *she* dare?

She practically ran all the way into the village. At the corner of Wildwood and Main Street, she cut through the path worn down through the bushes and saplings behind the Millers' house. It wound around to the right and came out in the alley between Kayfield's Bar and Grill and Trustman's vegetable market, enabling her to reach the action in the center of the village at least ten minutes sooner. It was already quite busy. All the stores were still open. They had these ten weeks of summer during which to make their year's income. Like most resort communities, the season was live or die. Putting in twelve or more hours of work was the norm.

But there was also that thunderous excitement in the air created by a weaving of the music, the laughter and the sounds of cars, their engines being revved up, their drivers and passengers taunting each other and girls on the sidewalk. It was as if all these teenagers had broken free, as if their childhoods were a form of enslavement of the senses. Unchained, they would rock the earth itself.

She had no way to explain why or how the normally sleepy little village took on the look of a Hollywood movie set. There were dogs sleeping on the sidewalk, their eyes half open as if they were just as curious about the changes in the hamlet. Cats peered out from under stairways, curious but afraid. Residents looked out their windows, some amused, some annoyed. The elderly men and women who were practically fixtures sat in front of Weintraub's department store reliving their own youth, just the way they did most any chance they had. There were no balloons, no spotlights and no extra decorations. It was her hometown, miraculously transformed into a place full of promise and excitement. Normally, it was the subject of jokes, a one-horse town where you could die on the street and not even be noticed by the undertaker.

Jena and Mindy were in front of George's, Mindy hiding a cigarette behind her, watching for anyone who knew her parents and then taking a puff, blowing the smoke with her back to the street. At the lake, no one would have to hide anything. They could wear the darkness as masks and lose their names in the shadows.

'Wearing your bathing suit?' Jena asked as soon as she saw her.

'Yes. What about you?' If it was difficult to see that she was wearing hers, it was impossible to know if Jena was wearing one. She looked as if she had thrown on her grandmother's house dress, something she would wear to wash floors or vacuum.

'Yes. I forgot to bring a towel, though. You don't have one either, Victoria.'

'We won't need a towel,' Mindy said. 'Jesus, Jena. This isn't physical education class.'

'Maybe Toby will have one,' Jena offered weakly. Mindy shook her head.

'If she does, it will be just for herself. Toby's not going to be here until eight thirty,' Mindy told her. 'No one's going to the lake before it starts getting dark anyway, so don't get your balls in an uproar.'

'What balls?'

'Victoria!'

'She's right. Relax, Jena,' Victoria said, trying to sound seasoned. 'We'll have fun.'

'I've only been there in the daytime,' Jena confessed, 'and never with a boy – only with my parents.'

Jena had a terrible habit of telling the truth, Victoria thought, especially in front of boys. She exchanged a look with Mindy, who rolled her eyes. On more than one occasion, sometimes not so subtly, Mindy told her the only reason she invited Jena to anything was because she was Victoria's friend.

Jena wasn't ugly, but she had one of those bodies that looked as if it belonged on a woman much older because of her wide hips and already sagging breasts. She was always dowdy and always wore what Victoria called *curtain clothes*, because they just hung loosely over her matronly figure.

She never did much with her dull brown hair either and, except for some lipstick, was afraid to put on makeup – not because her mother would be upset, but because she had no self-confidence. She clung to Victoria's friendship like someone clinging to a life preserver in the rough sea of adolescence. *Blind leading the blind*, Victoria often thought.

The three girls passed the time talking to other kids they knew. Victoria and Mindy were approached by some of the city boys who offered to take them to the lake, but they shrugged off the invitations, teasing with promises to meet up later. Toby arrived and the four of them set out with expectations for a night to remember. As if to emphasize that, Toby revealed a pint of rum she had taken from her home.

'Helps build courage,' she remarked and passed it to Mindy first who then gave it to Victoria. She drank less than a thimbleful and gave it to Jena who surprised them all with her long swig. Victoria remembered wondering if she wasn't a secret boozer after all and maybe that was why she couldn't lose weight.

Toby, on the other hand, was a tall, lean girl with one of those ironing board figures that suggested she'd been cursed at birth. Her brother Herbie was a stout fifteen-year-old in their class and often in trouble. Lately, he had flirted with Victoria, but she didn't even return a look. She knew her mother would never approve of her hanging out with Toby, much less her brother. Her father worked as a gas delivery truck driver and had a reputation for a wild temper when he got drunk, which seemed to be a frequent occurrence of late.

The whole night was fraught with forbidden danger. Every moment she seemed to sink deeper and deeper into the pool of jeopardy. Yet it was exactly that danger that made it attractive.

By the time they arrived at the lake, there were a few dozen kids and at least a half-dozen bonfires. The sun had just gone down fully behind the mountain and the veil of protection the darkness cast seemed to smother reluctance. The city boys they had met in the village spotted them quickly and invited them to their bonfire, where they passed around more whiskey and cigarettes. All but Jena went into the lake, the boys

28

surrounding them, splashing them, constantly trying to embrace them.

Mindy was the first to couple up. Two boys were courting Victoria. She entertained the idea of going off with the taller boy called Spike. He said he was a senior and lived in the Bronx. She didn't have to choose in the end. He practically elbowed his friend out of the way and she let him kiss her while they were still in the water, waist deep. She remembered feeling a little dizzy. She had sipped more alcohol than she had ever had before. When they stepped out of the water and made their way back to their campfire, Jena, who had drunk too much, was sprawled out and practically asleep. She hadn't even taken off her curtain clothes.

Victoria used her blouse to dry herself some. Spike had what looked like a towel that had been in the trunk of his car for weeks, and she refused it. He sprawled beside her and began to kiss her everywhere he could. At first, she thought it was just weird until he was at the inside of her thighs and then nudging his nose and his lips between her breasts. She looked for Toby or Mindy but didn't see them. Spike gave her some more to drink. She tried to refuse, but he practically pleaded until she took another sip and another.

She remembered seeing boys she knew from school pausing to look her way and smile and make comments to themselves that triggered laughter. Spike was trying to get her to drink a little more, but she resisted. He started to kiss her harder, kiss her on the neck, move his hands over her breasts, and then he tried to get his right hand into the bottom of her bathing suit. She held his wrist, but he pushed harder until she felt his fingers reach her pubic hair. She struggled to resist, and when he grew more aggressive, coaxing and pleading with her to relax, she pushed him away, leaped to her feet, grabbed her shorts and blouse and ran off.

She heard him laughing, but she didn't turn back, even though she realized she had left her sandals behind and Jena was still sprawled out and asleep just a few feet from him. For a while, she crouched in the darkness and watched him. He looked at Jena, shook his head and finally got up and joined some of his friends. As soon as he did, she swooped in, scooped up her sandals and tried to wake Jena, who groaned but didn't make an effort to stand. Victoria wasn't about to carry her away.

She wandered around for a while, keeping her distance from Spike. Some of the local boys approached her, but she was unresponsive, thinking now only of how she could get home. Toby was nowhere in sight and neither was Mindy. Where had they gone? She returned to the smoldering camp fire and shook Jena hard.

'I'm going home,' she told her. Jena sat up and suddenly began to vomit. After that, she lay down again and said she just wanted to be left alone for a while. The last thing Victoria remembered her saying was, 'My father's going to kill me.'

Father, she thought. *My mother would be the one to kill me.*

She rose, debated with herself about what to do next and then decided to leave. When she still couldn't rouse Jena, she left her behind. She started for the road that led away from the lake. Wayne Gerson, who was heading back with his friend Tommy Marks in Wayne's father's pickup truck, saw her walking. They were seniors in her school this coming year.

'You can't walk all the way back to the village,' Tommy said, leaning out of the truck window. He sounded pretty drunk, slurring his words. They paused and he stepped out. 'We'll squeeze you in. Hop in,' he said.

'Course, we'll need a can opener to get you out,' Wayne said. They both laughed. They knew her; she knew them. At least it wasn't like being with strangers.

She got in. It was tight, but she felt rescued as they bounced their way over the dirt road, smoking and laughing. She clutched her clothes against her breasts and held her breath as much as she could because of the heavy cigarette smoke and booze that churned her stomach.

'Have a good time?' Tommy asked.

'No,' she moaned and they both laughed.

'There's always tomorrow,' Wayne said.

Neither made any attempt to touch her inappropriately. They seemed happy in their own inebriated world as if sex was an afterthought. They'd get to it sometime probably.

When she saw the lights of the village, she breathed a sigh of relief. But she couldn't help feeling a little like a failure. Why were so many of the others, many her age, most only a year or so older, so ready to have fun, explore and take a chance?

How would she ever have any romance?

When would she grow up?

Her mind reeled with sobering questions about herself.

The last thing she had expected this particular night was a deep sense of frustration and self-doubt.

She almost decided to return to the lake.

In the end, she would have been better off if she had. Her whole life would have been different.

Two

'Your mother is a great teacher,' Bart Stonefield said as they pulled away from her house. 'I mean, she's tough, but she does make the work interesting, and I'll have to admit, she challenges you. You can't be lazy in her class. I regretted leaving her class more than the other classes I took. Whenever I saw her afterward, I felt like a coward. I would cross streets, turn away quickly, do everything I could not to confront her.'

'I do the same thing,' she said and he laughed.

He glanced at her and then turned back to the highway.

'Graduated college with high honors. Your parents are so proud of you. Really, what do you intend to do now?'

'Enjoy dinner,' she said.

He smiled. 'You have a little bit of your mother

in you, you know? Not that it's bad,' he added quickly.

'What's that expression – the apple doesn't fall far from the tree?'

'My father always adds *unless it's at the top of a hill.*'

She shrugged.

'I don't consciously try to be like her, or my father for that matter. I just try to be me, whoever that is. Mirrors are sometimes more like windows. You're looking at a stranger in another house.'

'Yeah, well I know what I see . . . a very nice, beautiful and obviously intelligent young woman.'

She smiled but wasn't sure exactly what to say. *Thank you* sounded so formal and even phony. How do you know when someone, especially a man, is sincere? Ever since that night, she was suspicious of compliments. Most were like band aids. Those administering them had good intentions, but she was hardened against good intentions. She didn't want the pity and she certainly didn't want to be handled. What she wanted, she knew she couldn't have: to turn back time and erase what had happened so she could be on an even playing field again.

And it wasn't simply solved by being someplace where people didn't know her well or knew what had happened. She had been in that place for four years at college. That was only half the battle, because *she* knew who she was and *she* knew what had happened. It was like walking over thin ice. It would break and she would fall through whenever someone new discovered the truth. They might suspect something in her

33

shyness or her introverted behavior, and then the questions might start. She had no confidence in her ability to hide the truth. She feared that other girls, especially ones who had *been around the block*, as her mother might say, could see through her excuses for rejecting a date.

How did Bart Stonefield really see her? Did she really look so different now? Had she matured, truly become beautiful? Was she at peace with her past enough to step into the future as a totally different woman and certainly not the wounded bird she had become, never flying, always grounded in sorrow and depression while watching so many her age soaring to new heights, finding a life for themselves?

She had to respond, say something. Silence could make him uncomfortable and she didn't want that.

'That's very nice of you to say so, Bart.'

'I'm a nice guy, even if I have to say it myself.'

'I'm sure you don't.'

'Well, I do talk to myself because I'm confident I'll convince myself.'

She relaxed. He had more of a sense of humor than she had imagined. In this way, he reminded her of her father who was adept at sidestepping controversy and unpleasantness with a joke. He was like a prize fighter who was so good at bobbing and weaving that he didn't have to throw retaliatory blows. He simply waited for his opponent to grow exhausted with the aggression and then retreat.

'My dad says if you don't convince yourself of something first, you won't convince anyone else, least of all a customer. No matter how tough that might be,' he added.

'You'll get no argument from me about that,' she said, immediately worrying that the conversation would drift into something depressing or cynical and lead to the inevitable questions. She was always bracing herself for the segue that would take her back down the dark path.

But he didn't seem to want that or was sensitive enough to know not to go there.

'So, seriously, what are you going to do now? Are you going to go into teaching, follow in your mother's footsteps, or what?'

'I don't know, Bart. I'm toying with going to graduate school, but I wonder if I'm not just looking for ways to avoid making choices.'

He turned and sped up as they reached what locals called the Quickway. The sky was partly cloudy, the early-evening summer sun blinding when it peeked out between the clouds. He lowered the visor.

They were headed for Monticello, about ten more miles. The mountains were plush with their deep green leafy trees and bushes. Like most who lived here and took it all for granted, she was oblivious to the natural beauty. This had been especially true for her afterward. It was as if a veil of fog had fallen all around her. Right now, she felt like a distorted version of Sleeping Beauty, woken and confused. She was still quite nervous and terrified of disappointment, but at least she was able to lower the drawbridge and let the world back in, if only for a little while.

Dr Thornton would take credit for this, she

thought – maybe deservedly so. It didn't help to resent the people trying to help you, even if they were being paid to do so. She had warned her many times. If you didn't move on, you could go through life demolished or angry or even both. She looked out the window.

Cars whizzed by. Because it was the summer resort season, there was heavier traffic, especially on a Friday night. The so-called weekend husbands were chugging up the mountain to join their families at bungalow colonies. Tonight and on Saturday night, bedsprings would sing something like *absence makes the heart grow fonder.* The image of such a symphony, the moans of pleasure and laughter resonating through the countryside, brought a smile.

'No reason to rush into the hectic world, I guess,' he said, obviously scrutinizing his responses before speaking.

'Is that the way you see it – hectic?'

'Spend a day at Stonefield's garage and then tell me,' he replied. 'Come by anytime.'

He had that impish gleam in his eyes she had seen many times, but not until recently directed her way. She thought about the comments her mother had made about him and his father perhaps pressuring him to work in their business.

'Don't you enjoy it? Your work, your business? I mean, you're doing what you want to do, right?'

'It's exciting to see how much we've grown over the last four years and how we could continue. Dad's talking about opening a dealership in Monticello – a fourth brand. Foreign cars,' he said and then, in a whisper almost as if it was profanity, he leaned toward her and added, 'Volkswagen.'

'Did you always expect to be working in your family business?'

'I flirted with doing something else. I was thinking of becoming an air force pilot. I was always fascinated by how the RAF stopped the Nazis during the Second World War. *Never was so much owed by so many to so few,*' he recited in his best Winston Churchill imitation. She laughed.

'Not bad,' she said.

He nodded and smiled. 'I actually took some flying lessons. Secretly,' he said. 'But in the end I decided I was a home boy. I haven't even been to New York City that many times. We take a Florida vacation every year, but other than that . . .'

'You still go with your parents?'

She didn't mean to sound disapproving, but his restricted experiences, self-imposed or not, surprised her.

He blushed. 'To please my mother, but I haven't gone anywhere with them for quite a while, actually.'

'You don't have the travel bug?'

He shrugged. 'I guess I should, working with cars. I do plan to drive cross-country one of these days. I don't mean in a day. I mean . . .'

'I understand. Like *Route 66*. I bet a lot of guys did it after they watched the television show.'

'We do sell Corvettes,' he said, smiling. 'Let me know when you're ready. We'll leave an hour afterward.'

Now she was the one who blushed.

The restaurant loomed ahead.

'I'd match Dante's against any of the New York restaurants. The owner had a restaurant in New York,' he said. 'We sold him a new car recently – Gino. Dad kidded with him, telling him he'd trade the car for a lifetime of his lasagna,' he continued. Suddenly, he seemed afraid of any silences between them. 'You've probably eaten here, right?'

'Years ago,' she said.

He pulled into a parking space, shut off the engine, but sat unmoving.

'I didn't mean anything when I said "when you're ready". I mean . . .'

'Now you're having second thoughts about the invitation? I was thinking how much luggage I would need,' she said. If she could do it, she would avoid even an innuendo. He looked at her and then smiled.

'OK, OK.' He raised his hands. 'Let's eat.'

He got out and hurried around to open her door. She had started to let herself out, not expecting it.

'Hey,' he said, 'when you give a girl a corsage on a date, you're expected to open all doors and pull out all chairs. Just so you know what to expect.' He closed the door and reached for her hand.

'I expected no less,' she said, making it sound as if she was used to it. He raised his eyebrows. Was she putting it on too much? Did he think she was measuring him against some college boyfriend? *My God*, she thought, *I'm analyzing every moment, every word spoken. Is this a result of years of therapy?* She was sure she was trying too hard not to offend him or make him feel uncomfortable.

They started for the front entrance.

'Actually, I can be quite sophisticated for a country boy. I watched enough Cary Grant movies,' he joked.

'I haven't been with that many sophisticated boys,' she confessed as he opened the door. 'And the last time any gave me a corsage was my senior prom.'

'Good for Jack Martin,' he said, stepping back.

'You know who took me to the prom?'

He had been out of high school for two years at the time. Why would he have any interest in her then if he had none when he was still a senior? He didn't answer. Instead, he led her into the restaurant.

Gino Dante's wife, who was the receptionist, stepped out from behind her high polished oak counter to greet them. She had a dark Mediterranean complexion and was buxom with wide hips. Strands of gray were woven through her licorice-black hair which was tied back into a neat bun. On the wall behind her were nearly a dozen portraits of comedians and singers who had played and still played the Catskill resorts. They had eaten here and had given their pictures with compliments for the food and service inscribed. There were also pictures of the Dante family, including pictures of the grandparents and aunts and uncles back in Naples and Florence.

'Good evening, Mr Stonefield,' she said, offering her hand.

'Mrs Dante. You remember Victoria Myers?'

It was just a small movement in her eyes and a slight tightening of her lips that revealed her surprise. *Did she think I had been sent away for the rest of her life or something?* Victoria wondered. *Did she think I would have developed some malformation, a hunchback perhaps, or shrunk into an anorexic?*

'Victoria, of course. Buonasera. I haven't seen you since you were in high school. What a beautiful young lady you've become!'

'See?' Bart said, validated. He straightened his shoulders. 'She graduated summa cum laude,' he said proudly. 'This year,' he emphasized.

'Oh, a special celebration. Congratulations. Your parents must be so proud.'

And surprised, Victoria thought Mrs Dante would add in her thoughts. After all, look what happened to Humpty Dumpty.

'They are. Thank you.'

A waitress approached them.

'Take them to table seven, please, Anna,' she said. 'Enjoy. And, again, congratulations, Victoria.'

They followed the waitress.

'I was here my first return trip during my first year of college,' she told Bart. 'Not that I would expect her to remember.'

He nodded. 'Well, she'll remember you tonight,' he assured her.

There was little change in the restaurant's décor from what Victoria recalled from that last time. The dominant color was still ruby – ruby

40

cushioned seats and ruby streamed through the light-oak panel walls. There were a half-dozen highly desirable booths, usually reserved for a party of four, but Bart had obviously asked for one. The booths offered more privacy, more intimacy. The tape of an Italian tenor singing 'Nessun Dorma', not loud enough to interfere with conversation, sounded like movie background music to her as she continued to the table. This evening was something like a movie anyway, she thought. Any moment the lights would come on and it would end. She'd leave the theater along with everyone else.

'So, do you like red or white wine?' he asked as soon as they sat.

'Doesn't it depend on what we order?'

He blushed a little again, closing and opening his eyes with an 'oops' expression. He was trying harder than she was, she thought. What a surprise.

'Of course. They have some great fish dishes and you'll want white with that. I usually order a Chianti, but we can order by the glass, too. We could have a cocktail first. I don't drink all that much, but I usually order a Rob Roy. What do you like?'

She smiled, remembering the first time her father had made her a vodka gimlet. That was his drink. He'd have one on Friday and one on Saturday night, but never during the week. She was only fourteen at the time he introduced her to it, but he believed it was better to have your child learn about alcohol at home rather than at parties or whatever. To her surprise, her mother agreed. They both expected she wouldn't like the gimlet, but she did.

'I'll have a vodka gimlet,' she said. He looked impressed. 'My father's drink,' she added. 'I've never had one outside of my house or unless I was with my parents at a restaurant. I think I had one here that night I returned from college. It was after my eighteenth birthday, but I had to show my driver's license.'

'You'll probably have to do that until you're in your seventies.'

'Watch out. You know what happened to Pinocchio,' she warned. It was one of her mother's favorites when Victoria was growing up. She was still capable of tossing it at her father when he exaggerated something.

'No fears. I wasn't lying or exaggerating as far as I'm concerned,' he replied and then gave the waitress their drink order when she brought their menus. 'So, you never had a gimlet on one of your big city dates either?'

'No.'

She didn't want to tell him she had never gone on a big city date. She wondered if she should make up something.

'So tell me what college life in the big city was like,' he said. 'Was it as intimidating as people tell me?'

'At first, yes, especially for someone who comes from a place where in the fall and the winter you could sprawl out on Main Street and feel safe,' she said.

He laughed. 'It does get like that in the smaller hamlets.'

42

'It was difficult to get used to just walking on the city sidewalk among hundreds and hundreds of people. And the noise, the lights at night, the traffic. Yes,' she continued, nodding slightly as though she was actually realizing it for the first time, 'it's intimidating. You think about crossing the street more, you cling tighter to your purse, and it takes a while to realize you shouldn't smile so much at other people – strangers. In fact, people in New York tend to avoid eye contact. When you go into a store to buy something, the clerks or owners just want you to tell them what you want. There's no *How are you? How's your mother, your father?* In the beginning, I actually waited for someone to ask how I was first or at least say good morning.'

She stopped, realizing she was going on too much. He had a look of amazement on his face.

'Sorry. I'm blabbing.'

'No. That was a great description. I feel like I've been living there a while myself now.'

'I don't mean to make it sound good or bad. I mean, I like New York City very much. It is exciting, but I'm not sure I'd want to live there.'

'You can take the girl out of the country, but not the country out of the girl – that sort of thing?'

'Maybe.'

'That's probably a fitting description for me. Whenever I have driven into the city, I'm always amazed at how hard it is to find a parking spot and how long it will take to go three miles. Here, it's about three minutes or so, but there it could be hours, I suppose. Maybe it's how your nerves are formed, although I do have classmates who live

43

and work in the city. Don Ritter works in the Empire State Building for some law firm. Remember Don? His family lives in South Fallsburgh.'

'Not much,' she said. 'I mean, I recall him, but I don't believe I said more than three words to him or him to me.'

'He was the class brain, but a nice guy. He took me to lunch once near the Empire State Building and then he had me go up to the top.'

'I've never been.'

'Never went up to the observation deck?'

She shook her head. 'Nor have I gone to the Statue of Liberty, and I can count on one hand how many times I've been to Times Square.'

'Well, I guess you don't graduate with honors if you're playing at college,' he said. Charitably, she thought.

The waitress brought their drinks.

'Give us a moment. We haven't looked at the menus yet,' Bart told her and she left. 'Well, welcome home,' he said, lifting his glass to touch Victoria's in a toast.

Yes, she thought, *I am home. In the end, where else would I go?*

She looked at the menu.

'Is your mother a good cook?' he asked. 'My mother's OK, but her favorite recipe is reservations.'

She laughed and thought. 'She gets a passing grade, but my father's actually a better cook, or should I say enjoys doing it more than she does. Actually, my grandmother has kept us in home cooking. She still sends over care packages from time to time.'

44

'She lives in Centerville, right?' he asked.

'Yes.' She smiled. She didn't know where any of his grandparents lived or even if any were still alive. How or why did he know about hers?

'She still drives. I've had her car serviced,' he explained quickly.

'Sounds like you know more about the residents here than the local newspaper does.'

'You can learn a lot about someone from the way he or she cares for their car,' he said. 'I have to tell you, though, men take care of their cars better than women, and I don't mean just the engine and stuff. They keep them cleaner inside. Of course, they're slobs at home. If I go by myself, that is.'

'Where do you live, Bart? With your parents?'

'No, I moved to a little apartment in Monticello two years ago. It's just one bedroom – nothing fancy, especially now that I've lived in it that long. You know, the bachelor pad syndrome. I'd have to fumigate before bringing you to see it,' he added.

Just the suggestion set a flutter under her breast. Should she tell him she had never been in a man's apartment? How much of her social failure did she want to reveal?

'My father's meticulous. He's more organized than my mother,' she said. 'My mother's the absent-minded professor actually. Except in her classes.'

'I'm pretty good when it comes to the garage. I pounce on stains and tools left out. Like everything, it's priorities, I guess.'

She looked at the menu again. She had nervously drunk most of her gimlet and the warm feeling actually frightened her. Since the Incident, she had rarely drunk any hard alcohol, unless it was with her parents. Would her life be different now if she hadn't done any drinking that night at the lake? She thought she had sobered up after she had left, but she had no way to measure herself, having never really been drunk. She was certainly not as inebriated as Jena was that night and nothing had happened to her.

'I'm going with the Spaghetti Bolognese,' he declared. 'I recommend the Dante salad first.'

'That's fine, but I'll follow your father's recommendation on the lasagna.'

He gave their orders to the waitress and ordered a bottle of Chianti.

'That all right? The Chianti?'

'Yes, fine,' she said and sipped her drink.

'Want another of those?'

'Not unless you want to carry me out.'

He laughed. 'One of these is enough for me, too.'

The waitress brought them a basket of home-made bread, half plain and half garlic.

Victoria looked around for the first time since they had sat down. Most of the people were summer residents and tourists, but she did recognize some locals. They were looking her way and speaking softly. Was she still that famous? Were they shocked to see her so well put-together and out with Bart Stonefield? Suddenly, she thought about his parents. Did they know he was taking her to dinner tonight? Would they have approved or disapproved? Would her mother had immediately said, 'Why do you want to get involved with that girl? She can't be stable. She's mentally wounded.'

'I see a couple of my customers here,' Bart said, following her gaze.

She nodded and glanced around again. One of them could be in here, she thought. He could be looking at me and smiling to himself, thinking, *I had her*. She had to stop thinking of that if she was going to stay here, at least for the summer.

'Have you stayed in touch with many of your high school friends?' she asked.

The question seemed to throw him, almost as though no one had ever asked it and he wasn't sure how he should respond.

'I see some of them – the ones who stayed here after high school – but very few – actually, no one except Don – of those who left. We're supposed to have a class reunion in four years – our tenth year since graduation. Charlie Sacks was class president and talks about organizing it. He ended up living down in Goshen. He went to work in the Emerson plant in Middletown after he served in the army and met a girl from the area. He's got twin girls, three years old.'

'You weren't drafted after you quit college?' she asked. This time he did wince.

'Politics,' he said cryptically. She didn't pursue it. 'I would have been a terrible soldier anyway. I've always had trouble following orders.'

The waitress brought their wine, opened it and poured some for him to taste. He nodded and the waitress poured them each a glass. He leaned toward her to whisper, 'I never know what to look for when tasting, but I do look like I know what I'm doing, don't I?'

She smiled, sipped the wine and stared at it for

a moment. 'It's not a cheap wine. Good clarity.' She smelled it. 'A little fruity, faintly floral. A Sangiovese?' she asked and looked at the bottle, nodding.

'Wow. You picked that up in the big city?'

'Yes and no. I was in a wine-tasting class one weekend. Something different to do. I didn't do much wine drinking afterward, so it was almost a total waste of time. Until tonight,' she added, smiling.

He laughed. 'Lots of beer drunk at college, right?'

'I never appreciated beer. I'm sorry. I must sound terribly dull.'

He raised both hands. 'Hey, I'm not much of a beer drinker either. I nurse one bottle or glass in the local watering holes. Maybe we have more in common than you'd think,' he said.

The waitress brought their salads, but his words echoed . . . *more in common than you'd think*. She started to eat rather than respond. It was almost on her lips to say, *Not unless you were sexually violated.* How many times had she thought that whenever any girls at school even hinted at getting to be a close friend because they seemed to like the same things?

'Just so you know, the time I did spend in your mother's English class didn't go to waste. I've been writing our company's advertisement copy and I came up with the slogan, *Stonefield, a car dealer solidly behind its customers*. Get it . . . stone . . . solid? Connotations – that's what I learned from your mother.'

'Why did you quit midway?' she asked.

'Couldn't you work and attend the classes?'

He looked as if she had struck some sore spot.

'There were pressures. As I told you, my father was going into a big expansion. He was going to hire someone else to manage the service department. To my parents, I suppose it looked like I was flailing about, purposeless. I mean, education wasn't purposeless, but without a definite goal . . .'

'Well, if you're happy about it, then you made the right decision.'

His smile widened, deepened. It was as though he finally had relaxed, felt relieved. 'I was right about you,' he said.

'What?'

'That you'd have a way of making me feel right about myself.'

He brought his wine glass to his lips quickly, as quickly as someone who might want to stop himself from saying another word.

He just doesn't want to imply that someone as wounded as I was could do something like that for him, for anyone, she thought.

What else could it be?

Three

When they arrived in the village that night, Tommy and Wayne realized that they were out of beer. That seemed to be the most important thing in their lives at that moment. In fact, Victoria thought they actually sounded a little

49

hysterical about it. She had been hoping they would volunteer to drive her home and not just into the village, but as soon as they turned on to Main Street, Tommy moaned, 'We're out!' He held up an empty beer bottle and burped.

'No way. We were robbed back there,' Wayne said. 'I hate those guys from Frishman's bungalow colony. They never buy anything.'

'Kayfield's is the only place selling it here now,' Tommy said mournfully.

'Shit. I ain't going home to get my father's stuff.'

She was following their conversation, but it all seemed surreal. She suddenly realized why they were upset. Neither of them was eighteen and could walk into a bar or store and buy a beer. Was Wayne even driving legally? You could drive at night at seventeen if you had passed driver's education. She didn't want to ask, but she doubted he had.

'There's Jack Morris,' Wayne said, nodding ahead. 'He's eighteen. We'll give him a few bucks to buy us six.'

They pulled to the curb. More kids had ended up in Sandburg as the evening had worn on. She saw some who she knew came from South Fallsburgh, Woodbourne and Hurleyville. Apparently, this weekend Sandburg was the hamlet to go to. Small crowds hovered around benches and the fronts of both George's and Fein's drugstore, which had closed. Only dim front window lights were on.

She glanced in the rearview mirror. Behind them, in front of Kayfield's, Mike Siegler, the township policeman who had Sandburg as his beat, was leaning against his patrol car and talking with some men who were all watching the gathering of teenagers with a disapproving eye, just waiting for some traffic or other violation serious enough to enforce. Checking on the ages of anyone seen drinking beer or horsing around wasn't worth the effort and might create more havoc than there already was. Some storeowner most likely would be the one to get into real trouble for selling it in the first place. The leniency seemed all right. After all, some businesses were making money, and these were the days and nights they had to do it. But Wayne and Tommy weren't going to chance it, especially since the only place open for beer was the bar and grill where the town cop hung out.

Wayne and Tommy seemed to forget her. They leaped out of the truck to head for Jack Morris. She stepped out slowly. She hadn't had the time or room in the truck cab to get her blouse and shorts over her bathing suit and now did it as quickly as she could. It felt funny dressing in the street. She would remember thinking that a number of the boys had been watching her, but rattling off their names later was not easy. Anyway, she couldn't be sure who was really looking at her and who was just looking in her direction.

She turned and walked slowly toward the alleyway between Kayfield's and Trustman's. A large gray cat leaped out of an opened garbage can as she approached and scurried through the opening in the foundation of Kayfield's building.

She hesitated, deciding whether to take the alley and the shortcut or go up the street, perhaps being noticed by someone she knew who was driving in her direction. They might give her a lift, but it was already ten thirty. She would have to move quickly to be sure she was home before eleven. Her parents could be home already. Her mother didn't like lingering at dinner parties once everyone was searching for something new or interesting to say, and when everyone obviously had had more than enough to drink.

She couldn't take the chance. The shortcut was the fastest way.

The night sky had grown quite overcast and there hadn't been any moonlight. Her eyes grew accustomed to the darkness. She had traveled this shortcut so often that she thought she could do it blindfolded anyway. Nevertheless, she stumbled over a tree root and nearly fell forward. She felt as if she might have twisted her ankle a little in the effort to stay upright, so she slowed a bit.

Behind her, the din of car horns, conversations and laughter began to dwindle. After a while, silence came rushing in like water breaking through walls on both sides. She could hear herself breathing hard. Her skin, cooled by her swim in the lake, was now dry and feeling itchy. Regret and then suddenly an inexplicable fear began to travel up her body like spiders. It was as if she had stepped into some pool of dark remorse and was sinking. She sped up, jogging now, chased by the image of her parents' faces when she came bursting into the house, hot, sweaty and panicky.

She felt a twinge in her right side, just below her ribs, and slowed up. At one point, she stopped and listened. Something was moving on her right. She strained to see into the shadows and make sense of the silhouetted shapes. The sounds disappeared. She began to walk fast and then faster. Just before she reached the Millers' house, she sensed something or someone behind her. She paused to turn and that was when it happened.

What she would later describe as some sort of sack was dropped over her head. At the same time, a rope shaped as a lasso fell along with it and was tightened quickly just under her breasts so that her arms were driven hard and snuggly against her sides. She screamed, but something else was wrapped around her face so firmly that it pressed the sack into her mouth. She gagged and choked, and then felt herself being dropped to the ground on her back.

There were no voices. It seemed like a ghost was doing this to her. She squirmed and kicked and froze in shock when she realized her Bermuda shorts were being unfastened and the bottom of her two-piece was being taken off her along with it. They were down to her knees and then with a powerful quick motion were brought to her ankles and completely off.

She was in a mad frenzy, squirming and kicking. Strong hands on her shoulders kept her from sitting up.

Those powerful hands left her shoulders but seized her ankles and pulled her legs up and then outward to the point that she feared they'd be ripped off. She thought she was being murdered.

The concept of being raped just wouldn't take the lead position in her stream of thoughts. She was fighting it back, but once she felt the hard, erect penis pressing into her, she sensed she was losing consciousness. She recalled thinking that it was better to let it happen. It was like being anesthetized for an operation. She didn't fight it. Her body collapsed seemingly into itself and all went black.

She emerged out of the darkness, gasping for air and in a sea of pain.

Every part of her body that had been subdued was screaming. Even her face and her mouth ached. The stinging in her groin and the insides of her thighs felt as if dozens of bees had attacked her. Her first moans were so low that she didn't think she had actually made a sound. Then her moans grew louder and louder, each one so deep and resonant that they sounded more like noises being made by some wounded wild beast. Gradually, she reached a higher pitch and the moans became shrill screams.

Warren Miller had fallen asleep watching television. He was in his big cushioned easy chair with its back to the opened living-room window. He woke with a start. His wife, Rose, had already gone to bed as usual, leaving him watching television and knowing he would fall asleep and then wake up to go to bed. It was a ritual especially followed on weekends. They did little else. Only sixty-two, he had retired from his job as a Centerville feed mill truck driver on a disability pension because his rheumatoid arthritis had not

54

only crippled his fingers but turned his back into a furnace the moment he strained to lift anything.

At first, when he heard the scream, he thought it had come from something on television, but there was a news program on and the commentator had moved to the weather report.

He sat up and listened harder. Then he turned to the window. Someone was screaming.

'What the hell . . .'

He rose slowly, walked through the short entryway and opened the backdoor. They had a small porch on the rear of the house built to provide for the four steps leading to the entrance. The floorboards squeaked and strained. Replacing them had been on his to-do list too long and now he was past being able to do it himself. He paused and listened. The screams were getting lower. Someone was straining to cry out. He went back into the house and found his flashlight in the kitchen drawer and then returned to the porch. At first he heard nothing and was about to conclude that it was probably some of those kids who were wild on weekends in the summer. Then he heard another scream and another and stepped off the porch.

Mumbling under his breath with threats if this turned out to be some prank, he made his way through a patch of birch trees and passed the wild blueberry bushes Rose harvested for her home-made jams. Their two boys, Rube, twenty-eight, and Jesse, twenty-four, had been out of the house almost the day they each graduated high school. Rube had, for reasons Warren still couldn't fathom, enlisted in the Coast Guard and was stationed in Rhode Island. He had never mentioned any interest in it until the last weeks or so of his senior year. Jesse got his high school girlfriend, Mary Williams, pregnant, married her and went to work for his father-in-law, who owned a lumber company in Hurleyville. Mary was already pregnant with their second child. Both he and Rose decided that Jesse had fallen into a good thing. He wasn't much of a student, but he was a hard worker.

One thing was sure: neither Jesse nor Rube would be out here tonight, drinking too much and raising hell, Warren thought as he paused again to listen. They had brought their kids up right. When he heard nothing, he concluded that it was over, that whoever was pulling the prank had moved on. He was about to turn to go back when he heard a distinct moan and some sobs. Now preparing himself for something possibly very serious, he cut through another patch of birch and waved his flashlight at the shadows from side to side as if he was trying to paint a wall of light in the darkness.

He lowered the beam.

The moment he saw her, he froze. She was sprawled on her right side, her naked ass and legs smudged with dirt. Her right arm was twisted back, her hand under her thigh and her left arm was extended, her hand grasping at the air. She looked as if she was trying to stand. He rushed forward.

'What's going on here?' he demanded, as if there was a group of teenagers and not just this half-naked girl squirming on the ground.

She screamed in response and he felt his heart stop and start. Then he knelt down slowly and carefully turned her body. The moment he touched her, she screamed again and again and again. Her eyes were closed. She looked like someone having a horrible nightmare. He gazed at her naked lower body and saw the blood on her thighs.

'Jesus, Mary and Joseph,' he cried. 'Don't move. I'll be right back.'

He turned and, despite the clawing pain in his lower back and behind his legs, he ran through the woods and to his back door.

'Rose!' he shouted the moment he entered. 'Come down! Hurry!'

He went to the phone in the living room and, before he dialed, shouted for her again.

'Get me the police,' he told the operator. 'Emergency.'

'What's going on?' Rose cried from the stairway.

'Girl . . . in the back . . . in the woods . . . raped, I think,' he said and shouted into the phone as soon as the dispatcher answered the call. He rattled off the little detail he knew, identified himself and where he was, and then told Rose to get a blanket. 'Hurry,' he told the dispatcher. 'She's hurt bad.'

The dispatcher said she would call an ambulance and a patrol car would be there as soon as possible. She repeated the information he had given her as if she had to be sure she was the one not dreaming. Rose, in her bathrobe and slippers, appeared holding the blanket.

'What is it, Warren?' she asked when he hung

57

up. 'What are you saying?' She was still dazed from being woken out of a deep sleep. Her thin gray strands of hair looked as if they were trying to flee her scalp. 'What the hell's going on?' she demanded. He was standing there, looking as if he had lost his senses.

'What? I told you. There's a girl back there, half naked, bleeding and maybe beaten to within an inch of her life. I'll take this to her.' He seized the blanket, gazed around madly for a moment and then brightened with a thought. 'I'll take another flashlight,' he said, handing the blanket back to his wife and rushing into his garage to get a bigger flashlight. He returned quickly, scooped the blanket out of Rose's hands again and told her to wait for the police and the ambulance and then direct them to the light in the woods.

'Who is she?' Rose asked as he headed for the rear door again.

He paused. 'I don't know. I really didn't look at her face,' he said. 'Maybe some city girl.'

Not realizing the cruelty of what she was saying, Rose replied, 'I hope so.'

He rushed out.

In the village, Mike Siegler, through his opened car window, heard the call coming in. Todd Berns and Randy Carr stepped back as Mike got into the car to listen to the dispatcher.

'I'm on my way,' he said. The two men with whom he had been chatting leaned in as he started the engine.

'What was that?' Todd asked.

'Young girl, attacked, maybe raped behind the Millers' house,' he said and hit his lights and siren as he turned the car around and shot off. Everyone in the street stopped talking. Laughter dribbled into silence. Only the jukebox music was heard. The moment held and then shrugs and laughter brought the festive night back to center stage.

Down at the fire house, three of the volunteer ambulance squad were playing gin rummy with Howard Gerson, the fire department chief. Howard was sixty and a lifelong resident. The fire department had been his whole life since his wife had passed away two years ago from the same esophageal cancer that had killed Humphrey Bogart. Attaching it to a celebrity gave it more meaning, for some reason. He practically lived in the firehouse now. All three of his children had moved away years ago.

When the phone on the wall rang, the four looked at it as if no one had known it was there. Howard rose quickly to answer. Charlie Morris, Jack's father, Carl Nichols and Pete Carnesi all waited, paused, their cards fanned in their hands. In the rather dim light of the firehouse, they looked as if they were painted on a sixteenth-century canvas, the colors around them fading, their eyes soaked in surprise. All three were in the mid-forties and, like most locals, lifelong friends. The chief hung up quickly and turned to them.

'Fire up Florence Nightingale,' he ordered, using their nickname for the ambulance. 'Girl was attacked in the woods behind the Millers' house. Siegler's on his way, as are the state police.'

'Attacked?' Charlie said, rising. 'What the hell does that mean?'

'Rape. What else?' Carl said.

'Who?' Pete asked.

'Don't know,' Howard said. He hurried to his car while the three ambulance volunteers slipped into their outfits quickly. Pete started the ambulance and, when the garage door opened, he hit the siren. Howard Gerson was already on the street, his tires squealing as he made the turn. Lights in houses along the way came on as the sirens woke the inhabitants. The hamlet was exploding with curiosity and concern. Some of the people living in these homes had heard too many sirens. They were refugees from the Second World War in Europe and the nightmares they had buried years ago rose like locusts eager to feast on their faith in this new world.

Victoria never heard the sirens and never heard the men rushing to her side. She felt herself being gently lifted, but she refused to open her eyes or speak. She was waiting for the morning light to confirm it had all been a nightmare, but that didn't come. Men were talking to her, trying to get her to tell them what had happened to her. She sensed her blood pressure was being taken. Cool antiseptic wipes were being used to clean up her face. Someone was saying, 'You're going to be all right. Don't worry.'

She felt herself falling back into the darkness. When she opened her eyes at the sense of being moved again, she saw the lights of the hospital emergency room entrance. Two nurses were rushing to the gurney and escorting Carl and Pete as they rolled her through the entrance and down a short hallway to an examination room where a young intern named Dr Friedman took over and had her placed carefully on the examination table. The ambulance volunteers stood in the doorway for a moment, all three of them with the same expression of pity and disgust. One of the nurses said something to them and they walked off.

The other nurse was cleaning her legs. 'Oh, my God,' she chanted.

Victoria felt her remaining clothes being stripped off as the full examination began. She remembered thinking she had been separated from her body and was off to the side, indifferent to whatever they were doing.

What seemed like hours later, she was still in the examination room, staring up at the sterile white ceiling. The pain throughout her body had receded like the tide. Whatever they had given her really had her floating. She heard the sound of her mother's voice and then her father's, but she didn't turn to look.

I'm home, she thought. *I'm in my room.*

I really did dream it.

Maybe she laughed with relief. Whatever the reason, it had a sobering effect on everyone else in the room. Everyone stopped speaking. The silence began to frighten her. She turned her head and cried, 'Mommy.'

Her mother shot forward to take her hand and her father came around on the other side. He held

her right hand and they looked down at her with
expressions she had never seen on them. They
looked very young, but in a great deal of pain.
She was going to laugh until she saw a tear escape
her father's right eye, and then she started to cry
and they were holding her, both of them, seemingly each struggling to get a bigger piece of her.
She wondered if the trembling she was feeling
was coming from her or her parents.

She heard the doctor say something and they
released her and stepped back.

'It's better she get a little sleep,' he said. He
wasn't smiling at her to make her feel better or
forget. He looked very concerned.

This is very, very serious, she thought, *and it's
happening to me.*

Four

'The food's really very good here. You're right.
It could stand up against any of the best New
York City restaurants,' Victoria said. 'Not that
I've been to that many or consider myself some
sort of gourmet.'

She saw Bart was pleased that she had agreed
with him about a hometown restaurant.

*Did I say it to please him or because I really
believe it?* she asked herself and then wondered
if everyone questioned the sincerity of their own
statements. Once again, she found herself
wondering. Was she doomed now and forever to

62

analyze everything she said and everything she did?

'You don't have to be a gourmet to know when it's good or go by the opinion of any professional food critic,' he said. 'Your opinion is just as important. That's what I think.'

'My mother would agree. She's always complaining about people following what's popular just because it is and not because they want to. Her motto is *Think for yourself.* You know, her and Descartes.'

'Descartes?'

'I think therefore I am?'

'Oh. Yeah,' he said, even though she could see he wasn't sure about the quote or who Descartes was.

'Only she adds *I choose therefore I am.*'

He nodded. She wanted to tell him about existentialism but thought it might be too heavy a topic. The danger was clear. She could make him feel inferior because he didn't have the education she had. 'Diminish the man and you demolish the romance,' her grandmother once whispered to her.

'That makes sense to me,' he said.

'If I counted how many times she's compared people to lemmings, I'd be counting until I was ninety.'

He laughed.

'I remember. She'd challenge any opinion or conclusion you had when you were in her class. I think her favorite question is *Why did you say that?* or *Why do you think so?* Am I right?'

'My father claims it was what she asked when

she was born. She looked at the doctor and said, "Why?" I told her she was never and would never be satisfied with the answer.'

He laughed harder. 'You have a good sense of humor about your mother.'

'That I inherited from my father,' she replied. 'But don't misunderstand me. There's no woman I respect more. She's . . .'

'What?'

'Got a firm grasp on whatever she needs to get through the day.'

Did he think that was odd, that she considered getting through the day such a big accomplishment? It had been for so long and, in her mind, it always would be.

He tilted his head and smiled. 'Isn't there more to life than just getting through the day?'

She looked away. She wouldn't say it, but she thought it: *not for me*. Tonight, however, she felt hopeful. Perhaps that would change, after all.

'Yes,' she said, looking at him. 'Of course.'

'Ah, Gino's come out of his kitchen cave,' Bart said. She turned to look.

Instinctively, she thought it was because of her. Surely Mrs Dante had gone into the kitchen and mentioned her being with Bart Stonefield. Gino came out to greet people, and although he worked his way through the restaurant, greeting the locals and the tourists, it looked obvious to Victoria that he was really coming out to see them. Every once in a while, he lifted his eyes from whoever he was speaking to and looked their way.

It gave her a cold feeling. She was still of the belief that no one who knew her history could look at her without some trepidation. Sometimes they looked as though they thought she was capable of suddenly screaming hysterically. The tension was palpable. Surely Bart would realize it, too, before this night was over, and regret ever even thinking about asking her on a date.

Gino paused at their table. He was in his mid-sixties, but his hair, full and thick, had turned into a cloud of white, creating a sharp contrast with his dark complexion and razor-sharp ink-black eyes. He was uncharacteristically slim for a chef. Bart seized on that immediately.

'Your food's fantastic, Gino,' Bart said, 'but obviously you rarely eat it. You haven't gained a pound since my parents first brought me here.'

'It's secretly made not to have calories,' he replied and looked at Victoria. 'And this is our little Victoria Myers. It's good to see you and see how beautiful you have become,' he said.

She felt herself relax. Gino Dante's smile was warm, his eyes full of sincerity. There was none of that hesitation and concern she feared. There were still people who actually stepped back as if she was radioactive.

'Your lasagna is still the best I've eaten,' she replied.

His smile widened. 'I make it only because his father would have the Mafia close me down if I didn't. He's in here, what, once a week?' he asked Bart.

'Sometimes twice,' Bart said, nodding. 'My mother had Gino sign a promise that once he retired from the restaurant, he would become her chef.'

65

'I would. So, are you here for the summer?' he asked Victoria.

'Maybe,' she said.

'My wife tells me you graduated college already. At this rate, I will soon be too old to cook,' he said. 'You kids are growing up so fast. This one used to hide behind his mother when I greeted them,' he said, nodding at Bart. 'That's how shy he was.'

'I still remember you pinching my cheeks. I think you called it a pinch of sugar and not salt.'

Gino laughed. 'I made a tiramisu,' he said. 'I'll send a portion over for you to share. Welcome home,' he told Victoria.

They watched him walk off to greet another table.

'He was always very nice to me, too,' she said. 'I didn't see him the last time I was here. I suppose he came out for you this time more than for me.'

'I doubt any man would come out more for me than you,' Bart said.

Was it possible to blush all over your body? That's the way she felt. One of the side effects of the Incident had been the turning of her into a little girl again in many ways. She had been on the verge of becoming sophisticated, confident, before she was so violently and abruptly sent to the back of the line. It was like learning how to smile and laugh like a woman instead of a girl all over again.

'They're nice to most people. They have three children, two boys and a girl, and none of them have anything to do with the restaurant. My

66

father's always comforting him about it even though Gino doesn't seem that upset.'

'They're all older than we are, right?'

'Yes. I remember Stevie. He was a good basketball player, terrific one-hand set shot from the corner,' Bart said. 'They all worked here when they were in high school, of course, but all three wanted to do other things with their lives. Maria married an executive from NBC television. His family used to come to the Catskills to vacation and that's how they met. I think he produces one of the morning news shows. They live in a fancy part of Manhattan – three kids, all girls. Stevie went to work for Kraft Foods. He's some sort of executive now, in Chicago. His uncle on his mother's side got him the job. He's married with two children, boy and girl, teenagers by now. Their youngest, Mario, was the one with the real wanderlust. He ended up with his own travel agency in Boston. Another uncle helped set him up. I don't think he's married. He was only two years ahead of me.'

She sat there, smiling at him.

'You really do know about everyone here, don't you?'

He shrugged. 'When you're in business here and you've lived here so long and your customers are mainly local people who talk about their families, you like to listen. At least I do. Besides, it's good salesmanship.'

'I don't mean it to sound as if I'm criticizing. I think it's actually very nice. That's what I think is missing in big cities,' she said. 'People live in the same apartment building, even right next to each other, and hardly speak to each other all week, if ever. They certainly don't know much about their lives, their families, unless there's some sort of trouble. I had some classmates who live in the city,' she said. 'I mean, I don't know anything first-hand. What I know, I know from listening to them.'

Now he was smiling with eyes full of delight and desire. 'You're probably more like me than you think – a hometown girl.'

She looked down quickly. If he only knew how trapped she was, she thought. Yes, she was a hometown girl; she wasn't fond of big city life. Maybe he was right; maybe it was the way their nerves formed, their temperaments. For her, though, home was a dark world, forever stained, a world where nightmares flowed freely, where every face was full of pity or even, in many cases, disgust.

Disgust didn't really surprise her as much as it should. There were those who believed in their hearts that bad things happened to people for a good reason, that we were punished on earth for the evil we committed. Another view that led more to disapproval than sympathy was that accidents happened to people who were careless or defiant. If you were scammed, it was because you were too trusting, downright stupid. You were robbed when you were in the wrong place and the wrong time. It was almost as if all the criminals had no-fault insurance.

Sympathy, if you could find it, was as valuable a commodity as gold or diamonds.

Pity was silver, but who really wanted to be pitied?

She recalled one of her grandmother Annie's Old World friends, Tillie Zorankin, a Hungarian woman who lived in Centerville with her unmarried son, Milton, a shy man who was satisfied working as a store clerk in Sanders hardware store for his whole life. If anyone had grown up asexual, it was Milton Zorankin. He looked as if he slept with bolts and washers and had erections dreaming of the perfect electric drill.

Tillie believed in the Evil Eye. She had warned Victoria about it when she was only ten and visiting her grandmother.

'Pride,' she said. 'Pride and joy are dangerous. You don't show what precious things you have and you don't brag. He's watching, waiting to pounce.'

'Who?'

'The devil, that's who. Mind my words,' she warned, waving her skinny, bony right forefinger at her. Her skin had a yellowish tint and her fingernail was blackened by the skin that faded beneath it. 'You be modest and humble. He hears the compliments and sees how you take them? Listen to me.'

She looked at her grandmother who shook her head.

'She believes in vampires, too,' she said, laughing.

'I've seen them,' Tillie declared, her eyes wide. 'In the old country.'

Victoria was actually more frightened of her than she thought she would be of a vampire. How many times had she thought about that day, those warnings, since?

'You all right?' Bart asked, reaching across the table to touch her hand.

'What? Yes. Sorry.' She smiled. 'You get me thinking deeply.'

'Is that good or bad?'

'I want it to be good,' she said. It was about as close as she had come to indicating interest in any boy or man since. His smile seemed to explode on his face. He was still touching her hand. She glanced at it, but she didn't move. When the waitress brought the tiramisu, he lifted his fingers away.

'OK, we're in for it. Those delicious calories. Coffee? They make a great cappuccino.'

'Yes, thank you.'

He ordered and then sat back. 'Go on. I know you're dying to take the first spoonful.'

She did.

'So good it's a sin, huh?' he asked.

She laughed, more to herself.

'What?'

'I was thinking about my father's expression every time someone says something my father has is good.'

'What?'

'Beats a stick in the eye.'

Bart laughed, leaned forward and took a spoonful. He stared at her for a moment, a moment too long and too intensely. He moved his eyes as if he was searching every pore on her face and his lips drifted into a soft smile.

'My turn to ask what you're thinking?' she said.

'It's good to see you happy, Victoria,' he said. 'Whenever I have seen you smile, like that time once when I saw you at the Down Under, you were smiling, but it didn't seem real. It was like you were putting on the smile mask because it was expected.'

'It was. And now?'

'This is real,' he said.

'Are you so sure?'

'Yes, and I like it. Very much.'

She was tired of blushing, tired of avoiding eyes, tired of retreating into some protective shell. Yes, it was taking a chance. Yes, she could be hurt so deeply and so severely that spinsterhood would become something to cherish. Every time since, when she had a sexual feeling or a romantic notion, she had clamped down on it and retreated either to her school work or some other distraction. If nothing worked, she went to sleep. She slept a great deal in the months afterward. The therapy was really just beginning, but she didn't trust it – or anything else, for that matter.

After her physical recuperation and once she had begun her therapy, she tried to fan her rage. Anger was at least an indication you were still alive. Jena was good at helping her do this. Jena would let her go into her rants, dreaming up her vengeance and punishments that were more in the line of torture than anything else. From castration to driving nails into their temples, she designed excruciating medieval penalties for the violators. It seemed to satisfy her more. Victoria began to wonder if Jena wanted revenge on all men because she had yet to have any give her the time of day.

'Maybe I'm finally relaxing,' she offered. 'Maybe it's finally sunk in that I have no term papers to write or tests to study for.'

'I was hoping *I* had something to do with it,' he said. His smile seemed to tremble on his lips.

'A little,' she said coquettishly. She hadn't flirted like this for so long that it felt as if she was doing it for the first time. His smile strengthened and widened.

'Well, I'll just keep working at it until a little becomes a lot,' he replied. 'Will that be all right?'

'Yes,' she said. She wondered if she would say yes to a marriage proposal with any more enthusiasm, whether it came from him or anyone.

'Did I mention that I have a boat on Echo Lake?'

'No.'

'It's nothing like a yacht or anything. It's a nice-size motorboat. We can go on a picnic on the water tomorrow. The weather report is very good, and service at the dealership is closed on weekends so I'm off. We can swim and I'll show you how to run the boat. Would you like to do that?' he followed when she didn't say anything.

The reason she hesitated was that it had suddenly occurred to her that she didn't have a bathing suit. Mindy Fein had invited her to their family pool twice after the Incident, but she had declined each time and after that because she didn't feel the invite was sincere. It was probably given at her mother's suggestion. *Take pity on the girl.* Mindy stopped inviting her. Her parents never went to any lake to swim, and although Jena hinted at it a few times during the summers that followed, Victoria never wanted to go. The truth was she hadn't gone swimming since that night. How foolish to assign any blame to that, but everything surrounding that day took on new meaning, brought a new feeling. She never traveled that path. She even avoided looking at the Millers' house.

How would she tell him she had no bathing suit?

'What time?'

'Is ten too early?'

She held her breath a moment. There was no way to get around it.

'I need a new bathing suit,' she said. 'I've been meaning to get to it, but . . .'

'Oh, no problem. I'll take you shopping and then we'll go from there. Where would you like to shop for one?'

The offer nearly took her breath away. She couldn't remember her father taking her to buy any clothes, much less a bathing suit. She never went shopping for her things with anyone but her mother. She never went with girlfriends, not even Jena, and her excursions in New York City were almost always alone.

'Will that be all right?' he pursued.

She was fumbling for the right words. She didn't want to sound dumb or unsophisticated about it, but she couldn't help feeling as if she would be doing something promiscuous.

'I know in some Middle Eastern countries you

have to get married after doing something like that,' he continued, 'but . . .'

'I'll take the chance,' she offered as a reply. He laughed.

'Then ten o'clock it is,' he said.

She sipped her coffee. It was so rare for her to be anywhere with anyone and wish it would last longer. She glanced at her watch and then looked at people who were leaving.

'It's a little early,' he said. 'To take you home, that is.'

Despite how she was feeling about him, she sensed a tightening in her body, a tightening she hated. What did that mean? *It's a little early to take you home.* Was he going to suggest his apartment? What would she say?

'I have a great idea. I'd like to show you something at the store.'

'Store? What store?'

He laughed. 'I'm like my father. I call the dealership a store. We just got this lovely Corvette. I'll hate to see it sold, but Ted Cross ordered it. He owns Cross Supermarkets. It's really a sweet-looking car.'

'Your store is still open?'

'No, but Dad trusts me with the keys,' he said with a wide grin.

'OK.'

She wasn't really into cars, but showing interest in things someone you liked enjoyed was probably a good idea. That was something she could truly say her parents had: they always took interest in what excited the other.

Mrs Dante thanked them and wished them well

74

as they left the restaurant. Her gaze was clearly fixed on Victoria, those silvery gray eyes like the eyes of a fortune teller holding back on what she really saw. Victoria wondered if that was something she imagined or if she had become super-perceptive.

Both she and Bart seemed to be afraid to start talking after they left the restaurant. She knew she was churning over possible things to say, including *Thank you for dinner*. It was the proper thing to say, of course, but tonight that seemed to have a finality associated with it or a formality she was trying to avoid. She reviewed her behavior, what she had said, not only to him but to the Dantes, scrutinizing it all as if it had been a one-act play and she was reviewing it for a romance magazine.

Just like in a play or a movie, after they had gotten into Bart's car and started away, they began to talk simultaneously, both beginning with that *Thank you*. They laughed.

'Go on,' he said. 'Sorry.'

'I was only going to say thank you for dinner. What was your thank you?'

'Thank you for coming to dinner. I've been in that place dozens of times, as you heard, but this time everything was really great.' He turned to her. 'It's definitely the company I was keeping.'

'You're going to have me saying thank you so much that I'll start sounding like that doll my parents gave me when I was five. You know, the one with a string you pull to make it say "I'm hungry". Then you'd take the toy baby bottle and start feeding it. I still have the doll and it still works.'

'Don't psyche me out by telling me you still feed it,' he joked.

'No, but I do look at it occasionally and wish I was five again,' she said, sounding her first deep note of sadness, a note that could quickly bring the conversation to the Incident and its aftermath. She held her breath, expecting him to say something about it.

'Believe it or not, I often wish I was five again,' he said instead. 'I miss being irresponsible.'

'Irresponsible?'

'Seriously. My father loaded me up with all these responsibilities just when I was ready to be reckless, wasteful and selfish.'

'Uneasy lies the head that wears the crown,' she said.

'I've heard that, but I don't know where it's from. Sounds like Shakespeare, right?'

'*Henry the Fourth, Part Two*,' she said. 'He's complaining about the weight of his responsibilities. A king is envious of lower mortals who can sleep free of worry.'

'That's for sure. Not that I'm a king, but my mechanics worry only about the car they're working on. When they're done, they're done, whereas my work's really just beginning. My father's a tough boss, too. I've got to be up on every detail in that shop. He'll challenge my purchase of a new wrench. Was it the best quality for the best price? Did we really need it? Stuff like that. But I'm not complaining. I mean, I am, but I'm not. Know what I mean?'

76

'Yes,' she said, laughing. 'Believe it or not, I do.'

He looked at her. 'I believe it.'

She remembered something Dr Thornton had once said. 'We all live in the gray area when we finally take control of ourselves,' she told Bart. 'Nothing's simply black or white anymore. You're constantly questioning what you say, where you go and what you do.'

'Yes. That's true.'

'The hope is you'll be satisfied with your choices – at least enough to live with them,' she said, again regretting the philosophical, somewhat mournful note.

He was quiet, too long for comfort.

'Sorry,' she said. 'I tend to get a little heavy.'

'You look absolutely perfect to me,' he said.

'No, I mean . . .'

She saw his wide grin and nodded. 'Serves me right.' She wanted to add that she was out of practice, but the truth was she was never *in* practice. This was the longest she had been alone in a man's company, not counting doctors or college teachers who held private conferences.

'So tell me more about yourself,' he said as they drove on.

Was this it? What she was waiting for? Questions about the rape and the aftermath and how she felt about the fact that the rapists had never been caught? How do you live with the violation of yourself, but doubly so, having no closure?

How would anyone know what that was like unless she had experienced it? How many times had she looked at a boy, a man, and wondered,

77

Were you the one? Are you looking at me now with some smug satisfaction, enjoying the fact that I don't know it was you?

It could have been any of them. All she knew was it had to be at least two. It didn't have to have been two local men, of course, but she had that sense, that intuitive feeling that it was. Maybe it was someone who had influence with the police and got away with it. Maybe someone was paid off. Of course, they might not be living here anymore. Maybe they left before they could be caught. There were so many maybes that nothing seemed too far-fetched.

Her silence was unnerving, but with a simple question he had sent her reeling back.

'What movies have you seen and liked?' he prompted. 'What's your favorite song these days? What's your favorite color? Where would you like to go on your dream vacation?' He fired questions at her like someone who was quickly trying to wipe up what he had spilled.

She relaxed.

'What do I get if I answer everything?'

'My lifelong gratitude,' he replied.

She was quiet.

'Isn't that enough?' he asked.

'If I tell you everything about myself in five minutes, you'll have nothing to look forward to,' she replied. She thought that was a very good answer and before he could respond, she congratulated herself.

Maybe I'm coming back, she thought.

Maybe I'll be Mrs Lazarus.

His response was pretty quick and sharp, too.

78

'Oh, I think I'll have something to look forward to every moment I'm with you, Victoria Myers.'

His words – the way he said them, the look in his face – warmed her in places she had long since thought had retreated deeply into her bones, those dead places that in the early days seemed to spread and seep into her. She feared she was turning into a shadow or at least no longer casting one. How many times back then did she look to be sure?

They didn't simply steal my virginity, she thought. *They stole my identity, my sense of self. They drained my ego and turned the day into a duller form of night, a form of it without stars.*

A short while later, they turned into his family's car dealership and garage. He drove around to a side entrance and parked.

'You're the first girl I've ever taken to this door,' he said.

'How many girls have you brought here on a date to see cars?' she countered.

He thought a moment. 'None,' he said. Then he nodded and turned off the engine. 'This is getting serious.'

She had to laugh, expecting him to laugh as well. But he didn't.

He got out and opened the car door for her. Then he took out his keys, unlocked the side entrance and flipped on some lights.

'Get ready to see the only competition you have,' he said, taking her hand.

He turned on another light and the showroom lit up. The red Corvette was center stage.

'We've got three days with it. He's away, so we figured we'd show it off and maybe draw in another customer or two,' he explained and then started around the car.

'It is beautiful.'

'Only solid colors are out this year. See the blacked-out grille and ribbed chrome rocker panel molding? It has an electric clock, dual exhaust, tachometer, seat belts, heater and defroster all standard,' he recited.

'I think you should be in sales, not service,' she said.

He paused and looked at her. 'I have to start doing all of it. I have to . . .'

He paused when another light went on. She saw the shocked look on his face and turned.

John Stonefield stepped into his office doorway. He looked as if he was finishing buttoning his shirt. At six feet two with broad shoulders and a full head of thick, dark brown hair, he looked more like Bart's older brother than his father. It was easy to see that Bart had inherited his striking movie-star facial features.

'What the hell are you doing?' his father demanded.

'Huh? I . . .' Bart looked at her and then back at his father. 'I just wanted to show Victoria the Corvette. Why are you here, Dad?'

'I had some work to catch up on,' he said. 'Finish up and get those lights off before we attract some worthless gawkers banging on the doors.'

'I didn't see your car in your parking spot,' Bart said.

'Parked behind the place. I didn't want to attract

anyone. Like I said. Next thing you know, some cops will be coming around to check.'

He looked behind him and then out at them again.

'Victoria,' he repeated as her name sunk in. 'Victoria Myers?'

'That's right.'

So his parents didn't know he was taking her out, she instantly thought.

'Oh. Well, finish up showing her the car,' he said and stepped back into his office, closing the door.

Bart looked at her, obviously very embarrassed. 'Sorry,' he said. 'I'll take you for a ride in one of these sometime,' he added quickly and hurried back to her side.

She said nothing.

He turned off the lights and walked her to the side door, flipping off those lights as well.

When they got back into his car, he just sat there.

'I didn't get you into any trouble, did I?' she asked.

He looked at her and then, without speaking, started the engine and backed up. Instead of driving off the property, though, he went behind and stopped.

His headlights revealed two cars.

He put his into reverse and turned around. Then he drove off quickly.

'Bart?' she asked as he drove faster. He took a deep breath and slowed.

'That other car is Shirley Barbara's,' he said. 'She's our bookkeeper.'

'Oh. Then maybe he is catching up on work,' she offered.

He looked at her. In the gleam of a streetlight, she caught the expression on his face. It was soaked in pain, the sort of pain someone would express if he or she had just stubbed a toe.

'Yeah, right,' he said. 'He's just catching up on work.'

He seemed to fall back into a coffin full of dire thoughts. He took deep breaths.

'I'm sorry, Bart,' she said. She nearly bit her tongue for saying it. There was no way to pretend. Bart's father was having an affair with his bookkeeper.

He looked at her and she held her breath, but then he slowed down and pulled up on the side of the road. He put the car in neutral and just sat there, staring at the steering wheel.

'I always suspected something,' he said. 'I don't know how long it's been going on, but it's been going on a while.'

'Does your mother have any idea?'

He thought a moment and then shook his head. 'I doubt it. With Florence Stonefield, you never know, though. I'm sure things will change between my father and me. There was always a little strain, but this is like a rupture.' He took a deep breath. 'It's all right. I'm a big boy now,' he said.

'It's never all right,' she said. She put her hand on his arm and he turned to her.

Maybe it was a cry for sympathy or the need to feel safe and secure, but he leaned forward and kissed her softly, and then, when she returned

82

the kiss, it was as if they were both lost and suddenly found. He kissed her harder, more passionately, and she welcomed it. His lips were all over her face, her neck and then back to her lips again.

The bright headlights of an oncoming car caught them in the windshield. He pulled back.

'Not the best place to park and neck like teenagers.'

'It's all right,' she said. She wanted to say they could find a better place, but she didn't.

She saw his smile. Then she leaned back in her seat and he shifted to drive away.

'So, more important. What did you think of the car?'

She laughed. 'Stunning,' she said.

'Yeah, stunning. Good word. Maybe hanging around with you, I can get credit for that class of your mother's I quit in the middle.'

'You still have to write that paper on *Huck Finn*,' she replied, eager to get back to the lightness they had been enjoying.

'Only with your help,' he said.

He drove her directly home, describing his aborted college days. If he had been afraid of silence between them earlier, he was absolutely terrified of it now. He talked just as much for himself as her, she thought. Before they reached her house, he talked about picking her up to shop for the bathing suit and then the boat and the lake.

When they pulled into the driveway, he got out quickly and hurried around to escort her to the front door.

'I had a good time,' she said before he could ask. 'I mean it.'

'I know. Same here. I'm going to make sure you have plenty of those,' he said.

She smiled and then he kissed her, softly, but still full of uncertainty. He held his face inches from hers, waiting to see her response.

She put her right hand on his waist and her left on his shoulder as if she was having dance lessons and they were about to do the foxtrot.

He brought his lips back to hers. The kiss was longer, stronger, reaching deeper.

It was the goodnight kiss she feared she would never have, the kiss she had dreamed about the night before she had gone to the lake. It was a dream lost.

And found.

'Night,' he whispered. 'See you at ten.'

'Night,' she said. She turned to the door. Her fingers were trembling on the handle. He seemed to sense it and reached past her to open it for her.

She didn't look back.

She was afraid she would turn to a pillar of salt.

Five

Every time Marvin Hacker had seen Victoria after that night, he experienced a myriad of feelings. The strongest was fear. There was always that lingering nervousness he hated to recognize in himself. He was the bravest, the most defiant and toughest son of a bitch in his whole class, wasn't he? His twin, Louis, resembled him, but was always weaker, meeker. Marvin could get him to do anything he wanted, but Louis whined a lot. There were times Marvin thought Louis would give away the whole thing. He was glad when Louis went into the army and, although he'd never say it aloud, relieved when Louis was killed in Vietnam.

To fight his fear, he would sometimes look directly at her and smile. Her gaze always shifted away quickly. It used to bother him, but then, in his senior year, he liked how he could frighten her. Even if she knew, she would never say, he thought. Under that basic worry lay his pride, his power. That was a feeling he would never surrender. It felt good to do what he wanted; it always did. Guilt was no competition. Maybe he didn't have a conscience. His mother often told him that.

'You're just like your father,' she'd say. 'When you do somethin' wrong, the only regret you have is that you didn't do it enough. Thank God Louis is not like either of you,' she'd often add. She babied Louis more. Marvin toughened him up or tried to, but what difference did it make now?

He still found her attractive, of course – cute in those days. He was amused at the way some of the guys thought of her as 'spoiled' or something. Of course, Bart Stonefield wouldn't so much as share air in the same room with her. For that matter, he wouldn't share it with him or

Louis anymore if he could. *Fuck him*, he thought. *Who needs him?*

He often thought while he was still in high school that he would love another taste of her. He wondered if it would be different, better – less frenzied, of course – but he put his lust into other girls. Why tempt the fates and bring trouble? But he always told himself that he could do it if he wanted to do it. He liked to strut. He didn't have a chip on his shoulder so much as he had epaulettes declaring him in charge.

When she had left to go to college, Marvin thought she had left for good. She'd meet some college guy and get married and move away, just like most of the well-to-do girls he knew from school. He had hardly seen her during the past four years – maybe only two or three times – but each time he had to look twice to be sure it was she. He didn't keep track of her. Of course, he knew when she had graduated high school, but he was smart enough not to ask anyone too much about her. What he knew about her, he had overheard. For quite a while afterward, she was often a topic of someone's conversation. Thanks to him, she was famous. Well, not just him, but it had been his idea.

It was almost six years to the day.

He didn't do anything to mark any anniversaries, of course, but, hell, he couldn't just look at a calendar and not realize what the date meant. Why, he would bet anyone that he remembered it just as much as she did. She, of course, would wish she could forget.

Marvin had seen her in South Fallsbugh the day after she had returned from college. He knew

86

she had to have graduated. He saw she had a new car, bought at Stonefield's. The plate frame advertised it.

'Son of a bitch,' he muttered. Did Bart make the sale? It's like water off a duck's back with these guys.

He seriously considered asking her out on a date. What a cool thing that would be!

He fantasized.

Maybe he would get her drunk; maybe he wouldn't need to. Whatever, when he screwed her, would her eyes suddenly pop open with the realization? He liked to think he had a unique dick, that there was something special about him that women appreciate. He knew how to get their rocks off, get them screaming for mercy. He had staying power. He heard he'd been nicknamed *The Drill*. Whether it was true or not, he loved it. Girls warned each other, 'Don't go out with him unless you want to be sore for weeks.'

Yeah, there she would be beneath him, maybe in the van or maybe at his place, and suddenly she would scream, 'It was you!'

'Me?' he'd claim, looking baby innocent. 'I don't need to force myself on any girl. Girls force themselves on me. If anyone in this place has been raped, it's me.'

'No, it was you,' she'd say. 'I couldn't forget *The Drill*.'

Oh, what the hell. Why deny it now? It's years later. Who gives a shit?

Yes, there she was coming out of that drugstore in South Fallsburgh, looking more grown-up than most girls her age. She was always cute, but now she was pretty. She looked like a woman and so different that he had to take a second and even third look. She was walking along, waiting to cross the street. He pulled over and watched her in his rearview mirror, and then he made a U-turn and followed her to her new car. He thought she might have glanced at him before she got in, but he couldn't be sure. She didn't look as if anything had frightened her, but, then again, how could simply seeing him frighten her? Or even talking to him?

For fun, he waited for her to start her car and drive away. It gave him a charge, so he turned around again and followed her. When she turned at Old Falls, he knew she was going home. He should have gone home, too, and left well enough alone, but he didn't. He continued to follow her. He liked toying with her. With all the time that had passed, he felt quite safe. Maybe it was past some statute of limitations anyway. One thing for sure, the police had long given up on solving it.

He saw her glance in her rearview mirror and wondered if she realized it was him. She knew he didn't live in her town. Maybe she was wondering if he was following her. She didn't speed up and he didn't pass her. He really did like teasing her. What would it be like now, he wondered, now that she was a woman? Surely, she'd got laid many times in college. That's what he had heard about college girls – loose, often drunk, in orgies, as wild as the boys. Those sororities were just clubs for girls to find new boyfriends.

That's what he'd been told. It almost made him wish he had gone to college, but, then again, what for? He could get plenty here always. Maybe they were occasionally girls you'd like to put a paper bag over their heads, but in the dark all cats were the same, weren't they?

She looked a little freaked when he turned along with her at the main cross street in Centerville a good ten minutes later. And when they left the village and headed toward Sandburg, she did speed up. He deliberately didn't, but he stayed on her tail.

I don't have to go faster to keep up with you, he thought. *I know where you live; I always knew where you lived, even before that night.*

How would he do it now? He would be alone, of course; he didn't need any help. Things would be different. What about crawling through her bedroom window late at night? He'd take off his clothes first. He could move like a snake if he had to. He'd slip in beside her naked and hold his new hunting knife to her throat and whisper, 'Scream and I'll kill your parents, too.' Shit, she'd give right in. Then he'd go at her, softly at first. No sense in making noise. He'd keep one hand over her mouth and then, there he was, *The Drill*. Sometime along the way, he envisioned her closing her eyes and enjoying it. She might even think she was lucky.

'Bet you never thought it could be like this. I got your sweet spot,' he'd say.

She wouldn't speak. She didn't have to.

'Oh, you're so much better,' he would say. 'Grown-up girls are definitely better, but then we didn't think you were a virgin. You sure weren't acting like a virgin. The way you stood out there in the street, not caring who was watching you. It was what we called a *fuckin' invitation.*'

He couldn't laugh too loudly. He might wake her parents and that would be nasty, very nasty.

When he was done, he would turn her over on her stomach and just lie there beside her, stroking her ass, calming her down.

'Go to sleep,' he might say. 'If you're good, I won't come back. Tonight.' He might even stay right there until he was sure she had fallen asleep or at least pretended she had. Then he'd slip out the window as quietly and gracefully as he had come in.

He'd scoop up his clothes and put them on a little ways from the house. He knew exactly where: behind an old oak tree. He knew everything about that house and those grounds. He might even have a cigarette before going home. He would be that confident. Why, she wouldn't even report it in the morning. And if she saw him somewhere days afterward, she would look away. Of course, he would smile. He might even be polite and make sure to say hello. 'How are you?'

He'd force her to look at him.

'Fine, thank you,' she would reply.

The fantasy was getting him so excited that it was becoming uncomfortable. The drill was demanding more room. He loosened his pants and unzipped his fly. A little relief, but no satisfaction.

He slowed up and when he saw her turn up the road to her house, he pulled over. He wanted to jerk off, but the heavy traffic kept him from doing it. People were looking at him, wondering why he was just sitting there. Frustrated, he made a sharp U-turn and sped off. He didn't calm down for miles and until he had to slow for traffic. Then he took deep breaths and sat back.

He wondered how long she would be here. Was she home for good? If she was, he would revisit that pussy. Then he realized he was acting nuts, pursuing her like this. Someone might spot him or she might even pull over and ask him why he was following her? One question could lead to another. Why put himself in this sort of danger?

What the hell was it about that girl that made him crazy? Why couldn't he just forget it all as he had for so long? Why the hell did she have to come back here anyway? Whatever happened would be her fault now.

Unexpectedly, he grew sullen. There was something about her that made him feel inferior. That was it. She was still too damn smug. She should look mousey, timid, unattractive. She was looking too damn good. She looked as if she had left him so far in the past that he was non-existent. He had no effect on her life after all. It was as if he was the one who had been violated.

For the longest time – years, in fact – he had felt powerful. Now he felt weak, and if there was one thing he didn't like, it was being put down by any girl.

This isn't over, he thought. Not by a long shot. *Maybe I'll make it a regular thing. Every five years or so, I'll be at her. We'll have an anniversary.*

He laughed and felt better.

Enjoy yourself while you can, he thought. *I'm coming back, sweetie pie, coming back for another taste and another and another.*

He turned on the radio and started to sing along until he made the turn toward his home and a flood of bad memories from those high school days came rushing back like a wave crashing over him. There were so many nasty things in that water. His miserable home life, the way his father treated him, diminished him with his wise-cracks. Even his mother didn't come to his defense. And being poor, having to shoplift to get the stuff others got easily. Then there was his brother's death, his mother's bitterness. And forget about thinking it was all in the way of punishment for evil acts. Except for Louis' death, much of it had happened before he was ten, for Christ's sake.

When he thought about it now, he concluded that he was just getting even with an unfair world. Why wasn't he dealt some of those free passes? Why did he have to work twice as hard as some of his classmates, the ones from the well-to-do families? What he did didn't stop the unfairness, but at least it made him feel better about himself. 'Hurt me, I'll hurt you,' he said out loud to no one in particular.

Or maybe God.

All his life, people were waving God at him like some sort of threatening whip, especially his mother. But he didn't fear God. There were too many so-called good people who had terrible things happen to them, like Dr Fairmont and his wife who were killed in a head-on two years ago on the Olympic Hill. He was minutes behind that accident and gaped at the sight. Both had hit the windshield so hard that it sent spidery cracks through it. If such a thing could happen to someone who helped people, saved them, what the hell?

He saw no good and evil.

There's just me and you, he thought, *and fuck yer, whenever I can.*

He laughed until he was in his driveway and had turned off the engine.

Then he looked at his life looming in front of him. He'd never be rich. The girls he went with weren't the sort that would make a good home for him and his kids. He couldn't even imagine kids now. He drove a crap car, lived in an old house and didn't have any real friends, no one really to depend on. Shit, now that he gave it some thought, what did he have to look forward to? He felt like punching someone in the face. Maybe he would tonight. Maybe he'd get good and drunk and do just that.

Got to celebrate somehow, he thought.

She's back.

And she looks better than ever.

Probably thanks to me.

After all, I opened her like a buried treasure.

Me.

The Drill.

He stepped out and walked into a shadow as if that was truly where he lived.

Six

Although the details of the Incident became painful to recall even with the passage of time, Victoria often vividly remembered every moment of the morning after. She never stopped questioning herself. Could she have done more to help solve it? Was it the fault of lazy, indifferent police or did she just want to forget so much that capturing the villains wasn't as important? How terrible would that be?

She was still in the hospital the day after, of course. Sometimes the scene would flash in her mind like the scene of a movie she knew she would never forget. There were other post-Incident scenes. For a long while, they would recur just before she fell asleep. It was why she hated going to sleep, being mentally unoccupied, even for a few minutes.

She was back there again.

'Lieutenant Marcus,' the policewoman had said when she introduced herself, and then quickly had changed it to Patty Marcus. 'I'm with the state police. Your local police department has asked us to step in and help with the investigation,' she added, emphasizing *local* as if it was derogatory.

Victoria's eyes were barely open. It felt better to keep them nearly shut when she was awake. Her bed had been tilted up the way it was when she ate the little she ate. Now she was dozing in and out. She had been in the hospital less than twenty-four hours, although she had no sense of time then. She wasn't even sure whether it was morning or afternoon. The tray of food beside her, however, told her she had been served lunch.

Her body still ached, but they had cut back on pain medicine. She wasn't aware that the main reason was so she could talk to this policewoman, who stood there with a clipboard in her right hand, held against the side of her body, looking more like a basketball or baseball coach. She reached for the chair nearby and brought it closer to the bed.

'I'm going to need you to tell me everything you remember, every detail no matter how small or insignificant you might think it is. Understand?' she asked. Without waiting for a response, she took a pen out of her breast pocket and rested the clipboard in her lap. 'Let's confirm some basic stuff first,' she continued. 'Your name is Victoria Myers and you're fifteen years old. Your birthdate is April seventh, 1947, and you currently reside at twelve Wildwood Drive, correct?'

Victoria stared at her. She was intrigued with the light but visible hair over her lip. Granted, it looked like peach fuzz, but why would a woman want it visible at all? Maybe it was the medication she was on, but suddenly she could see the smallest details in everything. It reminded her of Gulliver in that part of *Gulliver's Travels* when he was in Brobdingnag and he was the tiny one. All the imperfections in the giant people's faces were exaggerated. Skin pores look like deep holes and nostrils like caverns.

'Correct?' Lieutenant Marcus said, a little louder.

'Yes,' Victoria said, both happy and surprised at the sound of her own voice. She thought she had lost it.

'I know it's early on here, but we find it's best to interview victims as close to the event as possible. So . . .' Lieutenant Marcus improved her posture as though that really mattered now or as though she was preparing to go on some sort of fast ride, like a test pilot. 'You were walking home through the wooded area because . . .'

She waited.

Oh. I'm going to finish sentences, Victoria thought. *It's like a game.* 'It's a shortcut from the center of the village to my house,' she recited.

'OK. About what time was this? When you started out for home from the village, that is.'

'It was just a little past ten thirty. I have to be home by eleven.'

'And who were you with just before you left the village?'

Now she was going to get someone else in trouble, she thought, but she had a feeling that this policewoman knew the answers to the questions she was asking.

'Wayne Gerson and Tommy Marks. They go to my school. They gave me a lift from Sandburg Lake.'

'To the village?'

'Yes.'

She stared at Victoria a moment. 'Did you ask them to take you home?'

96

'No.'

'Did they know you were going home?'

She thought about it. 'I don't know.'

'Let's talk about the time you were at the lake. Were you with friends?'

'Yes.'

'And they were?'

'Mindy Fein, Jena Daniels and Toby Weintraub,' she recited. 'Mindy and Jena are in my class. Toby's a senior.'

Lieutenant Marcus looked as if she was checking things off.

'Now, at the lake, did you tell anyone about your shortcut home?'

'No.'

'Did Mindy, Jena or Toby know that was how you would go home?'

'Jena and Mindy knew I take the shortcut, but . . .'

'But?'

'Mindy disappeared with someone at the lake and Jena . . .'

'Drank too much and fell asleep?'

'Yes,' she said. She obviously knew that, Victoria thought, so why deny it?

'Did this Wayne and Tommy know that was your route home?'

'I don't know. I don't think so.'

'If you were worried about getting home on time, why didn't you ask them to take you?'

'They were interested in being in the village. I didn't have a chance to ask them,' she said. She didn't want to say that they were looking for someone to buy them more beer since they were

97

underage, but maybe Lieutenant Marcus already knew that, too?

Lieutenant Marcus had the sort of face that seemed devoid of expression most of the time. She couldn't tell if the policewoman was doubting her or thinking or what.

'Did they drink too much, too?'

'I don't know,' she said. She really didn't know what was too much.

'Did you? You drank at the lake,' she quickly added.

'I wasn't drunk when I started for home.'

'Have you been drunk?'

'No.'

'So how do you know you weren't?'

'I don't know.'

'Do you think it's possible you told the boys you were going to take the shortcut but forgot? Do you think you might have told someone at the lake but forgot?'

'No.'

Lieutenant Marcus looked down at her clipboard. 'OK, so you started out for home from the village. How do you get on to the path in the woods?'

She described the alleyway between Kayfield's and Trustman's and the turn where the path began.

'Did you look back before you were completely through the alleyway?'

'No.'

'Did you see anyone watching you go into the alleyway?'

'I don't think so. I mean, boys looked at me

when I got out of the truck, but I can't remember if any were still watching me.'

'How long were you in the village after you got out of the truck?'

'Just long enough to put my clothes on.'

'Clothes on?'

'I mean over my bathing suit.'

'Why didn't you put your clothes on before you got into the truck?'

'I was . . . just thinking about going home.'

'Were you running away from something or someone?'

'I was with someone but I didn't want to be with him anymore,' she said. 'Yes.'

This time Lieutenant Marcus's look was sharper. Although she showed little evidence of it, Victoria's replies were beginning to pique the Lieutenant's interest.

'Tell me what you remember about who you were with,' she said and sat back again.

'He's a city boy. From the Bronx. His friends called him Spike. We saw them in the village before we went to the lake and then they came to us at the lake.'

'Did he give you something to drink?'

'Yes.'

'All right. Describe him.'

'Describe him?'

'Tall, short, heavy, thin – what?'

'He was quite a bit taller than I am.'

Lieutenant Marcus looked at her clipboard. 'You're five six. So he was a little over six feet?'

'I guess.'

'Go on. Do you remember his eye color, hair

color, any distinguishing features, scars . . . anything?'

'He had dark hair, more black than brown. His eyes were more like . . . I don't know, gray or something. I remember thinking he looked a lot like Marlon Brando in *Mutiny on the Bounty*.'

Lieutenant Marcus smirked. 'So he wore what? A leather jacket?'

'No, just a black T-shirt and jeans with . . . yes, shoes that looked like boots, you know. Short boots. Oh. He had a watch with a silver band.'

'Did he tell you where he was staying?'

'No. We didn't get to talk that much.'

'But he gave you something to drink and then what?'

'I was getting a little sick and he was . . .'

'Getting too fresh with you?'

'Yes,' she said, grateful for the abstract description.

'So you did what?'

'I ran away from him, but I left my shoes so I had to go back when he wasn't there, and then I hurried to the road, and Wayne and Tommy picked me up.'

'So it's safe to say our Marlon Brando was dissatisfied?'

Victoria looked at her, not knowing how to react or what to say. 'I guess.'

'How many friends were with him?'

'A few – three, I think.'

'You said your friend Mindy disappeared. Did she go off with one of them?'

'I think so.'

She nodded and wrote on her clipboard. 'Did

you notice if this Spike or one of his friends followed you back to town?'

'No.'

'OK, let's get back to what happened. You got out of the truck, put on your clothes, went through an alley and were on the shortcut in the woods. How long before you realized you weren't alone?'

'A while.'

'The man who found you is Warren Miller. You were close to his house when he found you. About how long do you think it took for you to get there?'

'I don't know. Ten minutes the most, I guess.'

'Do you know Mr Miller?'

'Yes. Everybody knows everybody in Sandburg.'

'Did you hear someone behind you first or in front of you?'

'I don't remember. I heard something on my left, but then it stopped.'

'Did you hear voices?'

'No.'

'Even when you were attacked?'

'No.'

A nurse entered to check her pulse, blood pressure and temperature. She examined some of her bruises. While she did, Lieutenant Marcus stood and went to the doorway. She kept her back to her as if she was unable to watch or thought it was improper to do so.

Victoria noticed how wide her shoulders were and how thick her neck was for a woman. She didn't like her hair. It was cut too sharply behind her head. The uniform she wore looked a size or so too large. It was as if she had to wear a man's uniform because there were none made for women. The pistol on her right side looked awkward, the handle leaning too far away from her body.

When the nurse walked out, Lieutenant Marcus returned to her seat.

'OK. We're coming to the hard part,' she said. It was the first thing she said that indicated she was asking questions that could upset Victoria. Even so, she didn't seem that sensitive about it. It was a matter-of-fact statement. 'But you have to try to do your best. There were no witnesses. You're it,' she added, as though Victoria had been chosen and not been a victim.

Later when she began her therapy with Dr Thornton, the psychologist would tell her that policewoman did more harm than good in the manner in which she pursued the gruesome details. 'It's like scraping at a wound before there's even a scab.'

Victoria came to believe her psychologist was probably right. Lieutenant Marcus pursued each detail like someone trying to squeeze the last drop of juice from an already squeezed orange.

'Go on,' she said, 'tell me how it happened to the best of your recollection.'

She stared at her. She thought she had told someone all of it, but maybe that was a dream. She felt a little trembling in her body.

'Someone grabbed you from behind,' Lieutenant Marcus began, impatient.

Slowly, as if she was looking out from behind a protective wall, Victoria started her description. 'There was a sack dropped over me first and then the rope was tightened around me like a lasso.'

'You didn't raise your arms as soon as you sensed a sack being dropped over you?'

'I don't remember.'

'Was someone holding your arms so you couldn't keep it off?'

'I don't think so.'

'Did you feel someone grab your wrists?'

'I don't think so.'

'Was someone standing in front of you, too?'

'I don't think so. Maybe. Yes.'

'When the sack was brought down, did you try to get it off?'

'Yes.'

'And that was when the rope was tied around your arms. You said *like a lasso*?'

'That's what it felt like.'

'And then?'

'I started to scream and something was tied around my face.'

'Around your mouth?'

'Yes.'

'No one was talking?'

'I don't think so.'

'Think harder. Can you remember a voice, a word?'

'No.'

Lieutenant Marcus shook her head and wrote on her clipboard. 'OK, so then what?'

'I was pulled backwards and fell on my back. Something was sticking out of the ground. The doctor said maybe a rock. It hurt a lot.'

'Could you tell how many were there?'

'No.'

'But two, for sure?'

'I guess.'

'Go on.'

'Someone was undoing the buttons of my shorts. I tried to kick him, but someone grabbed my ankles and then they took off the shorts and the bottom of my bathing suit,' she said. She was talking about it now as if it had happened to someone else.

'When they were undoing your shorts, no one spoke?'

'No.'

'No sounds, no laughter, not even grunts?'

Did she think they were cavemen? Maybe they were. 'I don't remember any,' Victoria said.

'So describe what happened next.'

She started and then she stopped when she realized she was crying. The nurse was back in the doorway.

'Maybe that's enough for now,' the nurse said, stepping forward.

'Wait, one more minute,' Lieutenant Marcus commanded. 'Did you lose consciousness?'

'I guess.'

'The next thing you remember was Mr Miller turning you over?'

'I think so.'

'I do think . . .' the nurse began.

'OK, OK. I'll come back to talk to you – here in the hospital, if you're in much longer, and then when you're home, Victoria. Try to remember more. Every detail is important.'

She stood up. Where was the promise to get them? The vow to bring justice or even a simple 'Feel better'.

Victoria watched her leave.

The nurse fixed her blanket. 'Maybe take a little nap,' she said. 'Doctor Bloom will be here later.'

Victoria closed her eyes reluctantly.

Everyone is afraid of darkness after a terrible thing happens to them. Demons can't live in the sunlight. She heard herself sniffling. Adults could and do have nightmares, of course, but they usually don't wake up crying for their mothers or fathers. She felt thrown back to that. Her life was suddenly going in reverse.

She dozed off, and when she opened her eyes this time, she saw Jena standing there, looking out of the window. She groaned as she turned around and Jena turned to her. She looked almost as miserable as Victoria felt.

'I was sick or I would have come to see you sooner,' she said. 'And I got into trouble.'

Victoria boosted herself up on her elbows and sat back. 'Everybody knows about me, I guess.'

'Oh, absolutely,' Jena said. She went around the bed and sat on the chair Lieutenant Marcus had used. 'Everyone's been calling me. My father's so mad he won't talk to me. Toby didn't want to take me back to the village. She was afraid I would throw up in her car. I got a ride back with Denise Littlefield and her boyfriend, Mark Wheeler. Denise's family lives near us. I mean, we're not really friends, but she saw me and had Mark stop. I don't know what happened. I mean, why I drank so much.'

Victoria stared at her in disbelief. Why was she

talking about herself so much? She wasn't in the hospital; she hadn't been attacked. Apparently, Jena saw what she was thinking.

'I mean, nothing compares with what happened to you. What did the police say?'

'They're investigating,' Victoria said.

'Do you know who did it?'

'No.'

'Not a clue?'

'No.'

Jena nodded. Then she narrowed her eyes and leaned toward her. 'It was one of those city boys for sure.'

'I don't know, Jena. It happened so fast.'

'How? I mean, how could anyone do that to you and you not know who it was?'

As quickly as she could, Victoria summarized what she had told Lieutenant Marcus.

'Did it hurt?' Jena asked, grimacing.

'Are you kidding, Jena? I was attacked. Look where I am!'

'I know, I know. I'm sorry. How could any boy enjoy that anyway?' she asked. Victoria sensed that she was asking her seriously. It was as if she had suddenly become some kind of expert when it came to sexual intercourse. 'I mean, how hard can their thing be?'

'I wasn't exactly taking notes, Jena. I told you. I passed out.'

'And they still did it? How many times? Do the doctors know?'

'No one told me and I didn't ask.'

Jena embraced herself as though the questions had stripped away her clothes and she was hiding her breasts from someone standing on the other side of the hospital bed.

'My mother wondered if you needed stitches down there. She didn't say it to me. I heard her say it to my father.'

'I don't have any stitches. At least, I don't think I do,' Victoria said.

'You'd feel it, wouldn't you?'

'I guess.'

'Did they tear off your top too?'

'Apparently not.'

'Mindy's in trouble, too,' Jena said. 'Her parents found out we all went to the lake and were drinking. I heard more kids are being questioned and more are getting into trouble.'

'And blaming it on me?'

'No,' Jena said, but Victoria could see she wasn't being totally honest. 'How could they blame it on you?' she added. 'You didn't rape yourself.'

'You told them that?'

'Some of them get me so mad.'

Victoria turned away and looked out the window.

'When you're raped, you don't get a sexual feeling, do you?' Jena asked.

Victoria turned on her quickly. 'Someone said I did?'

'No, I'm just asking.'

'Why? Are you planning on getting raped, too?'

'No, silly,' Jena said, smiling. She shifted her eyes and pursed her lips.

She was obviously relieved when a moment

107

later Victoria's parents entered. 'Oh, hi, Mr and Mrs Myers,' Jena said, standing quickly.

Victoria's mother stared at her in amazement. Jena sounded as though nothing was wrong, as though they were meeting anywhere but in a hospital in which Victoria Myers was recuperating from a violent sexual attack.

'I didn't have a chance to get some flowers or candy,' Jena continued, obviously thinking that was what brought on Helen Myers' disapproving look.

'I don't think either of those would do much to detract from the situation, Jena. Have you spoken with the police?'

'Just Mr Siegler,' Jena said. 'I didn't know anything,' she added quickly. 'I wish I did. Honest.'

'I think your mother is waiting for you in the lobby,' Helen Myers said in a dismissive tone.

Jena nodded. 'I hope you get better quickly,' she told Victoria and then headed out.

'That girl's elevator doesn't go to the top floor,' her mother said as soon as Jena was gone.

'She's a very good student, Mom,' Victoria said.

'It will surely surprise many people to hear me say it,' her mother continued, taking the seat, 'but it takes more than just good grades to make you a complete person, especially an adult.'

'She means well,' her father said, stepping up and kissing Victoria on the forehead. He brushed away some strands of hair and smiled. 'How ya doin', Vick?'

'I feel like I'm in a daze. A state policewoman was here.'

'Yes, we saw her earlier,' he said.

She looked at her mother who seemed to be looking right through her.

'I'm sorry,' she said. 'I shouldn't have gone to the lake without telling you or asking your permission.'

Her mother raised her eyes toward the ceiling.

And then Victoria saw the tears streaming down her cheeks and felt herself weaken.

In moments, they were all crying.

Seven

After Bart had driven off, she entered the house on feet of smoke as if she was a child who had violated her curfew and paused like one anticipating the hysterical sound of an alarm going off. However, it was as quiet as a cemetery. Neither the television nor the stereo was on, but lights spilled a stream of pale yellow illumination out of the living room and over the dark gray Berber carpet in the hallway.

She closed the door softly, listening for her mother's or father's voice. She expected her mother would be stepping out to greet her with her standard set of questions, questions designed to determine how close to normal she really was. A real date was a good test. Did they talk much? Was she able to enjoy her dinner or was she too nervous to eat? Was he polite, which was code for did he bring up the Incident? It would be almost as if she was reading off a script Dr Thornton had provided.

One of the reasons Victoria avoided coming home when she was at college was the feeling that she was constantly on stage here, moving from one set piece to another. She knew her paranoia was most likely exaggerated, but she couldn't help feeling as if all conversations paused and everyone's attention, just like an audience's in a theater, was turned toward her the moment she had made an appearance.

Her mother didn't emerge so she walked to the living room and paused in the doorway. Only her father was there, reading a book. He was dressed in his blue robe and pajamas, with his slippers at the side of the recliner her mother had bought him two Christmases ago. It was licorice-black expanded plastic fabric with a tufted back and had a rich and elegant wood trim rubbed to a mellow walnut finish, with padded arms and a hidden footrest. The footrest was up and he was reclined, looking very comfortable. He was in it so often that it bore the imprint of his body. Neither Victoria nor her mother would ever sit in it. Her mother kidded him, calling it his throne. He did look royal when he sat with the back upright and his arms on the sides, a man holding court.

He looked up when he realized she was standing in the doorway looking at him. He closed his book and pulled back the footrest, sitting up in the chair.

'Hey, how was yer date, Vick?' he asked. To her it sounded like *Did the patient live or die?* His face was braced for bad news.

110

'It was nice, Dad,' she said. He widened his eyes, now hungry for the good details. 'The Dantes were happy to see us and the food was very good. I had lasagna. Mr Dante came to our table to talk to us and then treated us to his tiramisu.'

'Crowded?'

'Yes, very busy. I didn't speak to anyone else,' she added, knowing he was wondering how other local people had greeted her.

'Sounds like a very nice dinner. We haven't been there for a spell, but after ya left, yer mother dropped a hint as gently as the bomb on Hiroshima.'

She smiled. For as long as she could remember, she and her father had fun talking about her mother. He was never really critical, no matter what she had said or done, and her mother knew they shared the satire. Victoria believed – hoped – that she secretly enjoyed the attention.

'Afterward, Bart took me to see this new Corvette someone had ordered. It's a beautiful car,' she added. She decided not to mention John Stonefield's surprise appearance.

She hated how she sounded – like a little girl making a report. But then maybe daughters always sound like little girls to their fathers.

He smiled by tucking in the right side of his mouth. 'In ma time a young man would ask a young woman up ta his apartment ta see his new work of art.'

She was surprised at how casually her father referred to a man's apartment. Was he fishing to see if Bart had tried to get her to his? *There I go*

111

again, she thought, *smearing the paranoia around like peanut butter*.

'He thinks of the Corvette as his new art, I guess.'

'That's fer sure. I don't know him that well, but he seems ta have grown inta a very nice young fella.'

She knew he was fishing for more. If the date ended outside their home, it was a failure. Promises about calling soon were just another way to say it didn't work.

'He's asked to take me out on his boat on Echo Lake tomorrow for a picnic.'

'Oh, that'll be nice. I haven't been on that lake fer years.' He thought a moment, changing his smile to a gentler one, a smile of reminiscence. 'I usta take yer mother rowin' when I was first courtin' her. The year before you were born, I took her ta Oxford, England, and we rowed on the Thames. I mean, I rowed while she recited Shakespearean sonnets. She usta read poetry ta me before we went ta sleep, you know.'

'Really?'

'Oh yeah. She coulda been on the radio, don't ya think? She has such a strong voice, perfect enunciation. When she wants ta, she can be very . . . dramatic. Maybe I'll get her ta recite Browning's sonnet forty-three fer us one night.'

'Mom?'

'I know it doesn't seem possible, Vick, but we were young lovers once and she was more romantic than I was. I'd be talkin' P and L statements and the economy, and she would tell me great love stories, myths and otherwise. I think

112

I became her project. She was determined ta put some Casanova in me. The truth was I'd have changed species ta win her. Ya know that sonnet – Browning's forty-three?'

'It's practically in every high school English literature textbook, Dad. "How do I love thee? Let me count the ways."'

'Exactly. Without yer mother, I'd be as excitin' as a snail on the sidewalk.'

'You would not,' I said. 'You know a lot about wine and music, and talking about the economy and politics can be quite interesting, too.'

He laughed. 'Before I met her, I usta cure insomnia with ma conversation,' he insisted.

'Where is Mom?'

'Oh, she was tired and went ta read in bed. She'll probably be asleep with the book in her hands when I go ta the bedroom. I could never fall asleep with the light on,' he added. What he was really revealing was that he volunteered to be the one who would wait up for her. There probably weren't any parents of girls her age who would wait up for them. She was going to be twenty-two years old next birthday.

'I still can't fall asleep without a light on,' she said dolefully.

'Lots of folks can't. My father's mother burned two lamps.'

There was no way he was going to make reference to the Incident, even though before it she had been able to fall asleep without a light on since the age of four.

He looked at her, still smiling, maybe waiting to hear something else, something to keep up that hope he clung to as a passenger off a sinking ship would cling to a piece of drift wood. That's what she had been all these years – adrift.

'It was a very nice evening out, Dad. I like Bart. He's polite and considerate and he's not just about cars.'

'That's great, Vick. There'll be plenty more dates in store, I'm sure. Not necessarily only with Bart Stonefield – not that I don't like him, understand. I mean, once other men see ya out there in the social scene, the phone will ring off the hook and yer dance card will be full.'

'Social scene?' She laughed. She laughed quickly because she was afraid she might start to cry. This was her first date since the prom, which she didn't think of as a date. It had felt more like a doctor's appointment.

'Well, it's not New York, but it's pretty busy up here right now and there are lots of new places fer young people ta enjoy. I think,' he added. 'I'm really glad you had a good time, Vick. You deserve it. You've earned it, graduatin' with such high honors. We're very proud of you. Neither of us says it enough.'

'You don't have to say it, Dad. Anyway, you did – with a car.' She almost added that her car had led Bart to her or her to him.

She went over to him, hugged him, kissed him on the cheek and whispered, 'Good night.'

'Night,' he said. He watched her walk off.

Her parents' bedroom was before hers so she paused and looked in the partly opened doorway. There she was, just as her father had described, asleep with a book lying on her stomach. Her

114

hair was down around her shoulders. In the light, her face looked a little pale, but there was softness in her quiet sleep that reminded Victoria of her years ago, when Victoria was just a little girl. She looked more like the mother who would have no problem hugging and kissing her, comforting her and teaching and laughing with her. As she grew older, her mother seemed to find more distance. It was as if she believed it was necessary in order for her daughter to mature properly and become an adult faster.

She didn't kiss her goodnight as often and shook her head when her father treated her more like a little girl. In fact, she would say, 'Stop treating her like a little girl, Lester. Yer hear?' she would add, mocking his Southern accent.

'Yes, ma'am,' he would say and wink at her.

But as Victoria looked at her now, it suddenly occurred to her that she had never given enough consideration to just how much the Incident had damaged both her parents. She thought only of herself when she thought about the stain, the victim's mark on her. She never considered that even, without her accompanying them, the stain her parents carried as well would bring silence into a noisy room and steal away the attention. She never gave much thought to the idea that they would have a burden to carry as heavy as her own. But it was logical to think that if people pitied her and treated her like a leper, why wouldn't that spread to her parents? No one might come out and say it, but he or she would certainly be thinking, *Oh, you're the parents of that girl who was violently raped in Sandburg, aren't you?*

115

How is she? Did they ever catch the rapists? You must have such a burden.

How did they answer when someone innocuously asked, 'How is your daughter doing?' People asked that of parents whose children were attending college or away from home at a job or even in the services. Did they have to hoist their shoulders protectively to steel themselves in anticipation or search the faces of the inquirer to see if he or she was really thinking about only one thing?

'Oh, she's doing fine,' her mother would probably say. 'She's got an A-plus average and will be graduating with honors. She's in a top college, you know.'

No one could get the best of her mother.

Her father would offer a pleasant, appreciative smile and say she was fine – *Thanks for askin'* – and leave it at that.

Were parents of mentally ill children or parents of children who had committed crimes and sent for some sort of rehabilitation treated much differently?

Funny how she hadn't given this much thought until now. Surely, what had happened to her had caused changes in them, altered the way they saw themselves, too. Before this moment, she hadn't thought of herself as self-centered. She often thought about her parents' welfare, didn't she? Or did she?

Well, whatever, she certainly was thinking about them now. In a strange and yet exciting way, she was coming back to life, coming back in so many ways.

She had Bart Stonefield to thank for that, perhaps.

She started to turn away when her mother opened her eyes and called to her.

'Hi,' she said. 'Didn't mean to wake you, Mom.'

'That's all right. I thought you were standing there,' she said, pushing herself up to a more comfortable position. 'Did you have fun?'

'I did.'

'Good,' she said. Her mother gave her a look that told her she was studying her for the truth.

Victoria rattled off everything she had told her father with just as much enthusiasm. Her mother definitely looked impressed. No, *relieved* was a better description.

'Well, I wasn't kidding him. He showed a lot of potential when he was in my class, as short as that was.'

'He's happy about what he's doing, Mom.'

'Well, I guess that really is the most important thing when you get right down to it.'

'Did you always want to teach?'

'It just seemed to fit who I was, yes.'

'Dad thinks you could have gone into something dramatic, like radio or theater.'

She shook her head. 'He'll never admit it, but he's more of a romantic than I am, and despite his world of numbers and facts, he is more of a fantasizer.'

Could she be right? Victoria wondered. Do you ever really get to know who someone really was, even your own parents? It seemed as if time went by and you grew different eyes, and you peeled away more and more illusion. But didn't we need

117

those illusions? Cold reality brought on cynicism. A world without fantasy was far too black and white. Beautiful things fell back into weaker and weaker memories, including your prettiest features and light laughter. Who'd blame any woman for eventually wanting to live in a house without mirrors?

'Maybe that's a good thing,' she said. Her mother raised her eyebrows.

'Just be careful, Victoria,' her mother said. 'Wishing something or someone to be what you want is OK, but forcing yourself to believe it is another.'

'All right,' she replied.

'I have confidence that you'll know the difference, Victoria.'

'Night,' she said and left quickly. She didn't want to get into that mood of analysis.

Now she was the one creating more distance between them. What was she afraid of? Raw emotions? Honesty? Needing someone?

She stood before her full-length mirror and slowly, almost erotically, began to undress. She imagined her hands were Bart's hands. For the last six years, especially the first two, she was afraid of her sexual feelings. It was a key topic in her therapy. She sensed that girls in her high school had expected her to have that fear, and she knew that most of the boys who might have shown interest in her had hesitated because they had believed she was deeply wounded. They could see it in the way she avoided physical contact, in the way she closed herself up, sometimes looking as if she lived in a cocoon. They had avoided even looking at her. It was part of what made her feel invisible.

To be sure, there were college boys who, not knowing what had happened to her, flirted with her and even tried to date her, but she turned them all away. One of her dorm mates, Denise Samson, told her that everyone thought she was homosexual. But she couldn't change their impressions quickly. She couldn't bring herself to confide in Denise or anyone else at school for that matter and get them to appreciate her emotional struggles. She was afraid of how it would change the way they looked at her. It was easier to let them believe what they wanted to believe, even if they believed she was homo-sexual. Of course, no one could claim she had made any advances, but anyone could imagine it. Thankfully, she wasn't important enough or in any way a threat to them to be the center of their conversations. Eventually, she was just as invisible in college as she had been in high school, but for different reasons.

She might have had a romance, if only she could have permitted herself to take the first step, but despite her therapy and her own desires, she couldn't do it. What was different now? Was it because she was dating someone she once had a crush on, or was it because his dating her gave her the sense that it was over, that she had progressed enough to live a normal life after all? If she could do it here, she could do it anywhere. That's it, she thought. Instinctively, she knew it and thought that was why she had come home.

When she slipped her dress off, she stood there

119

daring to admire her figure. Her curves were natural and her skin soft and firm. She had no doubt that someday she would have to work at keeping this figure, but for now she could match herself against any other young woman Bart Stonefield might feast his eyes on.

She imagined him doing that now. She wasn't facing a mirror; she was facing him. She undid her bra and slipped it off her shoulders and down her arms, holding it against her breasts for a moment and then dropping it to the floor. She straightened her shoulders and lifted her bosom slightly, her nipples now erect with those slightly orange areolas. She closed her eyes and imagined him reaching out to touch and lift her breasts gently, appreciating her, breathless with desire. She pursed her lips and felt his lips just the way she had when he kissed her goodnight.

Then she brought her hands down to her panties and slowly slid them off, stepping out of them gingerly and dropping them beside her bra, stripping off all inhibition as well. Oh, she was ready. How ready she was. He was bursting with passion. He was coming forward again. He would put his hands just beneath her buttocks and lift her gently so he could carry her to the bed. She sprawled back, her head against the pillow, and then, throwing off that chastity belt that the rapist had locked around her that night six years ago, she spread her legs and welcomed Bart Stonefield to enter her and bring her back from the dead.

She was suddenly surprised by the sound of her own moans. It was truly like waking from a dream. For a moment, she was embarrassed and froze. Could either of her parents have heard her? She waited, her heart pounding, and then she got up from her bed quickly and went to the bathroom.

The sight of her flushed face frightened her. She looked back at her bed as if she thought Bart Stonefield might very well be there. She would have preferred that to the realization that she had just masturbated to a fantasy. Yes, fantasies were safer, but she was afraid she could become addicted to them to the point where she wouldn't want really to be with anyone.

Her therapist had once suggested that possibility. It was toward the last year of therapy. She had avoided a discussion about it and Dr Thornton had let it go. She shouldn't have, Victoria thought. She should have forced me to face up to it.

She prepared for bed and then slipped under the thin cover sheet. She still felt too hot even for that, but she also felt like snuggling, embracing her pillow and dreaming about tomorrow.

Would it last?

If she held back or stepped away, would he give up and agree with that part of him that was surely warning him about getting involved with a bird that had a broken wing?

She was determined not to let the doubts keep her awake. Instead, she relived almost every word spoken at dinner and smiled to herself as she remembered how proud he was when he was walking around that Corvette and explaining it to her as if he had built it himself.

Then she thought about his father in that doorway and the expression on Bart's face when they had driven around and saw the bookkeeper's car.

Everyone is broken in one way or another, she thought.

Maybe that was what really attracted him to her.

They were both wounded birds.

Unlike most every morning when she was home and had no college class to rush to, she didn't sleep late. She was up practically at the tip of the sun's head rising over the mountain to the west. She hadn't bothered to close her drapes. Not long after the Incident, her mother had redesigned her bedroom, one of the key new features being the bright pink flower-power vintage pinch-pleat lined drapes. It was as if she hoped to change the face of Victoria's world and sweep away any deep, dark depression. This was now a room that would look happy even on completely overcast days which cast dreary light in vain. She had her carpet changed to the pink looped and her bedspread and pillows matched the drapes. Even the light fixture was updated so it could be brighter. Her mother anticipated that Victoria would spend much more time alone in her room now, and she wanted to make it more difficult for her to fall into gloom and doom.

Maybe it helped. The moment Jena saw her redecorated room, she began to whine about her own and pressured her parents to update her dull cave, as she called it. Victoria was embarrassed whenever she was at Jena's home and she began to complain and compare her bedroom with

Victoria's. She could almost see Jena's mother's thoughts. *You weren't raped. You don't need to be treated like a mental patient.*

Victoria was never happier about the room changes than she was this morning. It really did enhance and complement her mood. She practically leaped out of bed and hurried to get dressed and into the kitchen so she could surprise her parents by making them breakfast, something she hadn't done for years. She wanted the table set and everything going before they opened their eyes. The aroma of the coffee would do that. She tiptoed past their bedroom and worked as if she were in a silent movie.

And when her mother appeared in the kitchen doorway, the expression on her face was worth her effort in spades. It was written clearly on her face.

Her daughter was back.

What had happened couldn't be completely forgotten, but at least it could be put in storage where it could wither into a skeleton and eventually decompose into dust.

Eight

It was raining hard the day she was released from the hospital after the Incident. *How appropriate that it is gray and dreary*, Victoria thought as her father brought his car up to the entrance where she and her mother waited with a nurse. It was

123

hospital rules that she be taken from her room to the door in a wheelchair. The nurse would escort her to the car and then the hospital could wash its hands of her. She was deposited back into the world and her bedding would be stripped away, her charts filed and the memory of her stay washed out with antiseptic cleaning fluid.

More serious patients needed attending: heart attack victims, cancer and stroke sufferers. They were fighting for survival. A teenage girl, sexually abused, would mend. In no time at all, she'd be out on the weekend having pizza and giggling with girlfriends. Those thoughts might just as well have been written on the instructions the hospital provided for care during recovery.

You'll live was written on their faces. *Get over it.*

Physically, she was on the mend. Her traumas were easing and the bruises were fading, but as her parents drove her away from the hospital that day, she felt she was leaving herself behind. The girl who had been brought there was not the girl leaving. Everything she looked at, tasted, smelled, heard and touched was different. Her mother had taught her that everyone sees the world around them differently. The differences could be slight or severe.

'Just look at how some of your friends and parents look at black people,' she pointed out as an illustration. At the time, there were only two in her class. 'This is far from the deep South – no Jim Crow here – but please, the discrimination and prejudice is palpable sometimes. You've invited Nina Williams to our house. Any of your girlfriends invited her?

'People even see shapes differently. Some love arches in their homes; others find that ugly, if not awkward. I've heard people complain about the Marxes' house color. It's too dark brown. On and on. Sometimes it's as if we're all different species.'

She always appreciated these instructive conversations she had with her mother. She thought they gave her an advantage over her girlfriends. Her mother was a college teacher, a woman who had graduated with honors, and someone whom people in high and powerful administrative positions admired or whose opinions they valued. Men didn't like to show their appreciation as obviously, but even when she was only eleven, Victoria could see it in the way they looked at her mother, listened and nodded.

'Your mother is like Eleanor Roosevelt or someone,' Jena once told her. All her girlfriends had agreed.

Is she? Victoria wondered.

'She should run for something,' Mindy said. 'Maybe governor. It's time we had a woman for governor and she could do it.'

This view of her mother as some kind of celebrity had an odd effect on Victoria. It wasn't that she loved her more or less; she found that she was more intimidated by her. Everyone's parents handed down edicts, set out rules and made decisions that were often unpopular, but her mother seemed to become more intimidating, her word gospel. Yet, especially when she was younger,

125

Victoria wanted to be more like her. She was conscious of her posture. She worked hard in school and achieved very good grades; she even took more care with her enunciation of words, and she was always aware of her mother's adage, *Think before you speak.*

'When you're with a group of girls who are all vociferous about their opinions on something, let them all speak first, Victoria. Try to be the last one to comment so you hear their opinions clearly and then sum up what they've said, choosing the best of each, if you can. It's difficult, I know, but don't let emotions drive you. Let them assist you.'

Her mother sprinkled wisdom around her like someone feeding chickens. She could peck at this or that, use this or that. There was enough to choose from. That was for sure. And she could see from the way her father listened to the things her mother said that he was in agreement with her most of the time. Unlike the fathers of most of her girlfriends, he relied on her mother a great deal and was not embarrassed if she took the lead in a conversation among their friends. Indeed, he looked at her proudly. She could see it in that small relaxing of his lips and that twinkle in his eyes.

Maybe they were a special family, but if they were, how could this have happened to her, to them?

She looked to her mother when she was released from the hospital. Her mother was the one who insisted on the therapy. Not that her father disagreed, but she was just the force behind it.

She didn't want to return to school in the fall, but her mother, more than the therapist, was responsible for her gathering enough strength to do it.

Her mother was present for every police interview. When Lieutenant Marcus suggested she not be, that perhaps Victoria would be more forthcoming, her mother nearly threw her out of the house, but her father calmed her mother and got her to go along with the policewoman's request.

'I know what she's up to. She's suggesting the girl brought this on herself and is ashamed to admit it in front of me,' her mother insisted. It was the truth, but something her father didn't want stated.

'Let's just let it run its course, Helen,' he told her. She looked at him and at Victoria and relented.

It was two days after she had been released from the hospital. The interview with Lieutenant Marcus was conducted in her room just before her mother began to have it redone. She sat at the work desk and Lieutenant Marcus sat on the tan fiberglass shell chair she had set back in the right corner. She brought it close and sat across from her with that clipboard she had when she had visited Victoria in the hospital.

'So,' she began, 'maybe you can remember the details a little better now?'

Victoria simply stared at her, but trembled inside. Did she mean the details of the actual rape?

'What did you do in the village before you went to the lake?' Lieutenant Marcus began.

'Just hung out with my two friends in front of George's.'

'Define *hung out*,' she said.

'Hung out. Talked.'

'Did you smoke anything, take anything?'

'I don't smoke.'

'You didn't take anything to have a good time?'

'No.'

She wrote something on her clipboard. *What did she write? That she didn't believe me?* Victoria wondered.

'None of my girlfriends do that,' she insisted.

Lieutenant Marcus looked at her blandly. 'None of them smoke pot?'

'No.'

'I'm not looking for you to get any of your friends in trouble. I'm looking to understand the whole picture,' she explained, but not in a tone of voice that had even an inkling of apology. It was cold, stated fact.

'Some of the city kids might have been smoking pot. I don't know. I don't even really know what it smells like.'

'OK. So, is there a special boy at school you liked or like?' she asked.

'No. I mean, no one I was going with.'

'But there's someone you like?'

'Sometimes. I mean, on and off.' What did she mean? 'You like someone but when you see he doesn't like you, you don't like him so much anymore.'

'Right,' Lieutenant Marcus said. 'What about the other way around?'

'What's that mean?'

128

'Was there or is there a boy in particular who has been trying to get you to like him, asked you out, pursued you? Perhaps more than others.'

Recently, Marvin Hacker had been asking her to meet him on weekends. He was a senior who, with his twin brother, Louis, worked in his father's garage just outside of Hurleyville. Both boys had grown up fast physically. They were six feet three and were good enough to be on the high school basketball team, but couldn't because they had to work in their father's garage after school. When they were only thirteen, they were driving, using cars left at the garage for service. Somehow, they had gotten away with it and now had their licenses and their own cars, jalopies and a pickup truck they had each resurrected, a perk for working so hard with their father.

Louis was shyer and therefore nicer in Victoria's opinion, not that either of them were attractive or interesting enough to want to date. They weren't grotesque, but they had long, thin noses and beady eyes. They always looked greasy, with their dull brown hair untrained. But they did other boys favors when it came to their cars, and when they were driving illegally, they were even more popular. Marvin wasn't coarse or particularly unpleasant. He was just a little more aggressive than his brother. His chief line whenever he suggested she let him pick her up was 'We could have a good time.'

She never gave him the slightest indication that he should have any hope, but right now his was the only name she could offer.

'Marvin Hacker,' she said.

129

'When was the last time he asked you out?' Lieutenant Marcus inquired.

'Maybe a week ago.'

'Was he in the village that night or at the lake?'

'I'm not sure. I thought I saw one of them at the lake.'

'One of them?'

'Him or his twin brother. It's not easy to tell them apart from a distance.'

'OK. Let's concentrate on the lake for a while. You admitted you drank more than you ever did. You said this city boy gave you the liquor. Did you make out with him?' she followed.

It sounded strange to hear that term from the mouth of a policewoman. 'A little,' she said.

'What's *a little*? You were in your bathing suit. Did you let him take any of it off?'

'No.'

'Did you encourage him to do more than just kiss you?'

'I didn't encourage him.'

'But you let him kiss you and then what?'

She stared at her. She wanted to cry, but it was strange how tears wouldn't form. Her eyes seemed to be freezing over instead. 'He went too far and I ran off. I think I told you that.'

Lieutenant Marcus made notes and then made her retell everything she had done after running from Spike. She brought it back to the moment she stepped out of the pickup truck.

'I want you to close your eyes and try really hard to picture everyone in the street. Then just rattle off slowly the name of every boy you recognized who was looking at you. Go on,' she ordered.

She did so, but she couldn't help feeling as if she was pointing an accusatory finger at each and every one she recalled.

'OK. I've left my phone number with your parents and I'm leaving it with you. If anything else comes to mind, I want you to call me instantly, even at night,' she said. 'Memory can be tricky. Your mind might be smothering something unpleasant, but it could be like a persistent itch that pops out as a pimple. That's when you call me. Understand?' she said, handing her the card with her telephone number. 'Keep it by your bed, in fact, because a lot of this occurs when we're alone, maybe starting to fall asleep, that sort of thing.'

She rose and, for the first time, Victoria thought she was finally looking at her not as just another victim to interview but as a young girl.

'Whoever did this to you wasn't stupid, Victoria. We've combed the area thoroughly and we didn't find any sack or rope or anything that could have been used to restrain you. They took it with them, knowing it might lead us to them. Maybe they read detective stories. The ground on that path was hard and covered with weeds and wild grass. There wasn't much of a footprint, and what we had was contaminated by all those rescue workers and the local police as well as Mr Miller. I told your parents all this just so they understand, and I'm telling you. This might take a while. That's why whatever else you remember is so important, OK?'

'OK.'

'You've been honest with me, too, right? There's no point in lying about anything you did now.'

'I'm not lying.'

There was a knock on her bedroom door.

'Yes?' Lieutenant Marcus called.

Her mother appeared. 'She is still in a sensitive period of recuperation,' she began. It was easy to see she had tolerated all she would.

'I'm done here for now,' Lieutenant Marcus said.

'Are you the only one working on this?' her mother asked.

'I'm the lead investigator now, yes. I have lots of backup if I need it. Forensics, for example. As I explained, though, we don't have much to bring to any laboratory. It's not a case where the perp left fingerprints, and there's not much we can do with what was left,' she added, referring to the sperm. 'Maybe there'll be scientific ways to use it someday, but for now . . .'

'Thank you. I think we got the picture,' her mother said sharply.

'I'll work with what I have. We'll do what we have to do to get them,' she said, but it sounded more like a defense of herself than a real promise for a satisfactory outcome. 'I'll be in touch,' she added and walked out.

'There's something about that woman that gives me the feeling she wouldn't mind being raped herself,' her mother said. She was that angry, but the remark not only shocked Victoria but also brought the first smile to her face since the Incident. In fact, she almost laughed.

Her mother realized too late what she had said and then embraced it with her own smile.

'Irritating,' she added. 'Just rest. Your father went to pick up some Chinese. He's getting your favorite and we'll have egg rolls, and after dinner we'll have your favorite ice cream – pistachio.'

She sat on Victoria's bed and looked down at her hands in her lap for a moment.

'You shouldn't have done what you did. If we had found out, we would have grounded you for weeks, but that in no way excuses or justifies what happened to you, Victoria, and I'd be lying if I didn't confess to having disobeyed my parents' rules from time to time. You'll see the therapist who will help you, I'm sure, but I don't want you to think for a moment that I blame you for what happened,' she said, raising her gaze to focus firmly on Victoria the way she could when she wanted her to listen and understand something she thought was important. No one was as steely-eyed. 'Understand?'

'Yes, Mom.'

'That policewoman might solve the case, but if she doesn't, she'll make herself feel better by convincing herself you somehow brought it on yourself. That's called rationalization and it's embedded in the human psyche. If some people didn't rationalize, they'd commit suicide. When you read Arthur Miller's *Death of a Salesman*, you'll really understand what I'm saying.' She took a deep breath and stood. 'Rest for a while. I'll call you when everything's ready, or your father will. Got to keep him busy, too, you know,' she added.

Then she stepped closer, put her right hand on the top of her head as if she was a bishop blessing her, before she knelt down and kissed her on the forehead. Victoria thought she saw those steely eyes begin to tear up before her mother turned quickly and walked out of the bedroom, closing the door softly behind her.

It wasn't until that moment that she realized this was the start of whatever recuperation she would enjoy. She wasn't hopeful or content; she was simply aware that, as people might say when they began something very important, this was the beginning of the rest of her life.

The days that followed were lonely and hard. Even though Jena could be very annoying at times, she welcomed her visits and her gossip, but about ten days later she brought her news she did not welcome. The police – Lieutenant Marcus with her rough bedside manner especially – were questioning so many local kids now, and everyone resented it. Some boys thought she was pointing a finger at them, and more than just Jena, Mindy and Toby were now in trouble with their parents for going to the wild party at the lake. An epidemic of various punishments was spreading. It was eating away at any compassion and sympathy her classmates and others would have for her. The thought of stepping into that atmosphere in the fall was almost as terrifying as traveling the shortcut behind the Millers' house again.

'But that's not fair,' Victoria said. 'They shouldn't be questioning the boys we know so much. It probably was those city boys. They might have followed me. I just didn't notice. I was too anxious to get home.'

Jena shrugged. She took a long sip from the Pepsi that Victoria's father had offered and she had accepted.

'Ralph Bud told Mindy that the police tracked down those boys. They were all staying at Klein's bungalow colony.'

'And?'

'The boy you were with, Spike – his real name is Carson Nadler – got involved with Delores Thomas right after you left the lake, it seems. They were there until midnight. Delores had to admit to it, so he had a solid alibi. Everyone is more or less convinced now that it was someone local.'

'Oh,' Victoria said. It seemed to inflame the wounds. It was easier to believe that someone out of their normal world would perpetrate such a crime. The intimacy of the small communities gave their inhabitants a sense of security. People could cheat each other occasionally, compete in economic business, lose their tempers and even have physical confrontations. They had families that didn't like each other – Hatfields and McCoys were everywhere in America – but lethal violence here was rare and, as far as they knew, this was the most high-profile sexual assault case in years. Realizing that someone whom she knew or who knew her and her family would attack her so brutally made the pill much harder to swallow.

'But I tell everyone it wasn't your fault, of course,' Jena said. 'I wish I hadn't gotten so sick drunk. I would have gone back to the village with you and maybe even gone to your house for an overnight. If I was with you, it wouldn't have happened. Or . . .' She paused, her imagination expanding. 'We both might have been attacked, I suppose.'

Victoria was silent. Oddly, if she disagreed, Jena might be insulted because it would be implying no one would have been after her body.

'Right?' Jena insisted.

'It's not an easy thing to do to two people at once. I told you about the sack and the rope and all. They would have had to have two of everything and two people means one could be a witness. Who knows what would have happened?'

'Yeah, you're probably right,' she said. 'Are you having nightmares every night?'

'I keep myself awake until I'm too tired for nightmares,' Victoria said.

Jena smiled. 'I'm sorry this happened to you, Victoria. You were one of the smartest and prettiest girls in the school.'

What did she mean? Was she implying that she no longer would be?

'I'm tired of talking about it,' she suddenly said. She understood better now why her parents avoided it so much.

'I don't blame you,' Jena said and began to talk about upcoming movies, a great song she had just heard and a surprising invitation she had received from Mindy. 'She just wants to spend some time, I guess,' she added.

Victoria understood. Mindy never liked Jena. She was inviting her over so she could delve into

136

what had happened more, pick up some hint as to whether or not Victoria had brought it on herself.

Her friends were flaking off like dead skin.

'Whatever,' Victoria said.

'My mom is trying to get my dad to ease up. I think they'll let me go for pizza or to a movie soon.'

Victoria didn't respond. Instead, she rose and looked out her window. How right her mother was about how different people saw the same thing, she thought. Eventually, girls as well as the boys wouldn't tolerate any more talk about her being attacked or the investigation and who could have done it. It was like shifting your eyes from some crippled person or a young person with Down syndrome. You'd utter the sympathetic words when you had to, but you didn't want to be reminded that such things existed.

Whenever any of her friends or even adults who knew her looked at her from now on, they would think only one thing and they would look away as quickly as they could.

How will I look away? Victoria wondered.

She turned back to Jena. 'Do you mind, Jena? I'm so tired all of a sudden. I think I need to take a nap.'

'A nap?'

The word didn't fit their teenage scripts. It was an older person's word or a word for a very young child. *It's time for baby's nap.*

'Yes,' she said. 'Sorry.'

Jena downed the rest of the Pepsi and smiled. 'No problem. I've got to pick up something on the way home anyway, and I can't break my new curfew or I'll never get out of Sing Sing,' she declared. She started to go to hug Victoria and then thought better of it and went to the bedroom door. 'I'll call you,' she said, and then she added as if she had to convince herself, 'Promise.'

For a moment after Jena left, it was as if all the air had gone with her. Then Victoria did sprawl out on her bed. She couldn't help it.

She clamped her arms against her sides and she tiptoed into the horrible memory, hoping maybe to come back with some detail, something that would help Lieutenant Marcus get the culprits and at least end the pursuit that haunted the world in which she lived, a world that was shrinking with every heartbeat.

Nine

The sound of his door buzzer jerked him around like an alarm clock might. Bart was just about to begin shaving. He had soaked his face in hot water and reached for the shaving cream. Normally, he wouldn't shave until early evening or late afternoon before getting ready to go out, but he wanted to be as handsome and desirable as possible right from the start.

He had laid out his white shorts with the wide white belt, a pair of blue boat shoes and his light blue short-sleeve shirt and matching light blue boat jacket. He had his captain's cap and his

Grand Seiko watch with the sky-blue leather band. Beside it was a sky-blue topaz pinky ring that matched. It had been a while since he had taken so much time and given so much thought to what he would wear to the lake. Most of the time he threw on some old jeans, sneakers and a T-shirt. He certainly didn't care about jewelry.

The buzzer sounded again.

'Just a minute,' he called. He was in his underwear and wrapped a bath towel around himself. He suspected it might be Thelma Stein, the building owner's wife.

His apartment was the top of a red brick-faced duplex built a little over a mile east of Monticello. Most of his friends thought it looked too much like a school. The Steins lived in the bottom apartment. Philip was sixty-six and Thelma was sixty-two. They had been buying their cars from Stonefield ever since Bart's father began the dealerships. They had two sons, both of whom had married and lived in Boston and Chicago. Mrs Stein missed her boys, who were both older than Bart, and he began to feel like a surrogate son. She was always bringing him something she had made for dinner or half a pie or cake. Recently, they had sold their dry-cleaning business and told him that they would be spending their winters in Boca Raton, Florida, but they had hired someone to look after the property.

What attracted him to the apartment was that it had its own stairway entrance. His floors were covered in thick Berber carpet so he didn't worry about being too noisy above the Steins, not that he had done much partying since he began renting. The truth was he rarely had anyone over. As he had told Victoria, most of the male friends he had in high school had moved on, and of those who remained, only two he cared to be with were unmarried, but both had steady girlfriends now. He wasn't comfortable socializing with them without a date for himself and he hated being fixed up.

'I'm going to go crazy,' his mother declared as soon as he opened the door.

He didn't step back, but she charged in and stood at the center of the small living room. He knew that Florence Stonefield, which was often how he referred to her when talking about his mother, normally never left her house without putting herself together as perfectly as a storefront mannequin. Her teased brassy light brown hair had rebellious strands on the side and the top, and she wore no makeup, not even lipstick. She was wearing the sort of baggy jeans she would wear when she had decided it was a morning to tinker in her flower beds, and she had thrown on a light pink cotton cardigan over her white blouse. She wore a pair of tennis sneakers without socks, which was also something she never did.

Florence Stonefield still had a lot to recommend her beauty at forty-nine. The truth was she really didn't need much makeup. She had nearly perfect facial features, with soft full lips and high cheekbones. Her green-blue eyes had an exquisite almond shape that gave her just a touch of the exotic. Unlike many women her age and even somewhat younger, she was nearly fanatical about keeping her figure. Her breasts weren't too large

140

or too small, and her hips absolutely refused to widen or thicken, even after childbirth.

The other quality that drew the envy of most of the women in the township, if not the entire county, was how photogenic she could be. It was impossible to take a candid shot of her and catch her looking awkward or unattractive. In all the local magazine pictures and the ads they occasionally did for the dealerships, she looked as if she had just stepped off the cover of *Vogue*.

Bart's first thought was that she had discovered his father's affair with Shirley Barbara or else he had decided to confess since Bart had brought Victoria Myers to the store and caught him. Oddly, the thing that depressed him as soon as he thought this was not that his parents might divorce and they would now be the subject of endless gossip, but that all this was happening on the morning he was preparing to take Victoria to the lake. It was going to spoil his day, upset him, and he would be unable to hide that from her. If there was one thing he was determined not to bring with him now or whenever he saw her, it was depression, negativity or unhappiness. That could easily revive her own, as it almost had the night before, and that could lead to places he did not want to go, not now, not ever.

'What is it, Mom?' he asked, closing the door.

She shook her head and backed up to sit on the Henredon sofa, lowering herself as slowly as she would lower herself into a hot bath. He knew what she thought of his pad. He had bought all his furniture in one afternoon and without her advice or assistance, which was

141

something she wasn't going to let him forget. However, in his mind the apartment was more of a stopover between his parents' home and eventually his own house. That temporary feel reduced the importance of anything he bought, including the dining table with pearl-white veneers and its chairs upholstered in tan linen seat fabric. She thought it belonged in a summer bungalow and even went so far as to say the food served on it would taste like plastic. He wasn't much of a cook, so he told her she had nothing to fear.

He held his breath as the seconds ticked by.

'What are you thinking?' she asked, nodding as though she was convinced those were the right words with which to begin. She looked down at the floor. 'And I have to hear about it from Cissy Levine of all people! She's like a bad news parasite who suckles off the tit of unhappiness. What's that German word? It's perfect for her? *Schadenfreude*,' she said, remembering. She looked up. 'Addie Lockheart, who's probably read the entire fiction collection in the public library, recently explained it to me.'

She waited for his response.

'What are you talking about, Mom?'

'Cissy was at Dante's last night,' she replied, pressing her lips together as if that had explained everything and was all she was capable of saying about it.

'So?'

'So? She couldn't wait to get on the phone this morning. Lucky I was already up and dressed, but I'm sure she woke your father. I ran right out and drove over here,' she added when he didn't speak. He remained silent, which was obviously more irritating. 'She saw you with Victoria Myers, Bart! You took out Victoria Myers,' she added, as if he had to be reminded.

He still didn't answer.

He walked across the room and went into the bathroom.

'What are you doing?' she called after him.

'Shaving,' he said.

She rose and stood outside the bathroom doorway. He lathered his face.

'Bart, you took out a girl who is quite a mess and has been for years.'

He started to shave.

'Are you listening to me?'

He paused, took a breath and turned to her. 'First, she is not a mess and she hasn't been a mess for years. She just graduated Columbia University with the highest honors.' He continued shaving.

'I don't care what she's done in school, Bart. She can't be normal.'

'You mean as normal as your friends – like Cissy Levine, someone who lives off the misery of others, or Janice Messenger who no longer speaks to any of her children, or Donna Basel who is suing her dentist for filling the wrong tooth? It's a wonder you don't hold your bridge game in the mental ward.'

'This is different from all that and you know it. You're an eligible and highly sought-after bachelor now. Other people, whose daughters you might take out and even hope to marry, would

143

question your judgment and certainly wonder what you were thinking, too.'

'I was thinking that she is a bright, intelligent and very attractive young woman.' He continued shaving.

'Where are you going? Are you taking her out again?'

'Matter of fact, I'm taking her to the lake today. We're going to have a picnic on the boat.'

'Well, you're just as stone-headed as your father. Stonefield's the right name,' she said and turned away.

He finished shaving and went into his bedroom to dress. His heart was racing, his temples beginning to pound. It was a cross between anger and disappointment, but when he gave it second thought, he realized he should have anticipated this. He had to stop ignoring who his mother really was, what sort of a person she was and what her priorities were.

She was sitting out there, nervous and upset. How was she going to react to his father's affair when that got to the ears and claws of someone like Cissy Levine? It worried him. His mother's physical beauty had nothing to do with her personality, her inner strengths. For as long as he could remember, she was almost another child in the house. She knew very little if anything about their finances. She was only on the surface when it came to their business. She liked to think she had better taste than most when it came to home decorating, but she wouldn't buy an ash tray without his father's consent and approval.

He was curious, of course, about her last remark.

When he was dressed, he stepped out and asked, 'Why do you say he's hard-headed?'

She was sitting on the sofa, looking so lost in her fears.

'Since I was sure the call woke him, I went back to the bedroom and asked him if he knew you were taking out Victoria Myers. He said no, but he didn't say another word. I told him he should speak to you about it and he said, "What for?"'

'So maybe you're making too much of it, then, Mom.'

'I know I'm not.'

'Are you worried more about Florence Stonefield or me?' he asked sharply.

She tried to widen those almond-shaped eyes, but the best she could do to show outrage was pull back her lips.

'That's a cold thing to say, Bart. I rushed out of the house to come over here to see if you knew what you were doing. It was for you. You're still my son even though you've moved into this . . . this place,' she said.

'Well, don't worry about it. Victoria is a charming young woman. You'll see so for yourself when I bring her around.'

'What are you saying? Bring her around? What is your intent here? How long have you been seeing her? How long has this been on your mind?' She fired her questions at him like an attorney cross-examining an unfriendly witness.

'Que sera sera,' he said. 'Thank you for worrying so much, but don't,' he said, reaching for her hand to get her to stand up. He knew the calm tone in his voice was like a knife cutting into her heart, but the anger was rising faster to the surface. 'I have to get going. I'm taking her shopping for a new bathing suit.'

'Bathing suit,' she said.

'Yes. Any recommendations? I was thinking about that new place in Monticello. You know, where you bought yours last year.'

She pulled her hand away. 'You know she has been seeing a shrink for years. Everyone knows.'

'A psychologist. I think people refer to *psychiatrists* as shrinks,' he said. 'She doesn't see her psychologist regularly anymore – hasn't for some time now.'

'How do you know so much about her, Bart? Have you been seeing her secretly while she's been at college?'

'Maybe I heard Cissy Levine's report,' he said and tried a smile.

His mother sighed. 'Why do I bother? You have your father's stubborn ways. You're two peas in a pod.'

'No,' he said sharply. 'We're different.'

She didn't pick up on it. She walked out ahead of him and then turned. 'She's damaged goods,' she said.

'Well, I'm the manager of the service department,' he replied. 'It's my job to repair things.'

She threw up her hands and pounded her way down the stairs.

He closed the door and returned to the bathroom to look at himself.

I really like her, he thought. *She's become so*

146

beautiful. She's everything I told my mother she was. Yes, he thought, raising his right hand fist to the side of his face. *Yes.*

Like someone being chased, he rushed out of his apartment, down the stairs and then froze when he turned to his car.

Marvin Hacker was leaning against it, his arms folded, smiling widely.

'What the fuck do you want?' Bart asked him as he walked toward his car.

Marvin didn't move an inch, nor lose his wide, shit-eating grin.

'That was your mother, wasn't it?'

'Yeah, so?'

'She's a fine-lookin' woman, your mother. I always thought she was quite the piece of ass. She looked pissed off.'

'What do you want, Marvin?'

'Playin' with fire, aren't ya?' he asked, straightening up.

'What I do is none of your business.'

'Oh, for sure it is,' Marvin replied. He smiled again. 'Course, I can't blame ya. Ya missed yer chance once and want another shot at it.'

'I think it's best you keep your mouth shut, Marvin.'

Bart opened his door hard, pushing Marvin back a bit. Marvin seized the top of it and held him from closing it when he got in. Then he leaned in toward him.

'Make it a wham-bam-thank-you-ma'am, Stonefield, and no chit-chat in the heat-of-the-moment shit. You wanna confess, go to church,' he added. He smiled again. 'When ya done, I'll

147

get my share one way or another. I'm sure you won't mind.'

Bart pulled harder on the door and ripped it from Marvin's grasp. He was trembling, but he kept control of himself and started the engine. He didn't look at him until he had put the car in reverse and began backing out.

Marvin was smiling widely.

The guy's very existence felt like a knife slicing through his heart, the heart that was pounding so hard that he could hear his blood thumping through his head.

He's bluffing, he thought. *He's not that stupid.*

He drove on, hoping the thought was comforting enough.

But he wasn't confident. Even though they had had little contact since that night, Marvin was always there in the shadows with that damn evil smile.

Victoria had taken a two-piece and a one-piece into the dressing room, both turquoises. She favored the two-piece, but she had been wearing a two-piece that night six years ago. However, when she tried on the two-piece, the memories of those great summer tans overwhelmed her memories of Sandburg Lake and the horror that had followed. Even before it was warm enough to go swimming, she would be out behind her house, sprawled on a blanket in her two-piece, reading a book or doing her homework. Sometimes she joined Jena and Mindy and they all sunbathed in late April and May. In the Catskills, you often had to wait until late June before the swimming pools were warm enough. And forget the lakes – even in the middle of the summer, they were easily ten degrees cooler than the average pool.

The three of them would put on their sunglasses, smear on their tanning lotions and listen to rock and roll. Other girls from their class sometimes joined them. It was easier to gossip, talk about boys, plan parties and interrogate each other as to how far they were willing to go. It was as if every fantasy was possible. It was all waiting for them just around the next corner, the next corner being the next summer, the next birthday or the next house party.

It was amazing how the sight of herself wearing a bathing suit again could arouse those hitherto buried and sleeping memories. It gave her hope as well. The choruses of laughter and the playful taunts were resurrected. She was peeling away time as she would peel an orange. It was lifting up the page of a magic notebook, erasing all the words and starting over with a brand-new *Once upon a time.*

Bart was waiting in the store. He had driven her to Monticello where she was confident almost no one would recognize her. The store he had suggested, La Femme Supreme, was only two years old. He told her his mother had bought a bathing suit there last year. An elderly lady with the richest-looking white hair Victoria had ever seen (she thought it actually glowed) and her middle-aged daughter owned and operated the store. How they had originated in St Remy, France, and ended up in the Catskills was probably quite a story, Victoria thought, but at the moment she wasn't interested in anyone else.

She hesitated, her heart racing, and nimbly stepped out. Bart was sitting in a chair and thumbing through a magazine. He looked up quickly. The look on his face brought a flush of heat into her neck. She felt as if she had stepped out naked, but his expression wasn't licentious as much as it was the appreciation of something truly beautiful. Instinctively, she had her arms up, her hands resting over her breasts and chest. Slowly, she brought her arms down to her sides.

'What do you think of this one?' she asked. She could hear the small trembling in her voice.

'Beautiful. You look great, Victoria. I love that color on you. It makes your eyes sparkle.'

'There's a one-piece in the same color,' she said.

'Why bother?' He put the magazine down and sat back, folding his arms over his chest and nodding.

The owner and her daughter stepped up beside him.

'*Très belle*,' the elderly lady said. She turned to her daughter and added, '*Il est un homme très chanceux.*'

'What did she say?' Bart asked Victoria. She shook her head. It was easier to pretend she didn't understand either.

'My mother said you are a very lucky man,' the daughter translated.

'Oh. Absolutely,' he said. 'Why don't you leave it on and put your clothes over it,' he told Victoria. 'We're going directly to the lake from here.'

She nodded and stepped back into the dressing room. For a moment she stood there. This was

150

what she had done that night – worn her clothes over her bathing suit. Would every detail of that evening resonate like this whenever it was repeated? How long would she remain emotionally crippled? She rushed to Dr Thornton's advice. 'You've got to put those memories in a box and lock it, Victoria. I don't want to diminish what happened to you, but it would help if you began to think of it as happening to someone else, someone you no longer are.'

'Yes,' she whispered, 'someone I no longer am.'

She got dressed, paid for the bathing suit and left the store with Bart. He held her hand and walked quickly as if he was afraid she would change her mind. They were practically running.

'I didn't steal it,' she said.

'What?' He paused. 'Oh. Sorry. My mind was flying ahead, going over the things I had to do when we get to the lake. I don't remember if I filled the tank last time. No big deal. The pump's right nearby. And I thought we'd get some sandwiches and sodas or beers, if you want, at the diner on the way. You know, Top's Diner?'

'I've driven past it but never eaten there.'

'It's good,' he said and reached for the car door. 'I've got sun tan oil on the boat,' he told her.

She sat back. He seemed to have everything under control. It felt good to put herself in the hands of someone else – a man in particular. It wasn't that she craved dependence, but she was always so nervous and concerned about every detail involved with everything she did, especially when she came home. To be just along for the ride and not have to plan anything was

151

something she hadn't done since she was a little girl going somewhere with her parents.

Bart was doing most of the talking today, sounding almost as nervous as he had on their way to Dante's last night. He talked about when he bought the boat, how he had always wanted one, how he took care of it and how lucky he was to be able to do that. Engines of all kinds, he explained, had fascinated him as a little boy. He liked to hang out with the mechanics when he was a kid and watch them at work. Most enjoyed him being there and his questions, but there were grouchy ones, too, he explained.

'At least I was out of my father's hair when I went with him to work. Back then, we kept the service department opened on Saturdays. I was with him whenever there was a school holiday, too.'

'What about your mother?'

'My mother?'

'Did she like that you were so occupied in the garage?'

'Oh yeah, but in the early days, my mother was at the dealership more, too. She was good at selling a vehicle to other women, pointing out things women would appreciate.'

'But she doesn't do that anymore?'

He winced. They had still not discussed coming upon his father. He liked that she wasn't bringing it up, but he knew it would hang out there and could not be ignored forever. Perhaps, after all that had happened to her and all she had gone through, she was much better at ignoring unpleasant things.

'No. Things changed when cars became a lot more involved,' he said.

They pulled into the parking lot for Top's Diner.

'Let's see what the special sandwiches are today,' he said.

She got out with him and entered. Suddenly, he paused as if there was an invisible wall in front of them. She heard him say 'Shit' under his breath.

He reached for her arm at the elbow and moved them quickly to the counter. The abruptness of his movements and the discernable change in his mood brought an unexpected feeling of trepidation. Because he was keeping his attention fixed forward, studying the chalk writing on the blackboard menu, she did the same.

They both decided on the fresh turkey. He ordered some sodas and chips as well. She noted that while the sandwiches were being prepared, he turned to pick up a copy of the *Sullivan County Democrat* and gazed at the lead stories. She sensed he wasn't as interested in that as he was in narrowing his view of the diner. She turned and looked to her right.

Top's Diner was classic 1950s style with its black-and-red checkered floor, its chrome, black vinyl counter stools, and its red faux-leather booths with jukeboxes on the sides for patrons to choose their favorite old and recent tunes. The kitchen walls were all silver metal siding and the grill was open. The waitresses wore pink-and-white dresses with black trim and Top's Diner logo over their right breasts. They were all wearing black-and-white saddle shoes as well.

She panned the long room with its oversized windows on the right and paused when she saw three boys in a booth second from the end. She recognized the man facing them. Marvin Hacker. The other two boys had their backs to them. She glanced at Bart again as he lifted his eyes from the paper.

'That's Marvin Hacker looking at us. He was in your class, wasn't he?' she asked.

He looked and nodded. 'Yes,' he said. 'His brother Louis was killed in Vietnam early this year.'

'Oh. I didn't know. They were twins,' she said, as if she believed when one twin died, the other had to and it was odd that Marvin was still alive.

'Marvin enlisted right out of high school and got out after three years. Louis was drafted,' Bart said. 'His father passed away last month. They still have their garage, but it's nothing like it was. I get a lot of their dissatisfied customers,' he muttered.

She looked back at him. He seemed to be staring, but he made no attempt to greet them. *He's probably angry at Bart for stealing away his customers*, she thought.

Bart paid for their food and drinks and scooped up the bag.

'OK?' he said. 'Anything else? Candy?'

'No, this is fine. Thank you.'

They started out. Bart didn't turn around to look again at Marvin. He seemed to want to leave quickly, too.

It's probably uncomfortable for him, she thought and kept his pace.

154

Less than a minute later, they were backing out of the parking space.

She looked toward the diner.

Marvin Hacker was staring out at them.

His face looked chiseled in granite, his eyes very dark – almost two holes full of ink. He looked angry. For a moment, she felt sorry for him having lost his brother and now his father. He was understandably bitter. It was impossible to go through life without some deep wounds.

The choice was simple: wail about it and layer on the self-pity or follow Nietzsche's advice and believe that what doesn't kill you makes you stronger.

I don't want to be pitied anymore, she thought, *but I'm not stronger. Not yet.*

And it's still up for grabs whether or not I will ever be.

Ten

Nobody still going to school wanted to rush the summer. Even those attending college wished days were thirty-six or forty-eight hours long instead of twenty-four. But probably no one wanted time to stand still as much as Victoria did that horrible summer. She dreaded the idea of walking into her high school after Labor Day. She had nightmares about it. In all of them, everyone was looking at her and whispering, and everyone else's eyes were twice the size. Even the teachers were standing in doorways and looking and whispering. In some dreams, all the boys were gazing at her licentiously, as though what had happened to her pulled back some blanket or opened some door and left her sexually vulnerable, easy pickings.

She woke in a sweat, battling back the urge to scream, her body trembling. If she had been hit by a car, broken an arm or a leg falling off her bike or had simply been seriously ill for a few weeks, she would be swimming in sympathy. Storekeepers would have given her little gifts. Her friends would have called frequently and visited. Why was the violation and abuse of a young woman treated so differently . . . or so *indifferently*?

She found herself in a prison of her own making. During the remainder of summer, she had left the house solely to go to see her therapist. Jena constantly tried to get her to do things with her, but she was always too tired or had a headache. Eventually, Jena stopped asking and even reduced her visits for a while. Victoria didn't blame her, and always accepted and went along with her obviously phony reasons for the longer intervals.

Nevertheless, Victoria welcomed her visits, however infrequent, because they were essentially her only connection with the world she knew. After some initial phone calls from other friends who seemed to call more out of obligation or sick curiosity, her phone was as good as dead. She never even called Jena.

She met with Lieutenant Marcus two more times before school began, and it was clear from the policewoman's questions and the way she responded to Victoria's mother that little headway had been made with the investigation. On the last occasion, her mother was interrogating Lieutenant Marcus more than Lieutenant Marcus had interrogated Victoria.

'How many boys have you questioned? Do you have any suspects at all? Why don't you have more help? How is the local police department assisting? How long will you be on this case? Have you found any evidence at all? Are the city boys completely exonerated? Summer's ending. How will you pursue any leads involving them? What else are you working on? Is this a priority? Were you given this investigation as some form of punishment?'

It got so that Victoria actually felt sorry for Lieutenant Marcus. As soon as she answered one question, she had to fend off another.

Her mother assured her – threatened her, actually – that she would go to the highest authority to get some results soon. 'It's not just for us. It's for this whole community,' she nearly shouted. 'Whose daughter can feel safe now?'

'I understand,' Lieutenant Marcus kept saying.

'Do you?' her mother finally said, her frustration palpable. 'I doubt it.' The way she said that made it clear she didn't think Lieutenant Marcus could sense or identify with a female's pain.

That seemed to put the seal on the discussion. The police officer left and never returned. When her mother inquired, she was told the findings were being given to the local police department to follow up, which, to Victoria's mother, was as good as saying, 'Don't stay up for results.'

The problem with not identifying and prosecuting the villains wasn't so much that justice wouldn't be served or revenge satisfied. For Victoria, it meant that she would never know if the boys looking at her, even talking to her, were the ones who had violated her. Naturally, that made her shy away from any attention, any conversations and certainly any romantic approaches in her remaining time at high school.

She told Dr Thornton that she felt as though her girlfriends believed that any association with her endangered them the way someone with a potentially deadly disease might. It was as if being raped was catching. More than one of her girlfriends asked her if she had suffered any sexually transmitted disease.

'We know that would be something only your doctor and parents would know, but you can tell me.'

No matter how she denied it, rumors spread that she had indeed contracted syphilis and had to be treated for that in the hospital as well.

The details of the attack were public knowledge now. At first, she accused Jena of spreading the information she had told her, but after a while she realized the interrogations led to conclusions and that someone in the local police department was leaking specifics. There was a big uproar in the school before Christmas that year when she found an ugly, nasty note in her locker. Someone had drawn a very graphic picture of her with a sack over her head and her legs spread. Her parents met with the principal and the police chief, Hal Donald. Her mother insisted that every student's fingerprints be taken, but, as it turned out, whoever had done it must have handled the paper with gloves. There were no discernable prints. The art teacher, Bob Dungan, was brought in to analyze the drawing to see if he could match it with the work of any of his students. The drawing was crude, so he didn't feel confident enough with his suspicions to offer any names.

The terror associated with talking to any of the boys, her now being afraid even to go to her locker, her grades suffering and her withdrawal from anything remotely social were turning Victoria into something of a pariah in the school. Slowly, she slipped further and further down to the realm of invisibility, like someone trying to go up a hill of ice. Many of the parents of other young girls were telling each other that Victoria Myers must have been hanging out with some very undesirable types. The emphasis shifted back to suspecting some city boys. City boys, by their very nature, were more exposed to such ugly events. Everyone knew that people were murdered, robbed and raped daily in the city. It had to be them and Victoria brought it on herself by having anything to do with them.

This idea made it difficult for any local girl to get romantically involved with a city boy the following summer and even the one after, and Victoria sensed that these frustrated girls blamed her. The unsolved sexual attack gradually took on legendary characteristics. When the story was told months and even years after, it was often embellished. It was a gang rape. There were more than two. She had agreed to let them walk her home . . . she was drunk . . . she was high on pot. Witnesses saw her half naked on the beach at the lake. On and on, the exaggerations built until there was no hope of ever returning to the actual event and facts.

For a while, Helen and Lester Myers toyed with the idea of sending Victoria to a private school. Dr Thornton wasn't in favor of that. She told them, 'Once you enable her to avoid reality, send her off as if she is the guilty party here, she'll drop further and further into withdrawal. More important, she might interpret it as assigning her guilt. Let's help her deal with it all here. She'll get stronger and that strength will help her when it's time to move on.'

All along, Lester Myers believed his daughter was too fragile to be sent away anyway and he grabbed on to Dr Thornton's logic. Helen relented, too, and the idea drifted away. Victoria did start to take baby steps and go places with Jena. Occasionally, one or two of her other friends from before the Incident invited her to something, and then there was her date to the senior prom as well as her gradual return to being an A-plus student. She continued to avoid any extracurricular activities and that was what solidified her association with Jena. They hung about with other outsiders who did little or nothing when it came to sports, plays and clubs. Victoria's grades were good enough to get most of the colleges to overlook this and she was accepted by four.

At first, her mother didn't want her to attend a college in New York City. The negatives of the city world were still quite compelling. Helen Myers had gone to Vassar, a school she believed was far more insulated. It was located in Poughkeepsie, and Poughkeepsie was more like a neighborhood than a city when one compared it with New York. Victoria did not want to apply to Vassar. She harbored the fear that everything she did there would pale in comparison with her mother's achievements. To her credit, Helen Myers did not push it. Victoria didn't know, but Dr Thornton had suggested the reason to her mother and emphasized that Victoria should go out on her own.

The summer before she left, her friend Jena suggested that they walk that old shortcut from the village to Victoria's house and they do it at night. She had, unbeknownst to Victoria, been doing research on rape victims. In fact, she had used the topic for her college admissions essay.

'It's a matter of confronting the demons that are in your subconscious,' she recited, quoting a psychology magazine and the author of the article, who had a trail of degrees as long as your arm.

The truth was that Victoria had herself toyed with this idea. More than once, in fact, she set out to do it, but fear of what it might do to the little progress she thought she had made stopped her.

'We'll start out from the same place you started that night,' Jena explained. 'We'll go slowly, and once you get through it, it won't have the same terrible meaning for you ever.'

'I don't know.'

'Don't you see? It's symbolic now. It's bigger than life. You've got to turn it and everything associated with it back to what it normally is. That's an exact quote.'

'The idea frightens me. I can't help it.'

'I'll be right by your side,' Jena insisted. Victoria couldn't recall her looking more excited about anything. *She really is living some exciting adventure through me*, Victoria thought. She almost laughed about it. 'Well?' Jena pressed. 'Shall we try to conquer this?'

'We?'

'Well, it's a little scary for me, too. I mean, I don't think this will happen, but what if you freak out or something? I'll get into a lot of trouble going along with you or urging you to have done it.'

'I don't know. You might be blowing it out of all proportion. It might not be that important anyway. Who cares about the shortcut?'

Jena's face of excitement seemed to lose air.

'On the other hand, I won't deny it's something I've thought of doing.'

'Right. That's natural. Deep inside, you want to conquer all these fears. It will help you heal.'

'OK. But maybe we shouldn't do it at night.'

'Oh, you have to duplicate the incident as closely as you can,' Jena insisted. 'That's what I read.'

'The *Incident*?'

'That's what I heard your mother call it once, and I don't want to say "rape".'

'We'll do it tonight,' Victoria said. An impulsive

162

decision was best. If she sat around considering it, she would never do it. She already knew that from her own toying with the idea.

Jena was driving now, something Victoria wasn't doing as much as she could. With her father's help, she had gotten her driver's license, and whenever he could, he let her do the driving, but without much incentive in terms of places to go, others to visit, parties or even going to school sporting events, Victoria just didn't push to do more driving as did most everyone else in her class. Some even had their parents buy them their own vehicle – mostly used cars, but nevertheless their own.

'OK. I'll come by at seven. We'll say we're just taking a ride to meet some friends to get a soda or something.'

'Just taking a ride is enough. My parents will be happy to see me go out,' Victoria said. 'No need to elaborate and lie.'

'Right. Whatever you say,' Jena replied. She was on fire with her idea.

Up until the time Jena showed up, Victoria teetered on the verge of changing her mind. In the end, she took a deep breath and decided that Jena was right: the demons she had to face were inside her and not on any path through the woods.

She was trembling when they cruised into the village. It was May and far from what the small hamlet would become in less than two months. Nevertheless, the warm spring night brought people out and stores were staying open longer.

This happened to be one of the nicest evenings of the year, with temperatures clinging to the low seventies.

'How are we going to do this?' Victoria asked. Now that they were in the village, the logistics played on her mind.

'I'll park my car where it will be inconspicuous, and then after we go through the shortcut, we'll have to walk back to town,' Jena said.

'I'm not sure I want anyone to see us go through the alley to the shortcut,' Victoria decided. She was thinking of pulling out now. 'It'll be too weird for them. This is weird.'

'We'll make sure no one sees us. Stop worrying so much. There,' she said, nodding at a parking space. 'We'll park across from Echert's garage. It's closed. No one will notice us.'

After she parked and turned off the engine, Victoria still hesitated. 'I'm not sure this is wise,' she said.

'It's wise.' Jena's enthusiasm was almost comical now.

Victoria shook her head. 'I don't know what you expect from this.'

'I expect to help you,' she said and opened her door. 'C'mon.'

She stepped out. Victoria hesitated and then got out as well. They crossed the street and, clinging to the shadows, they made their way back to the center of the village. No one was standing in front of Kayfield's or Trustman's fruit and vegetable market. Across the street, however, Billy Polland and Gerry Sussman were sitting on a stoop and smoking. Both were in their class.

Something caught their attention and they looked the other way.

'Quickly,' Jena ordered and practically jogged across the front of Kayfield's Bar and Grill. With her head down, Victoria followed. They reached the alleyway and practically dove into the darkness just outside of the glow cast by the streetlights. From the darkness, Victoria looked back at the boys and saw they were joined by another, Tommy Stratton. The three started up the street toward George's.

'Told you it would be easy,' Jena said. 'Lead the way and try to do it as closely to how you did it that night.'

Victoria began to talk to herself, telling herself that the darkness was no different here and the shadows cast by the starlight were shadows of trees and not monsters. She took baby steps at first, quite aware that Jena was watching every movement, even her breathing.

'Didn't you walk faster?' she asked after a moment. 'You've got to try to do everything as you remember it.'

'Yes, Doctor Daniels,' she said. Jena laughed, but it was a thin, nervous laugh. As they moved farther along, they were leaving the light and the sounds of the village behind them. The maple, oak and birch trees had filled out. There were walls of leaves and, in some parts of the path, the darkness did seem deeper, thicker.

After a few more minutes, Victoria stopped.

'What?' Jena asked instantly.

'I remember I stopped because I thought I had heard something, someone over there,' she said, nodding to her left. 'I waited and it became quiet again. I mean, it was a busy summer night so I could hear voices, cars and music, but off away.'

'Over there?' Jena asked, looking to her left as though it was happening now. 'Did you tell the police that?'

'I don't remember. The sounds stopped, so I continued anyway, maybe faster,' she said, walking faster and trying to avoid branches and tree roots. 'I stubbed my foot, but I kept walking and then . . .' She paused. There were lights on in the Miller house. 'I didn't see those lights that night,' she said in a whisper. 'I don't know why, and then I sensed someone was behind me, but before I could turn—'

'They dropped that sack over you?'

'Yes.'

She stood there. Neither spoke.

Suddenly, Victoria said, 'There was something else. Something I didn't mention.' She broke into a run and Jena hurried after her.

'What?' she called. 'Why are you running? Jesus, Victoria, I just scratched myself. There are berry bushes here,' she called. 'Shit.'

She slowed down. Victoria had disappeared in the darkness.

'Where the hell are you?' she called. She looked back. It seemed as though the shadows were closing in quickly. Her lungs ached. She was at least fifteen pounds too heavy. Mrs Helm, the girls' physical education teacher, was always telling her to lose weight.

Finally, she broke out of the woods and saw

Victoria standing by the road waiting for her. Her head was down and her hands were on her hips.

'What happened? Why did you just run like that?' Jena asked as she approached her.

'I don't know why I forgot,' she said. She shook her head but kept looking down. 'I don't know why. I was just so confused about it.'

'What? What did you forget?'

'When the sack was pulled over me, I smelled gas.'

'Gas?'

'Gas, gas – like you put in a car, gas. It must have been on one or both of their hands or on their clothes or something. Gas,' she said.

'Oh.'

'You go get your car,' Victoria said. 'I'm walking home.'

'What? But . . . I don't want to leave you alone,' she added, but what she really meant was that now she didn't want to be left alone.

'It's all right. I'm not afraid. You were right. I'm glad we did that walk. Thanks,' she said and started away.

'But . . . it's early,' Jena cried.

She watched as Victoria continued up the road, her arms folded just under her breasts, her head down, looking anything but frightened of what could lie ahead. She was walking at a fast pace and, in moments, disappeared in the darkness.

Jena uttered a small cry, bit down on her lower lip and hurried toward Main Street and the way back to the village where there were more lights

167

and people, and where the demons she aroused for Victoria would not be.

At least she hoped so.

Victoria, on the other hand, was not thinking about her demons. If anything, whatever was fantastical about the Incident had been diminished. Memories were supposed to get thinner as time passed. Could her crazy friend Jena have just done something more effective than her psychologist and all the police combined? It was as if a curtain had been opened for a few seconds and she was able to peer back through time and see through the fog.

She broke into a jog and then a run. Gasping, she burst into her house, took a moment to catch her breath and then went to the living-room doorway. Her father and mother were sitting on the settee as close together as two teenagers on the sofa in the living room of some house during a house party with the lights low and the music of some doo-wop song pushing inhibitions away as lips and hands began exploring.

'What happened? Why are you back so soon?' her mother asked, moving out from under her father's arm and sitting forward.

'I remembered something about that night, something I forgot to say,' she began.

Her father sat forward, clasping his hands. 'What?' he asked.

'When they attacked me, there was the smell of car gas,' she said. 'It was probably on their hands.'

'You forgot that? All this time, you forgot that?' her mother asked, incredulous.

'Yes. And when I remembered that, I remembered something else that I think just made sense to me.'

'What's that?' her mother asked, shaking her head.

'A sound that I think was the sound of a ring of keys,' she said. 'Like the school janitor wears – you know, jingling.'

They both stared at her.

'How did you . . . What brought back these memories?' her mother asked.

'Jena had an idea. It was something she read so we just did it.'

'What?' her father asked.

'I . . . we went on the shortcut from the village.'

Her mother sat back.

'Well, I'll be damned,' her father said. He turned to her mother. 'What do ya think of that? Jena Daniels comes up with somethin' the psychologist never suggested.'

'Out of the mouths of babes,' she replied.

Eleven

Even though he was having his lunch at Top's Diner, a popular place, Marvin took Bart Stonefield's bringing her here for takeout as an arrogant affront. Surely Bart had seen his truck out there when he pulled up with her, but he still

169

came in, and this just hours after he had confronted him. The arrogant bastard.

Marvin could barely control his rage, and he knew when he got like this, he was vulnerable in ways he despised in other men – that look of guilt, that giveaway. He would avoid looking directly at anyone, especially someone in any sort of authority – even a waitress in a restaurant, for Christ's sake, afraid she would take one look at him and know all his little secrets, know whom he had robbed recently and, in the past, knew when he had shoplifted, knew when he had put that snake in Mrs Rotter's top desk drawer in tenth grade . . . on and on, until the waitress would suddenly scream and point to him and shout, 'It was him!'

He hated looking meek and frightened, but he warned himself that raw anger, such as he was feeling now, put him at risk. Maybe that was what Bart Stonefield hoped would happen. He sat there in Top's, forcing the rage back like someone swallowing resurging bile. When he felt confident that he would not attract any interest or attention, he left. He didn't walk too quickly or rush to his car. He strolled like someone who had all the time in the world. He even drove more slowly than usual.

But when he was away from any prying eyes, the rage rushed back through him. Stonefield was so arrogantly confident. He hated rich people. He loved overcharging them whenever he could. He hated the way they were able to bypass the tough stuff of everyday life, like getting enough food on the table or paying the electric bill, just as much as he hated them for their expensive cars and clothes, the freedom they had to buy almost anything, the lack of worry about how much they spent, and especially their indifference to those poorer than they were.

He wasn't a communist or anything like that and he was far from being against making money. He simply hated how easily some seemed to be able to do it, even some of the electricians and plumbers he knew, and especially those smug accountants and lawyers. He hated their kids who had inherited all their privileges – a guy like Bart Stonefield.

When he was younger, he was good at hiding all this resentment. He couldn't recall the first time he had had someone from a family wealthier than his buy him lunch or dinner, but he was sure he had enjoyed it. In a way, it was like getting back at them, or at Fate for handing him a lousy hand at the card table of life.

It was easy to pull up to a gas station and have one of them pay to fill his tank. He didn't even blink when they took out their money and paid the restaurant bill or bought the beer. He started to borrow money from them, too, money they knew and he knew he would never repay. No one complained. No one dared complain or come after him.

Back in high school, he liked dating girls from well-to-do families. They didn't have to be all that pretty or well built either. They dressed better and he could spend time in their luxurious homes. He knew they went out with him because he was dangerous. He was smoking, drinking, driving well before most of the boys in his class. And he was tough, too. He had that wild look.

He knew there were snobby girls who called him greasy, even a degenerate, but he believed secretly, deep down, they wanted to be with him, to spend a night or two with him so they could brag. In a cool way, that gave them some extra standing. They had played with fire and not been burned – or maybe just a little singed.

Sometimes, just for the fun of it, he would take a girl like that on a date and deliberately act like a virgin – timid – just to see her reaction. He knew when she reported on her date to her girl-friends that few, if any, would believe her. In a way, that created more curiosity and he probably got to go out with a few more just because they were skeptical.

It didn't hurt that his parents were unambitious for their kids. He could probably count on the fingers of one hand how often his mother or father had looked at his report card. If they were called about something he had done in school, he might get a slap on the side of his head or simply cursed. By the next day, it was forgotten and he came to believe that he was promoted to the next grade or passed in a subject because his teachers simply didn't want to have to put up with him again.

That was fine with him. He never bought into the idea that the secret to success was to succeed in school. He saw too many examples of rich kids who had inherited positions in their family businesses – like Sammy Elkin who took over his father's wholesale plumbing or Tim Kaplan who became his uncle's partner in the natural gas company a year before his uncle died in a car accident. No, for guys like him, it was make your own luck your own way, and that meant fewer restrictions or obligations. Rules were for the weak.

Today, especially after seeing Bart and Victoria together, all those resentments came rushing back at him, reminding him that he hadn't really gotten even a quarter of the way toward that world of privilege. He wasn't just walking in his father's footsteps in some half-ass car repair business; he was walking in his own shoes and look what had become of him.

Nothing for some time had brought that home to him as much as seeing Bart Stonefield with her. Christ, was there anything Stonefield couldn't get? Talk about rules not applying . . . how the hell did he swoop in and get into that cockpit so quickly and so easily? Maybe Bart had less of a conscience than he did. Whatever. Stonefield was the one having a good time.

Whereas nothing I do, Marvin thought, *has any real effect in this world*. He was insignificant. Like engineering the most brilliant bank robbery and getting away with millions of dollars but no one noticing or caring. What would Bonnie and Clyde have been without their notoriety? Petty thieves, that's what. They would have died and been buried under blank tombstones.

Was he going to take this sitting down?

Would he ignore it and go on? Go on how? Little embezzlements – like charging too much for simple work or charging for new parts that were old and cheap – were suddenly unsatisfying.

He couldn't recall the last time he felt so damn pessimistic about his miserable little existence. And all this while Bart Stonefield paraded in front of him with his fancy car, fancy clothes and a beautiful woman.

Once, Bart Stonefield had seen him as a hero, looked up to him, wanted him at his side – not only for protection, but for the excitement he brought. He was the forbidden friend, the one you didn't tell your parents about, but you bragged you had done this or that with him. He made them look tougher, a little more dangerous. None of those types had anything whatsoever to do with him now. They would barely acknowledge him with a nod, and there was that smug, superior look on their faces. They always knew what he would become. He had been used, that's all.

For Christ's sake, in the end he was the one who was raped. They used his manhood, his courage, his wise-ass ways to make themselves feel as if they had all this, too. They sucked him dry. They were vampires. He was good enough under the cloak of darkness, but did any of them ever invite him to their homes for dinner? And after high school, when they went off to those expensive colleges, did they ever come by to talk old times? They didn't even bring him any business.

Would he even be invited to their class reunion now? And if he went, would they talk to him?

It really had been years since all these thoughts flew so freely through his mind. He had brushed most of it off, and if anything even slightly annoyed him, he drank it into the ground or fucked the brains out of some girl he picked up at Johnny's Dugout. He could wake up the next morning and feel restored. Wasn't that good enough?

Suddenly, no.

The sight of them looking so perfect together canceled out anything and everything he had done and could do to make him feel good about himself. That was it. They made him feel less manly. *Losers* raped people – not confident, strong, good-looking and bold men like him. He hadn't raped anyone since, had he? Not really. Taking advantage of a drunk-out-of-her-mind broad wasn't rape, was it?

But the reality was pretty damn clear now. The only way he'd enjoy a woman like Victoria Myers was to rape her. But not Bart Stonefield. He could date her, take her to expensive restaurants, buy her expensive gifts and sweep her off her feet with his charm. He wouldn't suffer a moment of guilt the way it was now.

You're an idiot to be surprised, he told himself. Anyone could have predicted this. Wasn't it his father who complained after their neighbors, the Temples, died in a house fire, 'The rich don't die in house fires. You can be sure the fire department gets there in fuckin' time.'

Well, this rich boy ain't gettin' outta this fire, he muttered as he drove along. *He'll pay. I'm not the fool he thinks I am.*

They were going on some sort of picnic, he thought when he realized they had bought takeout. Where would they go? He remembered Bart had that boat out on Echo Lake. He made a quick right and sped up. When he got there, he parked and looked out, at first not seeing them. Then he spotted them. As he watched them, he felt his body tighten and tighten. It was as if he was turning into stone.

It was too much. He started his engine again and drove away. He felt as if some creature was in his head, gnawing on his brain, getting down through his layers of memories until he was back there that night. Why the sight of her excited him so much more than the sight of any girl was a puzzle, but it did.

Yes, it was him who had come up with the idea when he saw how she was going to go home.

Or, rather, the idea just came to him. He remembered now. He almost couldn't breathe after he had thought of it, how easy it would be.

Louis was reluctant, but Marvin didn't care if he had to do it all alone.

Later, he remembered thinking that it was like a dream. He was exhilarated afterward. He felt so powerful. How easily he could control someone's life. Of course, he was the only one who felt that way. That made sense. Who else had his inner strength back then? Who else was so unafraid of punishments and unafraid of challenging God's wrath?

He could go back to all that. He was confident. His power was returning.

Let them think they lived in a protective cocoon never to be touched by someone like him. Let them be unaware, as unaware as she was that night.

He could come out of the darkness again, just as swiftly and firmly.

First, he'd get some sort of monetary satisfaction for sure. And then . . . his lips were salty wet with the images.

They'll never be free of me.

The thought energized him. Rage went away. He was happy again. Celebrations loomed ahead. He turned on the radio, and in moments he was back in high school, strutting through the hallways, aware of the eyes of girls who were watching and whispering about him.

'Would you dare?'

Giggles.

'I would,' she would say.

The others would look shocked, but then they would look at him again and they would wish they had the courage.

Was that his own laughter?

It seemed to catch up to him like someone or something he had left at the side of the road years ago.

'Welcome back,' he muttered.

Twelve

She shrieked when they took their first bounce. Bart was obviously showing off. His boat was really too fast for the small lake and she could see people in rowboats and small sailboats glaring at them with displeasure. He had shot off from the dock and turned so sharply that she fell against him. He, too, saw the way his driving was annoying some, so he slowed and they cruised for a few moments.

'I have to move this boat to a bigger lake,' he said. 'I've been thinking of an inboard anyway. You waterski on this lake with a boat like this and you do a full circle in ten minutes. By the way, you're going to waterski and you're going to learn how to run this ship so I can,' he said as if it was a fait accompli that they would spend weekends together.

She smiled and sat back. Now that they were cruising at a more comfortable pace, she closed her eyes and soaked up the sun and the scent of the water. She sensed he was close but she didn't open her eyes until after he had kissed her.

'Couldn't help it,' he said. 'You're too beautiful to resist.'

Am I? she wondered. He sounded sincere.

When, during the past four years – the past six – had she felt this comfortable, this pleased? There was nothing about Bart's attention that unnerved her. In fact, she was surprised to see and feel his vulnerability. He was the one who seemed nervous all the time, not her. Shows you really don't know anyone, she thought.

He got her to take the wheel and for a while, with his arms around her shoulders, his lips at her ear, he instructed her on how to drive the boat. It wasn't really difficult, but keeping an eye on where you were going and how close you were to other boats, waterskiers and even people swimming near their boats required strict

178

concentration. Finally, he pulled back on the accelerator and brought them to a stop at the east end of the lake.

'It's a little rocky in there,' he said, nodding at the small cove. 'We're better off anchoring here for lunch.'

He dropped the anchor and sat back in the rear of the boat on the cushioned bench. He smiled at her and then lay his head back, closing his eyes. Looking at him, without him looking back at her, she felt she could study him more intently. He was a very handsome man, very athletic-looking, with his broad shoulders and a tight waist. For years now, she had glided along on a shelf of low self-esteem. It didn't surprise her that she kept asking herself why he wanted to be with her. He could be with the most promising, best-looking women. Why wasn't he involved with someone? Could it be that he simply wanted conquests and no commitments, at least for a while yet, and she was just another interesting possibility, maybe even because of her history rather than in spite of it?

She was so tired of thinking the worst of everyone, especially young men. Couldn't she take a chance on someone, just once? So she'd be disappointed – so what? Look what she had survived already. *Relax, Victoria Myers*, she told herself. *Defrost*.

He looked at her and smiled. 'How about a dip?' he said. 'It's a pretty good place for it. We've got a little privacy.'

She nodded and slipped off her clothes, down to the new bathing suit beneath. He had taken his pants off when they had boarded and was in his suit. He took off his T-shirt, looked at her and then dove into the water, slicing the surface so smoothly that he hardly splashed. She recalled now that he had been on the school's swimming team. He bobbed and beckoned.

'It's great,' he said.

'I can't dive like that,' she said and sat on the edge of the boat. Then, before she could lower herself in, he reached up and put his hands on her hips to lift her and gently dip her in beside him.

She screeched with delight. 'It's cold!'

'Not after a minute or so,' he said.

She swam away from him and then back to the boat. She reached up to grab the side for a sense of security. He swam over and did the same.

'Happy?' he asked.

She was surprised at the question. It sounded as if he thought she might never be.

'It's fun, yes. I haven't swum for . . . a long time.'

'It's like riding a bike. You don't forget how.'

He moved closer. 'I don't mean this to sound bad in any way,' he said, 'but doing things with you . . . it's like doing them for the first time. Just like last night. I've been to Dante's often, as I told you, but it felt new.'

'I'm the one who's starting over,' she said. It was a terribly revealing comment. She realized it the moment she had uttered it, but he smiled and nodded.

'Start everything over with me,' he told her and kissed her, both holding on to the boat, his left hand on her shoulder.

'Hungry?'

'Suddenly ravenous,' she said. He boosted himself up and into the boat and then reached over to take her hand. Before she could try to get back in, he lifted her under her arms and for a moment held her there, smiling.

'Don't you dare,' she said.

He laughed. 'There's a toll to pay or else.'

'What's that?'

'Kiss me.'

'Blackmail,' she said, but she did and then he helped her aboard.

'You knew I was tempted even after you paid the blackmail, don't you?'

'I'm not a small fish you throw back in.'

'No, you're quite a catch,' he said. He handed her a towel and went for their sandwiches. He had a little table that folded out by the cushioned bench. The boat rocked but it wasn't uncomfortable. Behind them and to their right, other small motor boats were bouncing over the water, all staying their distance.

'Busy out here today,' he said, unwrapping her sandwich for her and opening a soda. Then he sat beside her.

She bit into her sandwich and nodded. 'Fresh turkey. It's delicious.'

'Yeah, I've always liked that place.'

She chewed and thought about Top's Diner. Marvin Hacker's hateful look gave her the shivers.

'So, Marvin Hacker really resents you? From what you told me, that is.'

'Whatever,' Bart said. 'I can't turn the customers away just to please him.'

181

'I remember him and his brother, of course. Weren't you friends with them?'

'We hung out for a while,' he said.

'Well, I guess you had something in common.'

'What?' he asked sharply, so sharply that it took her back for a moment.

'Cars,' she said, shrugging.

'Right. Cars.'

'Weren't they driving years before they were legal?'

'Yeah. So, how about we get you up on skis today?' he asked, changing the subject abruptly. 'I'll show you exactly how to do it. It's really easy and I know you'll love it.'

'I don't know. It looks hard.'

'It isn't,' he insisted. 'We'll go to a quieter, safer part of the lake after we eat. I want you to practice running the boat, too. I would like to get up on skis today as well.'

'Do you think I'll be that good that fast?'

'Victoria, you're that good now,' he said, smiling.

She laughed. *I'm a kid again*, she thought, *innocent and excited, and it feels wonderful*.

He took her to an area of the lake where she could stand while he went through the basics of waterskiing.

'All we're going to do today is get you up and going for a little while. You might fall once or twice, but don't get discouraged, OK?' he said.

She was nervous, but she went for it and, surprisingly, after only one fall, she was up. He took her on a small circle, going just fast enough to keep her standing. After that, he carefully

182

reviewed what she was doing wrong and they went at it again. This time she did do better. Maybe it was easy, but she had a terrific sense of accomplishment.

They spent the next hour on getting her better at running the boat. When he felt she was doing it well enough, he told her exactly where to go with him on the skis. She could watch him in the rearview mirror. They practiced his getting up and her moving forward three times before he said she was ready for the wide circle.

Nothing – not even learning how to drive a car – matched the excitement and self-satisfaction when she took him around the lake for what was a good fifteen-minute turn. When they returned to the starting point, he was all smiles.

'You're a natural,' he cried from the water. 'We're a real team now.'

She laughed and helped him get everything together.

'How do you feel?' he asked when they were ready to start back to where he kept his boat docked.

'Exhilarated,' she replied.

'I have an idea, if you're not too tired,' he said, practically shouting now as they were heading back quickly, the boat bouncing, spray all around them.

'What? And don't tell me another sport.'

He laughed. 'No, I was thinking we'd stop to get some Chinese on the way back and have it at my place. What do you think?' She hesitated. 'Unless, you think it's too much,' he added quickly.

'No. No, it's a great idea,' she said. She had come a long way. Turning back was not an option.

Her mother would be surprised when she heard, she thought and laughed.

'What?'

'Nothing. I was just thinking. I'll tell my mother I'm helping you with your *Huckleberry Finn* paper.'

His smile broadened and then he reached down for her hand and brought it to his lips as if she was a fairytale princess who had granted him a great favor.

Oh, please, she prayed to whatever guardian angel had taken on what had seemed to be a lost cause, *make this really happen.*

She helped him secure the boat, with him teaching her about ropes and knots and everything else that had to do with it. Every once in a while, she had the sense that he was talking to her as if he expected their little romance would go on and on. Was this the danger zone for a young woman – that place where she begins to have high, maybe unrealistic hopes, and then suddenly finds herself falling like someone in an unopened parachute? *Am I hearing what I want to hear and seeing what I want to see and not what is true?* she wondered.

When she really thought about it, she lacked the experience a young woman her age should have by now. She was leapfrogging from adolescence to maturity without making the required stops along the way. She had not had a single serious romance, not even serious dates.

I was raped once, she thought, *but I am still a virgin.*

184

And I am under the spell of a young man who might be able to instruct Casanova on how to win over a woman's trust and love. Am I going too far too fast?

She really didn't have time to ruminate about it. His excitement was infectious. As they drove back from the lake, he rattled off one story after another, telling her about his Uncle Frank, his father's younger brother, who had been the one to get him into boating.

'Frank and his family live in Philadelphia. That's where my father's family closest relatives are. My uncle used to take us all on his boat on Lake Winnipesaukee in the Poconos. When I was younger – eight or nine – I would spend part of the summer with him, my aunt and my two cousins. You'd love my uncle and my aunt. She's a little Bohemian and very sweet. Of course, my mother isn't crazy about her.'

'Why not?'

'They don't have much in common. My aunt Liz doesn't dress up, lets gray roots take hold in her dark brown hair and knows less about women's fashion than I do. She'd rather spend her day in her garden than at a garden party. What about your relatives?' he asked.

She told him about her father's younger sister and her mother's older brother, neither of whom lived on the East Coast now. She sensed that talking about their families candidly like this was adding another dab of glue to their budding relationship. *He can't be just a playboy*, she thought – or, rather, she hoped. *Unless, of course, this is all another ploy.* She felt like someone wearing

185

a blindfold and told to walk through a minefield.

But the lightness of the conversation and his excitement over things he was planning for them to do made her feel like a teenager again. The owners of the Chinese restaurant he went to for the takeout knew him well. Who didn't? He introduced her to the owner's mother, who he said was ninety-seven years old. She looked sixty. Of course, he ordered too much food. They walked out with two large bags filled with four different entrees, dumplings, egg rolls, a few pounds of rice, sauces and, of course, fortune cookies.

It occurred to her that she should call her parents and let them know she wasn't coming home for dinner, but she didn't. She didn't want to feel as if she was under any scrutiny or concern at her age. *They'll figure it out*, she thought.

'Ta daaaaa,' he sang when he opened his apartment door and stepped back. 'No checking for dust on the top of the refrigerator or anything,' he warned. 'My mother disapproves of everything in this apartment,' he added, almost proudly.

She laughed and looked around. It was simple, the walls bare, but not as messy as she had anticipated.

He started to organize the dishes and she went to work scooping out the food from the containers and heating what needed to be warmed. She didn't realize how quickly and easily she had taken control of his kitchen until she paused and saw him standing in the doorway, watching her, a wide grin on his face.

'What?' she said.

'I was afraid you might be spoiled and sit and wait for me to do it all.'

'I am spoiled,' she said. 'That's a warning.'

He laughed and stepped up to work beside her. 'Spoiled is my middle name. I guess we're a team in more ways than one,' he said. He kissed her on the cheek and began to bring the food to his dining table.

The two of them ate hungrily and talked as if they had both just been released from solitary confinement. They prodded gently at first at how each had spent the last four years. He confessed that when he had seen her that one time at the Down Under, he was an idiot.

'I guess you thought I was totally disinterested in you. I didn't try to start a conversation or anything.'

'I wasn't swept away,' she said.

He laughed, nodded and looked down. 'I know I have a reputation for being something of a playboy back then, and I'll confess that there have been girls I considered refundable.'

'Refundable?'

'Yes, return if dissatisfied. I knew I was investing only a night or two and returning them to the pool of available-for-fling young women.'

'Oh.'

'I knew immediately you weren't one of them. You were in a much higher class, and I just . . .'

'Wasn't ready for someone non-refundable?'

'Exactly,' he said, grateful for her finding the words.

'You made up for it,' she said. His smile was different. It was deeper, like the smile of someone who was waiting on pins and needles for approval.

She rose and started to clear the table. He sat there watching her and then, when she was in the kitchen, washing the dishes, he came up behind her, put his arms around her waist and kissed her on the neck. She paused, her heart fluttering, and turned into him. They kissed passionately, reaching deeply into each other to stir their blood so that every part of her warmed and welcomed his hands. Neither spoke except through their eyes. Then he gracefully knelt, put his arm under her legs and scooped her up as if she weighed nothing. She rested her head against his chest as he carried her from the kitchen to his bedroom.

Can I do this? she wondered.

Surely he knew the turmoil raging inside her, she thought, because he moved so slowly and so gently, like someone testing every touch, every kiss, to see if he had gone too far, moved too fast. She watched him undress her and then himself, feeling at times more like an observer, almost scientific, researching to see how she would do.

But his passion was real and demanding. She could feel herself easing into her own, pushing aside all fears and inhibitions, stamping on the ugly memories. This was as different as could be. The only thing forcing her was her own desire.

When he brought himself to her, she tightened for a moment and he waited. Then she closed her eyes again and relaxed, gently opening her legs wider, inviting him, welcoming his lips on her hard nipples, clinging to his waist as he pushed gently into her and began a slow, rhythmic, pulsating stroke, pressing into her own rush of passion that was more like a hunger now, a need to restore the woman in her. *Yes*, she thought, *I can do this. I can be normal, be loving, satisfy myself and a man.* Her joy spilled out in her tears, tears he kissed. He was saying so many things, declaring how strongly he felt about her, how much she fulfilled him and, strangely, how sorry he was he had waited so long to ask her out.

Sorry he had ignored me, she thought. *What did he mean? When could he have taken me out? While I was still in high school?* No one was really trying to take her out then. She couldn't even recall times she had seen him. Where or when would they have had the chance to meet while she was still in high school? And yet he had known who had taken her to the prom.

Oh well, she thought, who could blame her for being oblivious to what went on around her back then?

She wasn't oblivious to what was going on around her now. The orgasms she reached seemed to lift her body higher. She let her head fall back and welcomed each rush that flooded every part of her with a warmth she had thought beyond her forever. He lifted himself to look down at her and she looked up at him.

'I swear,' he said, 'you're as non-refundable as any girl could be.'

She studied him as best she could, searching his face for some deception, but he looked younger, more like a boy swearing and promising.

I can't survive a betrayal, she thought, but she had gone too far.

She was dangling over a cliff and he was holding her hands. If he let go, she would fall forever and ever and never trust another kiss, much less a promise.

It would be as if the world had finally closed up around her and left her to whatever she could find in the darkness.

Afterward, they took a shower together. She didn't realize how much sun she had gotten until then. Somehow, she had neglected the sun lotion. He rubbed some lotion on her while she sprawled on her stomach on his bed and then they made love again, more slowly, more controlled, moving like people who now knew the road they were on and could anticipate every turn.

He collapsed beside her and she curled up in his arms. They closed their eyes, which was a big mistake because neither awoke until it was a little after one thirty in the morning. Her first thought was she hadn't done anything remotely like this since the Incident.

'I'm sorry,' he said, when she moaned at the realization. 'Are they going to be waiting up for you or something?'

'Something,' she said, rising to dress quickly. He did the same.

'I guess your mother will have me washing blackboards.'

She paused, the panic broadcast in her eyes.

'There's nothing you can be blamed for, Bart. I'm a big girl.'

'Oh, sure. Sorry,' he said. 'I was just joking.'

190

They didn't talk much on the way to her house. No matter what she said or how she said it, she could see he looked guilty and sorry.

They saw a dim light through the living-room window. She wondered if her father would be in his chair, waiting and worrying. He started to get out when he pulled into her driveway, but she told him it was unnecessary. He kissed her and she started out, but he grabbed her arm and she turned around.

'I don't want anything to get in the way of our seeing each other again and again and again,' he said. He was so firm about it that she had to smile. 'I mean it, Victoria.'

'OK.'

'I'll call you some time after twelve or so.'

She nodded and got out. He waited until she had opened the front door. She looked back and he waved and backed out. She watched him drive off and then entered. She paused in the living-room doorway and was happy to see that neither of her parents had waited up for her. She turned off the light and made her way to her bedroom. Her parents' bedroom door was not fully closed. She smiled to herself. Either her mother or father had left it that way so either could hear her walking to her bedroom. Maybe they both were listening.

What were they thinking?

Were they really, deep down, happy or were they simply nervous wrecks?

She'd know sometime today, but for now she couldn't be happier.

And she knew it would take her only minutes

to fall asleep again, eager for the first time in years to start a new day.

Thirteen

Victoria recalled that she could see what Chief Hal Donald was thinking on his face. His deep wrinkled forehead might as well be a television screen. *Are you kidding me? Nearly two years after the fact, you walk in here with additional clues? How could you not recall these things for so long? How do I know you didn't dream all this? And really, what does it add to what we have?*

She was sure her mother saw the same thoughts as they sat in the office of the town's police chief, an office that was spartan with its dark cherry-wood desk on which there was simply a phone, a small note pad beside it, some papers, neatly stacked, and a ballpoint pen. The office had very dull pale white curtains. They looked faded from the sunlight. A framed three-by-four picture of President Kennedy, two brassy plaques, one seemingly for a golf tournament, were on the walls. A simple black file cabinet was in the far right corner. The window behind Chief Donald looked out on the dull backyard of the police station, where bushes overtook the remnants of the Ontario and Western Railroad tracks, a rail-road that once had been a prime contributor to the establishment of this part of the Catskills as a resort area. The memory of it in its heyday was drifting away like some dead relative.

Victoria and her mother sat on two hastily gathered yellow wooden chairs. The floor itself was cement painted a dark green.

'And you just remembered this?' he asked and tapped his pen on the pad after he had written down what Victoria had told him.

'Do you know what a repressed memory is?' her mother asked him.

Hal Donald's face seemed made of clay for a moment. It looked as if his lips were rolling from one side to the other. His cheeks went in and out like fireplace bellows and his eyes widened as his temples tightened. He cleared his throat.

'Well, I don't think I could give a definition that would satisfy a college professor,' he said, tacking on as harmless a smile as he could manage.

'Let me do that for you. Repressed memories are memories that have been unconsciously blocked due to the memory being associated with a very high level of stress or trauma.'

'Sure. I know that,' he said.

'The point is this new information is not diminished because of the time that's passed. In fact, the time that has passed helps bring it to the conscious mind.'

'Makes sense,' he said, nodding, but he looked as if he was about ten feet under water.

Helen Myers couldn't prevent a disdainful smirk. Hal Donald corrected his posture instantly. After all, he was the chief of police.

'I hate to even suggest this because I was far

193

from satisfied with her,' Victoria's mother continued in the same condescending tone, 'but maybe you should pass the information on to that state policewoman who was in charge for most of the investigation.'

'Everything she did or discovered is in the file here,' Chief Donald replied, nodding at the file cabinet. 'Lieutenant Marcus has moved on to other things, I'm sure.'

'We haven't,' Helen Myers countered.

He nodded, but avoided eye contact. 'We'll look into it,' he said, tapping on the pad.

She closed and opened her eyes as though she was enduring a sharp pain.

'Well, we'll see,' she said. She looked at Victoria and then stood.

Chief Donald turned to Victoria and smiled. 'How are you doing?'

'All right,' she said and stood quickly, too.

Her mother nodded toward the doorway. 'Please keep us informed,' she told him.

'Will do,' he said as they turned to leave.

Victoria's mother muttered under her breath and marched ahead of her. The air around her was electrified with her frustration. She practically lunged at the car's door handle, but then paused and looked back at the station.

'If it had happened to a man, they would have turned the world inside and out by now,' she declared. She shook her head. 'Get in, Victoria.'

They started away. The hamlet of Fallsburgh was just awakening. It wasn't yet the resort season, so store owners and merchants weren't rushing about to make every minute profitable.

194

Unenthusiastic hands pulled up window shades slowly and unlocked doors that they inched into open positions as if they were fighting the decision to work. Near the end of the town, Ted Kerry lifted up the service area door of his gas station and garage, revealing the two automobiles that waited like wounded soldiers in a surgery to be mended. The fifty-four-year-old stood as still as a statue for a moment, as if the effort to open had taken all his available energy for the day. He watched them drive by.

To Victoria, it seemed as though the small town was yawning, unhappy to admit it was morning. The poster on the movie theater had not been changed. Last week's showing of *Lolita* hung like the headline on a vintage newspaper – old news. Empty boxes of popcorn and candy still littered the front, waiting to be removed like the dead on a battlefield. You could see the flies circling with glee.

She had been to the movies only once since the Incident, and that was when she went with her parents because her mother wanted to see *To Kill a Mockingbird*. She was very self-conscious sitting between them as though they were bookends keeping her upright and protected, which she thought made her look pathetic. To their right and left and in front of them, girls who were on dates were snuggled closely to their boyfriends, and if she let her gaze drift from the screen, she could see some kissing. The giggling infuriated her mother who declared she would not go to the movies on a weekend ever again. When they left, Victoria kept her head down. She didn't want to greet anyone or see the disdain in their eyes. Who goes with their parents to the movies on a weekend? Who goes with them after you are seven or eight years old anyway?

This sense of having regressed only grew stronger as time passed, and she found herself either left out or retreating from social activities attended by almost everyone else in her class, even Jena. She couldn't help the trembling when a proposal with the potential for some promiscuity was made in her presence. 'We're just going for a ride with some boys, but who knows what will happen?' Or 'Everyone's going to Darlene's house this weekend. Her parents are visiting relatives. It's a BYO party,' which meant you had to bring your own booze.

She wasn't even participating in a glass of wine with her parents at dinner anymore. Every time her father offered it, she glanced at her mother who looked as if she was waiting for her decision as some sort of test. She knew what troubled her. Was Victoria capable of ever doing what she had done, of putting herself once again in that compromising situation and letting down her guard? Was she doomed to be forever the vulnerable one? How could she even think to spread her wings and fly with her flock? It was easier to turn down invitations or ignore suggestions.

I'm in a form of social hibernation, she once thought. *Will I ever wake?*

On the way home from the police station that day, her mother wondered aloud why no other girl these past few years had suffered such a sexual violation. Unbeknownst to Victoria, her mother had, through her own connections, tapped into police business. She was aware of criminal activities in just about every hamlet in the township. On Sundays, she would scour the local paper which listed police department reports. It had become an obsession. There had been plenty of domestic violence incidents, the usual petty robberies, an occasional car theft, some burglaries, two murders of passion without premeditation, drunk-driving arrests and the like, but the crime she searched for had yet to appear, even during the resort season. In a way, she was hoping for at least one or two, some modus operandi that might track back to Victoria's assault.

However, when her mother voiced her astonishment at the absence of a similar crime, Victoria didn't see it that way. Instead, her complaint seemed to indicate that, yes, Victoria had done something in particular to bring about this crime, something most girls would never have done. Here was the proof. It didn't happen to anyone else her age.

'I'm sorry it's happened only to me,' she said bitterly. It brought tears to her eyes, tears that would freeze there and then, somehow retreat to wait for another, better opportunity to spend themselves.

'That's not it. You're missing my point, Victoria. What this indicates to me is that it is more likely that it very well was not committed by local men. I hate to use the word "men". I mean, by local animals.'

'If that's true,' Victoria said, 'then my additional

197

details really won't make any difference. Maybe they've never returned.'

Her mother was silent. *Whom does it bother more that they will get away with it*, Victoria wondered, *my mother or me?* Would the capture and conviction of the perpetrators change the way everyone viewed her? Would that bring the sympathy she longed to see in other people's eyes? Would it somehow wash away the stains? Would she return to the world?

She had little hope it would happen anyway, even now, even with the revelation of repressed memories.

Before they reached home, her mother looked at her and, sounding more like Dr Thornton than ever, asked, 'How could you have walked that path?'

Was she referring to the first time or now? It sounded as if she meant the first time.

'I never felt in any danger walking it. I didn't imagine Norman Bates dressed as his mother was hovering in the shadows or anything.'

'No, no, I don't mean the first time. I mean now. To me, the emotional and psychological trauma would be overwhelming. That would take a lot of inner fortitude.'

Was she proud of her now? Victoria wasn't sure.

'I told you. Jena read this article about how that would help make a victim stronger. You defeat . . .' She swallowed back the remaining words like someone afraid that merely saying them would bring the evil back.

'Defeat what?'

'Ghosts,' she replied and looked out her side window.

For the past two years, there hadn't been very much discussion about the Incident at home and she was grateful for that, even though some would think her parents were fleeing from reality. Her mother had even stopped grilling her about her sessions with Dr Thornton. They simply asked, 'Is it helping?'

Even though she wasn't sure it was, she said so just so she wouldn't have to go on and on about it.

Why did I go on that path again? I should have left it, she moaned to herself. *All I've done is tear off a scab*. It was all back. It was all Jena would talk about again, and her mother would surely go into some sort of tirade about the police when they were home and with her father. He would say something that might sound as if he was defending them and that would shatter the ceasefire that lay quietly over it all. Her father would retreat to his chair, to the television or to a magazine or book, and her mother would mumble to herself as she went through the house, the complaints dropping and shattering around her in every room.

Of course, Victoria would retreat, too.

She wished she and her mother had not stirred up the hornet's nest, and, again, she regretted going with Jena to retrace her steps. She was always worried this would keep the Incident fresh and her name would return to gossip and chatter. She'd been seen the way she was those weeks and months that followed, and she feared she would never be free of the memory.

The first time she felt she might breathe again came when she received her confirmation of admittance to Columbia University. The letter took on the power of a passport or the famous letters of transit in her father's favorite movie, *Casablanca* – permission to leave that even the Vichy French government couldn't rescind. There it was. She pinned it to her wall so she could treat it with the reverence that other people showed a religious icon.

Finally, she had something she could brag about, something that brought a true, deeply felt smile to her face in and out of school. When teachers and administrators congratulated her, she felt redeemed, blessed, cleansed of any sin. She could walk with straighter, prouder posture and hold her head high. Jena was the only one who seemed wounded by the news.

'I thought you'd be happy for me,' Victoria told her.

'Oh, I am. I just thought you said you applied to New Paltz, too.'

'Not far enough away,' Victoria told her. 'Don't worry. We'll see each other on holidays and keep in touch,' she pledged, but secretly harboring the hope that she would unload Jena and the baggage that accompanied her. In the end, she didn't. If there was one thing about Jena now, it was that she was safe. Jena knew when to remind her of the Incident and when not to. It was simply that Victoria wanted a clean break from it all. Was that possible?

In fact, she was disappointed to learn that their class valedictorian, Dave Stein, had been accepted to Columbia, too, and even though he was also accepted at NYU, he decided to attend Columbia. There would, after all, be someone who knew her history, not that he was particularly someone who cared. In fact, he surprised her by congratulating her personally and carrying on a long conversation about it at lunch.

It wasn't often that one of the boys in their class joined Jena and Victoria at their table, but on this particular day, Dave did. He ignored Jena entirely and talked about all the things he knew about Columbia and places he had visited in the city. She thought – dared to think – that he was actually happy to have someone from their school going to Columbia, too – even her.

However, she was aware that having his attention and interest wasn't an enormous accomplishment. He was referred to as one of the class 'brains' and was not on any sports team or even in the drama club. He was in the chess club and wrote for the school newspaper. In fact, journalism was the career he wanted to pursue.

He was also a good two inches shorter than Victoria, stout, with habitually unruly dull brown hair. As far as a girlfriend went, he occasionally took Barbara Kenner to a movie or to a school party. She, too, was considered one of the class 'brains' and had been accepted at Bennington. She dressed like someone's mother and barely brushed her reddish brown hair. Most of the time it looked as if it was on its way to becoming a bird's nest.

'Lucky you,' Jena said when Dave left them.

'He's all right,' Victoria said. Jena's opinions of boys often amused her.

Why was it, she wondered, that girls who had trouble attracting any boy's interest were the most critical of them? It reminded her of one of her father's favorite films, *Marty*, in which these male losers were always denigrating the women who were available. Jena would instantly change her opinion of Dave Stein if he had asked her out, she thought. It was on the tip of her tongue to say so, but she resisted. She resisted anything and everything that would in any way diminish the light of hope and happiness piercing her dark world. Concentrating on college helped her ignore all that she was missing at the moment. Better days were ahead. What she didn't anticipate was the weight of what she would still carry with her when she left.

Paranoia was a stubborn companion. It refused to leave her side or stop talking. It was especially loud during those first years. Every time a male student approached her, even stopped merely to talk about the class that they were sharing, she would feel herself tighten and step back. No matter how well she tried to disguise it, she was sure that anyone who took a really intense look at her would see that she was someone who was wounded deeply in her sex. It was only a matter of time – minutes actually – before one of them would ask, 'Did something terrible once happen to you or something?'

What would she do? Say no and rush off? She certainly couldn't say yes.

Like someone watching a close friend or

relative in a coma, she waited for some sign of an awakening. Weren't there people who suffered the loss of a limb, facial scars, even blindness who had recuperated enough to live normal lives? They could fall in love and have someone fall in love with them, couldn't they? Dr Thornton often had made such analogies, always qualifying that she appreciated how deeply Victoria's wound was. 'However, you can't give up the hope that you will get past it,' she told her. 'I promise. It will happen.'

What else was she supposed to say? *You'll never be the same? You'll never have a normal relationship?*

A few times when she had come home and gone out with Jena, she had a good enough time to think perhaps it would happen. She felt some subtle changes coming over her. For one thing, she was taking more time and more interest in her appearance. She was shopping for more attractive clothes, clothes that complimented her figure. During her senior year in college, she could sense that more men were attracted to her. It was this that gave her the courage to return home after graduation and challenge herself. There was the thought that if she could succeed here, she could succeed anywhere. When she analyzed herself, she concluded that was probably the main reason she had put off a decision about graduate school.

Her mother wasn't happy about it. 'In my experience, young people who put off their future end up having none. Education is not so very unlike training for a sport, Victoria. You've got momentum now. You start to get rusty when you just loiter.'

'I'm not loitering. I'm stepping back and being more thoughtful – something you're always preaching. Haven't you told me time and time again that impulsive behavior is responsible for most failure?'

Her mother nearly smiled. She actually appreciated the way Victoria could toss her own words back at her now.

'Well, what about teaching?' Victoria's expression prompted an immediate addendum. 'Not here, necessarily,' she added quickly. 'Perhaps even some college or community college. I have some good contacts. You could begin as an adjunct instructor. There are all sorts of possibilities if you wanted to go that route.'

Teaching? Standing up in front of an audience of girls and boys who were my age when all this happened? It was difficult enough to stand in front of a college class and make a report. And what would happen if someone in her class learned about her past? She could easily imagine an innocent ten-year-old girl approaching her after the bell to end class rang and asking, 'Is it true you were raped, Miss Myers?'

Who was being more unrealistic now? Victoria wondered. She didn't even respond.

The conversation had put her into a funk. Rather than remain in her room and sulk about it, though, she took walks along the road heading in the opposite direction to the village. One afternoon, she reached the bungalow colony and watched the *invaders*, as her father jokingly referred to them, going about their daily summer lives. They looked happy, like people who had gotten a reprieve. The women were laughing together, and the children looked excited about swimming or playing the games organized by the young camp counselor. She almost felt like crossing over, stepping into their world and asking, *Can I put my real life on hold like you're doing, too?*

She was staring so hard that she didn't hear someone come up behind her until a voice said, 'Hello, there.'

She spun around to face a lady whose body looked aged beyond her years because she had somehow clung to a child's brightness. Her features were diminutive and she had eyes the color of blue hummingbird eggs. She wore a flowery dress and thick-heeled black shoes with stockings nearly up to her knees. Her still thick perhaps premature snow-white hair was tied in a bun, but not severely.

Victoria's gaze went to her right arm, which, like her left, had a puffy forearm. Under her arm, she held a small pot filled with blueberries. Just visible because of the way her arm was turned were the tattooed numbers that Victoria knew too well meant this lady had survived a Nazi concentration camp, thus explaining the contradictions in her appearance.

'Are you the owner of the property?' she asked, indicating where she had picked the berries.

'Oh no. I think that's the Baxters', but they won't mind. They have many berry bushes.'

The lady widened her smile. 'Going for a nice walk?'

'Yes. I live about a half a mile toward the village.'

'Beautiful. I lived in a village even a little smaller in Hungary. You're a very pretty young lady. You have a boyfriend?'

'No,' she said, smiling.

'How old are you if I may ask?'

'Nearly twenty-two.'

She shook her head. 'What's wrong with the young men here? I was married four years by your age.' She patted Victoria on her left arm gently. 'But you're probably smarter. Wait for the man who thinks you walk on water,' she added.

She started to walk away.

'Can I ask?' Victoria said. 'Those numbers on your arm?'

The lady looked at her arm. 'What numbers?' she said, smiling. She walked on.

Victoria watched her being greeted by a young girl who could easily be her granddaughter, excited about the berries and what she would do with them. She could probably already taste the pie.

Victoria smiled but also felt a sudden wave of shame. Look what that woman had survived. How many times had she been raped, abused, beaten? How close had she come to death? From where did she get her smile now?

From today, she answered herself.

She walked on, laughing at the elderly lady's advice. *Wait for a man who thinks you walk on water.*

And then, a few days later, she had brought

206

her car for service at Stonefield's. Bart came out to greet her, and it was as if someone had cleaned the blackboard, erased her entire history, and she really could be reborn.

She could smile like the elderly lady, too.

Fourteen

Florence Stonefield had barely touched her chicken salad, served in a scooped-out half of papaya. It was her weekly luncheon with her two closest friends at Patsy's in Monticello, a more upscale restaurant where they could get a decent mimosa. Occasionally, they had a fourth join them if none of the three put up any resistance. It had become something of an understanding among the three, however, that whoever was lucky enough to be included was not to become a regular. It was the exclusivity of their friendship that made becoming one of the Yalta Three – so nicknamed by the three husbands, jokingly comparing them to Churchill, Roosevelt and Stalin – so valuable and desired.

Natalie Newton believed with the fervor of a religious fanatic that you needed only two real friends, friends being differentiated from acquaintances. There was nothing friends couldn't frankly discuss, and friends always told each other the truth. Friends were as reliable as mothers – good mothers, that is. Sisters were not reliable. There was that nagging sibling envy thing. Real friends bonded, went out with each other, took vacations with each other and were frank about everyone their friends knew. They weren't envious of each other; they were happy to learn something new, especially when it came to fashion, nails and hair. They never gave each other false compliments. Friends didn't ingratiate to earn friendship. They paid for it with honesty and sincerity.

'Good girlfriends, married girlfriends,' Natalie declared with an air of prophetic certainty, 'annoy husbands. They are not only jealous of their wives' relationships, but fearful, if not respectful. No secret should or could be sacrosanct when it comes to real girlfriends. Real friends share misery as well and as quickly as they share pleasure and success.'

And these three had plenty of success to share.

Natalie's husband Henry was a county judge and had been for close to twenty years now. Her two sons, Theodore and Paul, Theodore a year older, were both accomplished attorneys. Theodore was in Scarsdale, New York, and Paul in Albany, both recently married to girls they had met in college – girls from accomplished families, one girl's father also an attorney and the other's father a cardiac surgeon. Theodore's wife was pregnant with the delivery date only four months away. She'd be the tight group's first grandchild.

'But I'll insist my granddaughter or grandson call me Nana or something and not Grandma,' she declared, pronouncing *Grandma* as if the word came along with the taste of sour milk.

Natalie was Florence's oldest friend. They had attended high school together and then both married local men. They were double-dating as far back as their junior high school year. Both husbands knew they had to win over their wife's best friend as well as their wife.

Bea Sommers, the youngest of the three, was married to Karl Sommers whose family owned and operated the county's biggest home heating oil company. They also distributed propane to heat swimming pools and run barbeques. Bea and Karl had two daughters – Sally, now attending Skidmore as a sophomore, and Janice, who was a high school senior. Bea was also the shortest of the three, just five feet four. She was often compared to the actress June Allyson because she was soft-spoken and had those diminutive facial features, as well as the light brown hair.

The three were on all sorts of charity boards, often went shopping in New York City together and, when attending large gatherings, always ended up clinging to each other's reviews of what was happening around them. They believed with sincerity that they didn't gossip; they discussed and their comments, about other women espe-cially, were not petty. They were simply more perceptive.

Natalie was elaborating on her opinion of sili-cone breast implants that had suddenly become the rage. 'The question every woman considering it has to confront,' she concluded, 'is whether she's doing it to please herself or her husband or boyfriend. I'm tired of all the sacrifices we women make for our men.'

Bea was about to offer an opinion when Natalie

practically spun on her seat to face Florence. 'All right, Flo, enough.'

'What?' Florence asked, looking confused. Was she supposed to answer a question or offer an opinion after Natalie's diatribe?

'You're sitting there like a Buddha. What is bothering you today? And don't tell me it's nothing or not really important. Don't even try it.'

'Natalie,' Bea said with the tone of a gentle reprimand. Although the three were honest with each other, they were also very protective. Natalie and Bea were quite aware of the rumors about John Stonefield and his bookkeeper, but neither had the heart to bring it up. They had an unwritten agreement not to discuss it until Florence alluded to it.

Florence looked at Natalie and then Bea.

'You two know about all this, I'm sure. You're just being kind, too kind. But don't either of you worry. You won't tell me anything I didn't know or express feelings I don't share about it.'

Bea's face softened as her gray-blue eyes filled with compassion. Natalie pressed back the sides of her dark brown hair so hard and abruptly that she unhinged her orange-and-white Ronettes-style clip-on right earring. It fell to the table. She plucked it off the stark white table cloth and put it back on without saying a word. Of the three, she was the one who was more intense about looking well put-together. She was nearly five eleven, a good ten pounds overweight now, but still cut a striking figure in her favorite black crepe, beaded chiffon lace-bodice dress.

'Neither of us takes any pleasure in it, Flo,' Bea said. 'I'm sure you know that.'

'Of course I know that. I was going to tell you myself,' she said. 'I was just trying to find the right words, the words that wouldn't set me screaming.'

'Neither of us would blame you if you did,' Bea said.

'The truth is we're glad you're ready to talk about it,' Natalie added.

'She's not stable, you know,' Florence began. 'He doesn't see that, I'm sure. Men unfortunately see with one eye – the eye between their legs.'

Her bitterness forced both her girlfriends to look down for a moment. No one spoke anyway because the waitress, a woman who Natalie was sure was nowhere near the age she appeared to be, was too close. She was surely much younger, but worn and tired living with some miserable bastard. She passed them by, pausing to see if any of them wanted anything. The morgue atmosphere she sensed sent her off without asking.

'He's a damn fool,' Natalie muttered. 'He doesn't have any idea what he's risking.'

Florence nodded. 'Yes. I always hoped the example you and Henry set for your boys would by proxy influence him.'

'None of us has it that perfect,' Bea suggested. 'We're open and honest about ourselves, but sometimes, I'm sure, each of us felt we could so depress the others that we kept our disappointments to ourselves. In my mind, you have to look at the entirety of it and not judge yourself and what's happened on the basis of one or even two incidents. Too many boats are sinking and we're still afloat.'

'Afloat but taking in water very quickly in one case,' Natalie said. She pursed her lips again. It was as if the gesture sealed the words she had spoken.

'What can we do to help you, Flo?' Bea asked.

'I doubt there is much you can do about it if I can't,' Flo said.

They both nodded. Bea instinctively reached out and put her right hand over Florence's left. 'The worst thing is to get yourself sick over it,' she said.

'*He* won't. That's for sure,' Natalie added.

'Why should he? He's happy. That's what's so hard about it,' Florence replied. 'He thinks he's found the perfect love. He sounds like a lovesick teenager, in fact.'

'Does he?' Bea asked. She shook her head. 'Men never really stop being boys.'

'And the worst part of this is how alone I am. I mean, John doesn't . . . he doesn't seem to care. Oh, I know he was always carefree about things that your husbands took more seriously, but he's not exactly oblivious. He knows what's happening, what she has to be like.'

Natalie narrowed her eyelids. 'Are you saying that he doesn't mind your talking about it?'

'Oh, I can talk myself red in the face, talk until the cows come home. He just looks at me as if I'm speaking a foreign language or he'll simply get up and leave the room.'

'That makes it all so much more difficult for you,' Bea said. 'It's downright cruel.'

'To say the least,' Natalie added. The three were quiet for a few moments. Then Natalie leaned forward as if she wanted the other two to do the same, just like three children sharing a secret. 'When . . . how did you find out exactly?'

'Oh, I knew from the get-go,' Florence said. 'He never mentioned anything, of course. He surely knew how I'd react, but Cissy Levine saw them together.'

'Cissy Levine?' Bea said. She looked at Natalie. 'Did she say anything to you? She speaks to you more than she speaks to me.'

'Not a word,' Natalie said. 'She'd know better. I assure you, I would have taken off her head if she so much as showed the first signs of glee. You know how she is.'

'She's a parasite,' Florence said. She took a deep breath. 'Anyway, it came to something of a head this morning. Of course, he's been seeing her almost daily since that night Cissy saw them at Dante's.'

'They went to Dante's together?' Bea asked quickly.

'Yes. You'd think he would have been a little discreet in the beginning. I mean, it could very well have worked out that he knew he had made a mistake. Why be seen with her so quickly?'

Neither of them spoke. They stared at Florence.

'The last thing I expect is for either of you to tell me I'm being unreasonable.'

'How could we?' Bea asked.

'Exactly. Anyway, to get back to what I was saying. At breakfast this morning, he announced he was going to give her a ring.'

213

'What kind of ring?' Natalie asked, pulling herself up, her eyes widening again.

'An engagement ring! What else? Well?'

The two stared with one astonished face.

'You know who I blame for this? I blame John. Two days ago, unbeknown to me, he decided to go forward with the Volkswagen dealership in Monticello and he told Bart he would be the manager – at a much higher salary, of course. So Bart felt he now had what he needed to go forward. He hasn't even been dating her that long. Well? What do you really think about it all?'

Bea looked at Natalie and then back at Florence. 'You're talking about . . . the Myers girl – Victoria Myers – Bart and Victoria Myers?'

'Of course. Don't tell me you two didn't know Bart was seeing her regularly. I didn't mention it because I didn't want to admit it was happening, but it's happening. Oh, is it happening,' Florence said.

Suddenly, setting free all she had pent up also released her trapped appetite. She dug her fork into her salad and began to eat.

For the first time in a long time, Natalie Newton was speechless. Bea said nothing either. The three returned to their food, and to all three this lunch had turned into a wake.

Meanwhile, across town in the county's newest restaurant – and its first Mexican restaurant – Bart couldn't stop talking. He pulled out the chair for Victoria. He had told her the night before that this was going to be a special lunch. For the last

214

three and a half weeks, they had been seeing each other every day, spending both weekends at the lake boating and swimming. If it rained, they went to a movie and dinner. One Saturday, he took her to New York City to eat at a restaurant one of his customers had raved about and arranged reservations for him. Three times, she had gone to his apartment for dinner, a dinner she insisted on making. She had impressed him with her cooking skills.

'When I was younger, I was drafted into it,' she explained. 'Both my parents were working jobs that kept them often until nearly dinner time. In the beginning, my mother would leave something for me to warm up, but gradually I began to take charge. My father loves pasta, so I took out an Italian recipe book and began experimenting. By the time I was fourteen, I was making lasagna, manicotti, spaghetti and meatballs, or vegetarian dishes with eggplant and zucchini, as well as casseroles. I make a killer meatloaf,' she added.

Bart was sincerely impressed. She could see it in his face when he ate what she had prepared.

'You're the whole deal,' he told her. 'Brains, beauty and the path to a man's heart – his stomach.'

Gradually, during their dating, she began shedding whatever inhibitions and insecurities she still endured. Her confidence had been resurrected from some grave dug immediately after the Incident. It rose with a vengeance. She bought new clothes and shoes, went to the beauty parlor to sharpen her style, paid almost scientific

215

attention to her makeup, chose a new perfume and, for the first time, cared about and did up her fingernails.

It felt as if the air had changed around her, especially in the house. When she did spend time with her parents, they each brought up amusing stories from their work, something she hadn't heard them do for years. And, as if her new attention on herself was infectious, they seemed to spruce up as well. Her father, who could put off a haircut for weeks after he needed one, was right on it. He and her mother bought themselves new clothes as well, and her mother had her hair done, too, choosing a more fashionable style. Because Victoria was out and about every free hour, they were spending more time with each other, going out to dinner, seeing a movie or just taking a drive.

Jena called often and was obviously upset about her friend not having any time for her. Victoria kept promising to find an evening for them to spend together, but had yet to do it. Meanwhile, more people had seen her out with Bart. The gossip was flowing in around them as if some dam holding back any reference to her had been breached. She found people were smiling at them, eager to say hello. Many were Stonefield car customers.

The result was she was once again comfortable in her own skin. She put off her yearly follow-up session with Dr Thornton and even began to think that she would never return. Did she dare be that confident?

The Mexican restaurant had three mariachi

singers at lunch and dinner. They moved around the room, singing to couples for extra tips. As soon as their waitress brought their margaritas, something Victoria never really drank, Bart signaled to them and they came to their table and sang the Richie Valens hit, 'La Bamba'. Everyone in the restaurant was moving to the rhythm and it established a party atmosphere immediately. As soon as it ended and Bart had tipped them, they ordered their food.

'How are you going to be able to return to work after this?' she asked, laughing.

'I'm not. You have me for the day . . . and the night,' he added and tapped his glass against hers. They sipped and gazed at each other.

'OK, I can't wait any longer. What caused all this?' she asked.

'Well, first, say hello to the manager of the new Stonefield Volkswagen dealership. Construction is beginning tomorrow.'

'Oh, Bart, that's wonderful,' she said. She tapped his glass again and sipped some more of her margarita. Three good sips had already begun the merry-go-round in her head. She ate some chips. Drinking on an empty stomach was going to turn the restaurant into a ship on the high seas very quickly, she thought. 'Mr Manager,' she said, and then she had the horrible thought that his father was paying him off to keep quiet about his affair. She chased that thought out quickly. Better to believe Bart's father knew he was capable of the job and deserved it as well.

'Did I tell you yet how beautiful you are, Victoria? I want to be sure I tell you every day, because I made a vow to myself never to take you for granted,' he said.

She knew she should be smiling, but all she could do was soak up the moment. She was probably looking incredulous and she didn't want that. She didn't want him to think for an instant that she doubted him or believed he just quoted lines that had brought him romantic success with other women. She finally managed, 'Thank you.'

'Aw, don't say thank you,' he said. 'I'm the one who's trying to say thank you. Thank you for being beautiful for me every day. Thank you for being so amazing to be with. Thank you for making me care about myself, for making me ambitious and, most of all, just plain happy, Victoria.'

The waiter brought them their food and Bart ordered two more margaritas.

'If I drink another of these, I won't hear anything you say,' she warned.

'Oh, then don't take another sip,' he said, smiling. 'Eat something.'

They began. The food was delicious and something she had never really eaten before.

'Right now, it's more of a West Coast thing, but I think it'll catch on. Maybe we should invest in the place,' he said, looking around.

'Your father would invest in a restaurant, too?'

He paused. 'I didn't mean my father. I meant us.'

'Us?'

The waiter brought the two new margaritas.

'Don't touch that yet,' he warned.

She started to laugh, but he put his hand in his

jacket pocket and brought out a small box, a box that could only be for a ring. He put it in front of her. She looked up at him. He thought she looked terrified.

'It won't bite,' he promised.

'Bart . . .'

'At least open it before you speak,' he said.

Her fingers were trembling. She reached for it and then opened it slowly. For a moment, she simply stared at it. She knew it was rather size-able, but she didn't know how big it really was. All she knew for sure was it was bigger than the one her father had given her mother.

'Victoria Myers,' Bart said, 'will you marry me?'

She was holding her breath. She looked at the ring again, glanced at him and then looked out the front window that faced Main Street. Of course, she felt more for him than she had felt for any boy or man, excluding her father. Why was she so lucky? How had this happened so fast?

'Victoria?' he said, his voice now sounding his fear of rejection.

She turned to him and smiled. 'Are you really sure about this, Bart?'

'I spent a lot of money,' he replied. 'No. Of course I'm sure. I'm about as sure of it as I've been about anything in my life.'

She took the ring out of its box. 'How did you know my size?'

'I'm not giving away all my secrets,' he said.

She tried it on. It was a perfect fit.

She thought about what her mother would

probably have said. 'Well, since the ring fits, I guess the answer is yes.'

His smile broadened. Then he lifted the new margarita. 'To us,' he said.

She lifted hers and they clinked their glasses.

'You'd better eat. You'll need your strength,' he said, nodding at her food.

'For what?'

'The start of our honeymoon,' he replied. 'Right after lunch. You didn't think there was any chance for me to do anything else, did you?'

She laughed and then started to eat again, expecting to hear a bubble pop and find herself back in bed dreaming.

Fifteen

Her first thought when she had got her parents to take a seat in the living room and shown them her engagement ring was that they look relieved – as relieved as parents of an ugly duckling might feel.

'That's an impressive ring,' her father said. He held on to her hand, looked at her mother and then, as he let go, added, 'I'm sure you know whether or not Bart's the right guy for you.'

'It is rather quick,' her mother said. 'It took us six months to get engaged, but I suppose that was because your father was too bashful.'

'That's not true,' he said. 'I wasn't bashful. I was cautious.'

Her mother rolled her eyes. 'The eye sees not itself but by reflection,' she offered.

'Don't start quotin' Shakespeare, darlin'. You know I was and always have been cautious.'

'Right,' she said with a flick of her right hand, her favorite gesture of dismissal. 'So how have Florence and John Stonefield reacted to this news?'

Her mother always went right for the jugular, Victoria thought. She wasn't sure whether that was good or bad. The opposite approach – circling the real issue, which was the way most people handled controversial things – could be frustrating and a waste of time, too. It was amazing. Here she was in her twenties and she was still wondering if she wanted to be more or less like her mother.

'I don't know,' Victoria said. She had never told her mother or father about what she and Bart had come upon that night at the dealership. He hadn't mentioned their reaction to his giving her an engagement ring and she hadn't asked. She just assumed that they didn't know yet.

'Have you met Florence Stonefield since Bart's been taking you out?' her mother asked.

'No.'

Her mother folded her hands together, pressed her forefingers against each other and brought them to her lips as she thought. The tightness at the corners of her eyes spread tiny lines into her temples like hairline cracks in a window. Victoria knew that meant her mother was having a troubled thought.

'I'm going to meet them tomorrow night. Bart's

arranging for us all to have dinner at Dante's,' Victoria quickly added.

Her mother looked up. Her eyes were sharp, that familiar look of confidence and authority firming her posture. When she was like this, Victoria thought, she seemed regally beautiful. It was harder to ignore her than it was to ignore a queen.

'Florence Stonefield is one of those women who believes there's a caste system in America similar to the one in India,' she said.

'I'm not marrying Florence Stonefield,' Victoria responded.

'Let me give you one word of advice, Victoria. When you marry someone, no matter what the man might tell you, you marry his family, too.'

'And vice versa,' Victoria countered. Her father smiled.

'Just so you're aware of it,' her mother said.

'How could I not be? Bart works with his father. Which brings me to the other big news. His father's going forward with the foreign car dealership in Monticello and Bart will be the manager.'

'Well, that is good news,' her father said.

'When do you plan on this wedding?' her mother asked. 'Or I should say, when do *we* plan on it?'

'We were thinking we might just elope,' she replied.

'Elope?' her father said.

'I see. Who came up with that idea?' her mother asked.

She shrugged. 'We were talking about an

elaborate wedding and Bart just said, "Why don't we just run off and do it? We could always have a ceremony later." I thought that made sense.'

'Nothing impulsive ever makes sense,' her mother said. 'But you're both adults and in charge of your own lives. Is this happening very soon?'

'We haven't decided on the exact date yet, but it won't be too long.'

'Seems like a waste to buy an engagement ring,' she quipped.

'No, it's not. You still wear yours.'

'Yes. Well, keep us up on the details, such as what day you're running off,' her mother added and rose. 'We're supposed to join Gerry and Miriam Kaplan for dinner tonight. I'm going up to shower and dress,' she said and walked out of the living room.

Victoria watched her leave. 'I'm glad she's so excited for me,' she muttered.

'Well, mothers look forward to their daughter's weddin's, Vick – all that plannin' and shoppin'. In a way, it brings them closer just when they're about to separate, don't ya think?' he asked softly.

'I suppose,' she said.

'I would be lyin' like the fox to that hen if I didn't say I was lookin' forward to walkin' you down the aisle and givin' you away, darlin',' he added.

She nodded.

'I mean, why do you guys hafta run off in the night as though you were doin' somethin' underhand or forbidden?'

'We don't have to,' she said. She saw the disappointment in his eyes. 'I'll speak to Bart. You're

223

right. I was just . . . overwhelmed and didn't think it out.'

He smiled.

'There's nothin' wrong with that, Vick. I'm really happy for you and so's your mom.' He rose and gave her a kiss. 'Got to get dolled up or I'll be whipped in the tool shed,' he joked and walked out.

She sat there thinking a moment before going to her bedroom and calling Bart.

'Hey,' he said, 'how did you know I miss you already?'

'Let's see if you say that in five years – even two.'

'I'll say it. You can take that to the bank.'

'I have a problem,' she said.

'Oh?'

'My parents are really very disappointed about our not having a wedding. I didn't realize how much it meant to them. I'm sure it will mean the same to me when our daughter gets engaged,' she added.

'Right, right.'

'I mean, you don't mind, do you?'

'When were you thinking?'

'I haven't gotten to that yet. What do you think's a good date?'

'Sooner the better or I'll force you to live in sin,' he said.

She laughed. 'OK. I imagine your parents will want to have their say.'

'Let your parents take the lead,' he said. 'My mother can be . . . overwhelming. It will be a coup de tata or something.'

She laughed.

'Tata? *Coup d'état*. Not if she meets mine,' Victoria said and he laughed. 'Maybe this will be more fun than we know,' she added hopefully.

'It could be as much fun as being on the Titanic,' he said.

After she hung up, she went to tell her parents about the reversal of their decision.

'I hope you're not doing this for my benefit alone, Victoria,' her mother said. 'It has to be meaningful to you more than to anyone else. There are times when being selfish is not only OK, but it's necessary.'

'No. I really gave it some thought, Mom. I realized I want a real wedding. I want to come out of the closet,' she said. Her mother widened her eyes and looked as if she was going to laugh or at least smile.

'I like that,' her mother said and did smile. 'Lester?'

Her father, still holding his razor with shaving cream over his face, stood in the bathroom doorway, listening.

'I heard it all. Of course. It's great. I'll even buy a new tuxedo – a real penguin suit.'

'Oh, you'll buy more than that,' her mother told him.

He looked comical in his lathered face, smiling.

'You can be such an idiot sometimes, Lester Myers,' she said and then added, 'But a delightful one.'

The three looked at each other and then, for the first time in a long time, they all laughed.

225

They laughed together and suddenly she felt that they were really a family again.

How ironic.

It was happening just when she was planning to leave them.

The following day, Victoria's mother and father explored some possible venues for the reception. Their best hope for the closest date was a moderate-size hotel called the Olympic, just outside of Woodridge.

'I hope Florence Stonefield won't hold us to Emily Post rules and regulations,' her mother told her. 'This is quick. The pressure will be on to make some big decisions. We can do the wedding right after Labor Day. The hotel will be available, obviously. I'm hoping the Stonefields don't expect they'll be able to invite every Stonefield customer. It's not intended to be a business write-off,' she added.

Uh-oh, Victoria thought. *Now I see why Bart was hoping to elope.*

Actually, it felt good to be concerned with the issues that confronted any two families when their children were marrying. They all looked quite surmountable to her. When she had told her parents she was coming out of the closet, she wasn't kidding. She knew the wedding would revive the memories, the infamous Incident, and for that reason both she and Bart would be in a bigger spotlight. She was depending on her love for Bart and his love for her to carry her above it all. The wedding might be just the way to put it finally to bed. After all, she was marrying a respectable young man with a successful business. Girls who didn't carry her wounds weren't doing as well.

She was more nervous preparing for their dinner with Bart's parents than she had been on her first date with Bart. Bart's own descriptions of his mother underscored the view of Florence Stonefield expressed by Victoria's own mother. That alone set the stage for a complex evening.

She had read enough novels and even some psychological research on the relationship of mothers-in-law and daughters-in-law to know there was a natural distrust, even a resentment sometimes. This young woman was taking away her son. She was no longer the number-one female in his life, and when and if there was conflict between them, her son naturally would support his wife. That was who he would be living with now; that was whom he would pledge to keep happy and safe until death do them part. It would help if they liked each other, but it wouldn't prevent eventual conflicts and disagreements about everything possible, from the furniture she chose to how she and Bart raised their children. All this was double pressure because they were both only children.

Bart would face some of the same issues with Victoria's mother and father. Her mother especially, she thought, was a very strong personality. She was that famous Sagittarius who would say exactly what she felt or believed. Sagittarius personalities were not good politicians.

Now, added to all this, was what she knew

about Bart's father and what he knew she knew. Apparently, Bart had chosen to see no evil and hear no evil. She would follow his lead, of course, and pretend she saw nothing out of the ordinary that night. However, she anticipated his father searching her face for signs of disapproval or disdain at dinner. *Just for tonight*, she thought, *I will try not to be my mother's daughter.*

Bart arrived a little earlier than usual to take her out, knowing he would have to spend a little time with her parents. They greeted him warmly. Her mother was even funnier than she had been the first time.

'Don't think you're getting a pass on college credit by marrying my daughter,' she told him.

'I expect she'll have me reading more,' he said. 'I've already improved my vocabulary,' he added. 'But she knows the importance of a carburetor now.'

'Don't believe him,' Victoria said. 'I've never looked under a car hood.'

He took her hand. Her parents could see the deepening affection between them and exchanged glances.

When her father mentioned that Victoria had told him about the new dealership, Bart went into it in great detail, describing his plans to crack the market for foreign cars, the publicity ideas he was conjuring and then the plans for the business management – something he thought her father, being a business manager, would appreciate. They were off and running with a conversation that left both Victoria and her mother only observers.

'It all sounds quite sound and excitin',' her father told him. 'You've prepared yourself well for the move, Bart. I wish you all the best.'

Bart was beaming. She had the sense that he was getting more support from her father than he usually received from his own.

They were flying on a magic carpet when they left for Dante's.

'Your parents are great,' he said. 'I wish my father had more of your father's Virginia ham in him.'

'Oh, you should see how they go at each other over the way he pronounces words and some of his Southern expressions. But she was charmed. You were right to compare my father to Randolph Scott. She used to call him her Randolph Scott. She never told me. He did in front of her one day and you should have seen her blush.'

'That I would like to see. My mother doesn't blush; she burns.'

'Oh, Bart, surely you're exaggerating,' she said, hoping.

'Let me prepare you for my mother,' he began. 'She's capable of asking embarrassing questions. I'll play referee, but if she gets out of hand, don't hesitate to let her know. She's actually a pussy cat at heart, but, like most cats, she'll lord it over you until you show your own claws.'

She sat back.

Maybe she wouldn't get through this unscathed after all. Maybe this whole thing was really impossible. Perhaps she should have gone off to a graduate school in another state and met a

229

different young man whose parents didn't know she was a rape victim who had returned to the community where the perpetrators could still be living.

What really had brought her back?

What secret was she yet to discover?

By the time they arrived at the restaurant, it seemed as if everyone there knew why they were having dinner. Bart suspected his father had let them know. He wanted extra-special treatment. Mrs Dante practically leaped at her engagement ring.

'What's this I see? How beautiful. Special night tonight. Thank you for spending it with us.'

His parents were already there, waiting. His father rose as they approached the booth.

'Hi, Victoria,' he said, reaching for her shoulders and kissing her on the cheek as if they were already father-in-law and daughter-in-law.

Bart's mother remained seated, looking up at them. She sat stiffly, her eyes lit with defiance. It was as if she had an invisible electric fence around her. Bart moved quickly to kiss her and then made what sounded like a formal, even awkward introduction.

'Mother, this is Victoria Myers.'

'I think I know she's Victoria Myers,' his mother said. She looked at her husband. It was clear that they had discussed and decided exactly how they would behave. 'Please join us. I imagine there's a great deal to discuss.'

'Thank you,' Victoria said. She and Bart would sit opposite his parents, she directly opposite

Florence Stonefield. They had been here a while. Both had martinis.

'I was thinking we'd have a bottle of champagne,' his father said. Something he read in Victoria's face told him he had nothing to fear concerning his indiscretion.

'Great,' Bart said. 'Thanks.'

'I'm not going to drink this martini and then a glass of champagne,' his mother said.

'Oh, we'll handle the bottle of champagne, I'm sure. Won't we, Victoria?'

'We'll make an effort,' she said and he laughed. Bart smiled, surprised at how cool she was being.

John Stonefield ordered the champagne and sat back. 'So, we're all ears,' he said.

'What do you think of the ring I chose, Mother?' he asked.

'I think I already told you. It's very nice, Bart.'

Victoria looked at him. So he had told her. She must have had a reaction, a reaction he obviously didn't want to describe.

'I suppose Bart's told you about our plans for our dealerships,' John said. The champagne was brought to the table and the waiter and the busboy set up the glasses quickly.

'None for me,' Bart's mother said. She pushed the glass away.

The busboy reached out and took it back as if he was picking up something in the ocean and feared a shark might bite off his hand.

'He did,' Victoria said. 'It sounds very exciting.'

'First really big foreign car dealership in the county,' John declared. 'It's like landing at Normandy.'

'There are a few thousand American soldiers who might be upset with that analogy,' Florence Stonefield quipped.

'We're not going to actually use that, Mom,' Bart said. 'It's just a figure of speech.'

'Never mind,' John said. He lifted his glass of champagne. 'To the newest Stonefield couple in America.'

The three clinked glasses. Victoria sipped her champagne and watched Florence take what looked more like a gulp of her martini.

'Well, good news,' Bart began as the waiter brought them the menus. 'Victoria's parents have already begun looking at wedding venues and have found a great one for our purposes. The Olympic.'

His mother sat back, her mouth falling open like the mouth of an actress in an over-the-top silent movie.

'How long have they known about this?' she asked.

'What? A day or so?' Bart asked Victoria.

'About,' she said. 'My mother originated the saying, *A rolling stone gathers no moss*,' she said with pride.

'That's for sure,' John said. He continued to look delighted. Victoria couldn't help liking him, despite what she knew. Another voice inside her was defending him, especially now that she was facing his wife. She almost justified adultery.

'The Olympic. Why? We could get the Concord or Grossingers for sure,' Florence Stonefield said when she regained her composure. 'We should at least discuss it. That's the way things are done.'

'We want it to be as soon as possible and they're available immediately after Labor Day,' Bart said.

'After Labor Day? You're talking about less than six weeks – if that. People are supposed to be given decent notice. Some will come from out of the state.'

'We don't want it to be that big an affair,' Bart said. 'Smaller is cozier.'

'How small?' his mother demanded. Both Bart and Victoria nearly smiled. First, she was obviously against the marriage and now she was worried it wouldn't be big enough to fit the image she had of the Stonefields.

'We thought maybe two, two fifty,' Bart replied.

'Each?'

'No, Mom, total.'

'Ridiculous. We'll insult so many people.'

'We can cull out those who aren't true friends and important enough relations,' he said softly.

'The bride's parents handle the wedding,' John Stonefield added, happy most of the work would be done by someone else. 'We can have a helluva rehearsal dinner. I'll take over this entire restaurant. There's no better place for it.'

Florence Stonefield's eyes electrified as a thought shot through her with lightning speed. She fixed her gaze on Victoria like a pin spotlight. 'Are you pregnant?' she demanded.

The ceiling could have fallen on the table with less of a wham.

The waiter approached them and Florence turned on him. 'Not yet,' she snapped and looked at Bart and Victoria.

Bart nudged her with his knee.

Victoria took a deep breath and leaned forward. 'Only with my love for your son, Mrs Stonefield,' she replied.

There was a pause, a true pregnant moment, and then John Stonefield roared. He signaled for the waiter.

And the dinner officially began.

Just like most young women her age, Victoria had done her homework when it came to weddings. From time to time, when she was fantasizing about falling in love and marrying, she had perused magazines and read articles. She had never had a detailed discussion about it with her mother, but occasionally she had brought up one wedding concept or another to hear her opinion. She would never confess it, but soon after she and Bart had begun their second week of dating, she even began looking at wedding dresses. That was why she had been somewhat disappointed with his initial idea of eloping. He had promised a ceremony later, but her parents' reactions gave her the chance to revisit her dreams.

Despite her mood, Florence Stonefield was impressed with Victoria's knowledge about flowers, wedding music, food and even invitations. She kept shaking her head, now wondering just how long this romance had gone on. Had her son been seeing Victoria Myers secretly for months and months?

Reluctantly, she had to admit that Victoria sounded quite organized. She didn't hide her surprise and before their dinner ended – after Gino Dante presented them with a special chocolate swirl angel food cake, glazed with chocolate syrup – she got in her sharp dig, a comment through a question that left no doubt as to her reason for being unhappy about her son's choice.

'Despite how quickly this is all happening and the preparations you have done,' she began, 'a wedding still imposes great pressure and tension on any prospective bride. Is your therapy complete? Are you in a good place for this big life-changing decision? I'm asking only out of concern for you, dear,' she added with as plastic a smile as Victoria had ever seen.

Both Bart and his father looked as if they were holding their breath.

'Bart has made that question unnecessary,' Victoria said. She looked at his father, too. 'None of us underestimates the restorative power of sincere love.'

Florence Stonefield sank with defeat and looked down as John called for the bill. He and Florence remained behind after the obligatory thank yous and quick kisses good night. Victoria told Bart's mother that her mother would be calling her the next day.

Bart took her hand. They made their way out of the restaurant, navigating good luck wishes from other local people who had inquired about the elaborate dinner and learned about the occasion.

They burst out of the restaurant and both paused to take a breath.

'My God,' Bart said. 'You were fantastic.'

'I was, wasn't I?' she replied, laughing, and

then stepped forward with him toward his car, feeling more confident about her future than she had ever thought possible.

She was glad she had come home.

Sixteen

Detective Rob Luden sat back in his desk chair and for a few moments felt sorry for himself. He had studied for a criminal justice degree at the Bronx Community College in New York City and was one of the best students they had processed to date. His prospects and the expectations of him were very high. The more he was complimented, the bigger his ambitions grew. He would put in the years he needed to build his resume and maybe he would move on to join the FBI. That was his original plan.

His first job was a very prestigious one. He worked in Yonkers, New York, and almost from day one found himself working high-profile murders, as well as the usual embezzlements and armed robberies. Despite coming to the job with great recommendations and impressive academic achievements, however, he had to overcome a physical obstacle. Rob was the kind of man who would be burdened by his youthful appearance most of his life. He was in a profession that required an air of authority that came from a look of maturity.

Most everyone had a movie and television

image of the typical detective. He was usually dark-haired with an unkempt appearance, a man who drank and smoked too much. He was good-looking in a dangerous way, but also hard, worn and radiating cynicism. But Rob Luden's reddish blond hair, resembling a soldier's cut, his soft, somewhat chubby cheeks with freckles that looked tossed on to them, and his greenish-blue eyes made him look more like a character out of an Archie Andrews comic book than a Sam Spade movie.

He felt he had to work harder, become an overachiever almost from the get-go. Sometimes he even looked for and welcomed a physical confrontation just so he could prove himself on the job. He had had extensive self-defense training and kept his body tuned with vigorous exercise. He was doing fairly well, despite being called The Kid, and regardless of the fact that even the uniformed patrolman knew him as that. There were plenty of in-jokes like 'Does he faint at the sight of blood?' or 'When did he get the braces off his teeth?' Rather than get angry, he battled back with insights and achievements that wiped the teasing smiles off faces.

Then he fell in love. He was so smitten by this ravishing redhead who had just started teaching elementary school that he found himself often cutting corners to spend more time with her and be able to make every date. He was actually afraid that if he did miss dates or frustrate her, she would soon find another beau, no matter how much she seemed to be falling in love with him as well. They had an intense two months before

237

he woke up one morning determined to pop the question. In the back of his mind was the fear that, no matter how passionate their romance was going, she would in the end hesitate out of fear of being married to a policeman.

As he was wisely told by his father, 'A policeman, perhaps a homicide detective more so' – which was what he was hoping to become – 'is truly like a soldier always on the battlefield. There's never a period of peace, never a truce, Rob. You're always at war. Your mother hates to even think it, but in few other professions does someone have the realistic possibility of not coming home at night ever again.'

It would take a special woman to want to marry into that, but Becky Clancy was that woman. To find someone so beautiful and willing was truly like hitting the jackpot when it came to a relationship and a life. Why hesitate? Fortunately, she felt the same way. They married and, within the first year, had a child, a daughter they named Megan.

His career and his ambitions took an unexpected backseat. Family concerns raged to the top of his priorities. His wife's family lived in upstate New York. They were a close family. Becky was especially close to her mother since her brother had joined the navy and then married a girl in the Philippines where he now lived. When his father-in-law suffered a stroke and died, Rob and his wife and Megan, now three years old, moved to the upstate hamlet of Woodbourne to live in the big home with her, and he was able to get the job at the Fallsburgh police department,

238

a small town police force that had just taken on the task of developing a respectable detective unit. He was given carte blanche to organize it, which was the most attractive aspect to a job that threatened to bore him to death.

Almost every serious capital crime usually brought in the county and state units which more often than not ended up taking command. It wasn't unusual to feel like the unwanted child in this police family – someone tolerated, but hardly respected, despite his 'big city' early experiences. Detective work in the more rural upstate world was clearly different. The urban mentality wasn't a good fit. Adjustments had to be made. There wasn't the surrounding professionalism he was used to having. Everyone moved more slowly and found it harder to accept the evil that lived in so many hearts.

The other problem he was finding was internal. The former police chief, Hal Donald, retired the year he began working there, and he wasn't terribly fond of the new chief who was a political appointee with hardly any experience necessary for the job, in Rob's opinion. Chief Skyler was the brother-in-law of the county's district attorney. County government was incestuous, Rob thought. Skyler was the epitome of the 'if it ain't broke, don't fix it' philosophy. He would use that expression for avoiding requests or he would simply ask, rhetorically, 'Why rock the boat?' Making innovations and bringing in some of the techniques and procedures Rob had mastered and used in Yonkers was sometimes like introducing electricity to Aborigines. His father always advised, 'Swim with the current, not against it, and you'll get farther in life.'

How much farther could he swim here?

Rob looked at his current cases, if he could call them that, on his desk. At the top he had a man named Flip Kasey who claimed someone had deliberately set his pet's doghouse on fire. He was apparently having an argument with both neighbors concerning his dog's constant barking. 'One of them for sure did this,' he said when he came in to see him. Rob tried to look as concerned and efficient as he could, keeping his head down and taking what looked like copious notes but were really doodles. In the end, he suspected some kids in the neighborhood were pulling a Halloween prank early.

The second case was a burglary in Hurleyville that he had investigated. An elderly lady lived alone on a street with houses on both sides and across from hers. No one had heard or seen anyone breaking into her house, but most of her jewelry was gone. Nothing else was disturbed. After less than an hour of questioning and inspection, it was clear to him that the woman's grandson had done it. He was waiting for a call resulting from a lead he had picked up from the owner of a hardware store who had the grandson arrested for shoplifting only six months before. He told him where the boy would fence the jewelry in Middletown, New York, something he had picked up from the assistant postmaster who seemed to know every closet that held every family skeleton. In this case, the Middletown police chief was his cousin who had told him about an earlier incident with the old lady's grandson. He assured Rob he could get the information for him to arrest the seventeen-year-old boy. Rob felt sorry for the grandmother.

The third case was a car theft, and for that he did need the help of the state police. The victim, as was more the rule than the exception in this quiet country world, left his keys in the ignition. There was an APB out on the vehicle.

He sat forward and stared at the file cabinet that had been moved out of Hal Donald's office and put into his two by four. There was one thick file of cold cases. Seeing some of the 'hot' cases, though, he wasn't very motivated to re-examine anything. Nevertheless, out of total boredom and self-pity, he rose, opened the drawer and took out the files. As he sifted through them, he grew more depressed. He was about to put it all back when he came upon and read the first page of Victoria Myers' case. The initial segment was quite professionally completed, he thought, realizing at the end that it had been done by a state police officer. The details of a seven-year-old case, as gruesome as the description read, didn't give him much hope for solving. This Lieutenant Marcus seemed finally to have concluded it had been committed by perps out of the area, long gone and forgotten.

He sat back and skimmed some of her interviews. As he reviewed them, he could almost sense her frustration. She had cast a wide net over all the potential persons of interest, obviously hoping to stumble on something. All her more probable suspects had good alibis. She had little else to go by. The victim's story left so few possible leads. It was as if ghosts had committed it. From the description, though, he also concluded that whoever the perps were, they weren't dumb. They had left nothing behind. He had to credit Hal Donald with at least doing a thorough job. There were even volunteer police personnel who went through the whole wooded area and every approach to it. Someone had done a very good drawing of the vicinity scoured.

He was about to close it up when he saw the slip of note paper stuck in behind the last page. He took it out and read Hal Donald's notes: *Scent of gasoline and sound that could be a ring of keys.* Rob noted the date and then looked back at the date of the crime. A little over two years later, the victim and her mother had brought in the additional information. At the bottom of the page was scribbled *Repressed memory* and a question mark.

He smiled to himself, thinking the chief had absolutely no clue. He was reminded of a serial rapist case he came in on when he worked in Yonkers. They had a forensic psychologist in to report on his interviews with some of the earlier victims, and information extracted from repressed memories was significant. It actually led to the solving of the crimes and the arrest of an assistant librarian. With his thick-lens glasses and his thin physique, he looked incapable of collecting a fine for an overdue library book, much less committing rape, or seven rapes to be exact.

He thought about the additional clues and then looked at the file again. Apparently, Hal Donald had not used the information to reinvestigate anything. There were no follow-up interviews. Had he passed it on to the state perhaps? He checked the contact number and reached for his phone.

It took a little over a half-hour, but amazingly he was able to locate Lieutenant Marcus who was now in administration in Albany. She took the call and from the sound of her voice seemed happy to be talking about something happening in the field and not in conference rooms.

'Yes, I remember that case well,' she said. 'I was never so frustrated. Getting anything out of the victim was worse than pulling teeth.'

Rob mentioned the additional information.

'Oh, I had moved on before then, but no, no one passed anything on to us that might have brought me back. Is the victim still living there?'

'I don't know, actually. I just started rifling through our cold cases and came upon it.'

'How nice to have some time on your hands,' she said. She didn't mean it to be sarcastic. It actually sounded more loaded with envy.

'Yeah, well, I might just get into it.'

'Oh, please keep me informed. Failure is usually not in my vocabulary.'

'Understood. Thanks,' he said.

He returned to the beginning of the file. The little experience he had with cold cases had taught him to go about it subtly. The worst, most cruel thing he could do was give the victim and her family a sense of real hope that they would have closure. They had already suffered through disappointment and frustration. He wasn't going to

243

have them relive it until he had something to offer.

However, he recognized that, in a small community like this, the moment he asked someone a question, it could move through the township with electric speed. He'd be driving under telephone wires that were reporting his latest move, and, eventually, he would have to come face to face with this family. Should he even start?

He held the file up almost at arm's length and debated with himself. Then he looked at the first pages again and gazed at the black-and-white picture of the girl. It wasn't the bruises around her mouth so much as the vacant look in her eyes. It was as though a vampire had come and sucked out her future. She was obviously still alive, but inside she was dead. He couldn't help wondering if she had recovered at all.

He got up and, with the file in hand, walked out to the lobby to speak to Lillian Brooke, the dispatcher. She was a tall, slim woman in her early sixties who he knew had been working here for over fifteen years. A widow who now lived alone and was childless, she had what Rob thought was the perfect dour personality for someone who had to be the first to hear desperate cries for help or complaints. Although it was true she wasn't any poster woman for compassion and sympathy, she was good at picking out what was serious enough to take up police time and what could linger in some waiting room. According to her, if the complaint hung out there long enough, it dried on its own and was forgotten. Most important, she appeared to be

244

knowledgeable enough about the local people to serve as town historian. She always referred to some relative, dead or alive, who might shed light on the issue. He was tempted to put her in for assistant detective pay.

'Hey, Lillian,' he said, approaching her. She turned, her light gray eyes and lean face expressing a mechanical look of attention, 'I was looking through this old file and wondered if you had any memory of this case.'

She took it from him without speaking, glanced at it and handed it back.

'It was quite a splash,' she said, 'mainly because of how vicious and violent it was. There was a lot of fear for a while, but nothing like it happened again, at least not until now. Who knows about tomorrow? That's not to say some girls weren't forced to have sex on dates and probably still are. I can tell you, quite a few mothers over the years asked my opinion about lodging a complaint for their daughters.

'This,' she said, nodding at the file in his hand, 'is the touchstone or, if you like, the best example of not only how futile it often is to pursue a complaint like date rape but, maybe more important, what it does to the victim and her family.'

'It didn't go down like a date rape,' he said.

'No, but a rape victim is a rape victim. It's like wearing a scarlet R instead of an A,' she added, her thin lips dipping so deeply at the sides that it made it look as if she had been sliced across the mouth.

'Scarlet R,' he said, smiling. 'Clever. So, what about this girl?'

'What about her?' she replied with a shrug.

'Did she, is she . . .'

'She suffered through her remaining high school years. Her mother is a highly respected college teacher, you know, and her father is still the high school business manager – a very, very nice man. She attended college in New York – Columbia, I believe – and, from what I've heard, graduated with honors.'

'Oh, that's great to know.'

'There's more,' she said. The phone rang. She lifted the receiver and with a clear, sharp voice snapped, 'Please hold.' Then she turned back to him.

'This morning, I heard that she is engaged to Bart Stonefield, the son of one of our more successful businessmen, John Stonefield.'

'The car dealer?'

'Yes. So,' she added, 'I'd think twice about resurrecting that ugly corpse. It's not like bringing up old crimes in a city where people don't know who their next-door neighbor is,' she added and lifted the receiver. 'Sorry. Town of Fallsburgh police department. No, we haven't had a report of a broken parking meter. Where is this?'

He looked at her a moment more and then returned to his office.

He could hear Chief Skyler say, 'Let sleeping dogs lie.'

Would he do more harm than good by looking into this cold case? The girl was or had recovered enough to do well in college and now start a happy new life. What would he have accomplished if he ran an investigation down the same

246

dark road and hit the same dead end? He would only revive the misery for two obviously happy families. He'd even lose the respect of Lillian Brooke.

He shook his head and put the file back in the cabinet. He perused a few others before he took the call from the Middletown police chief and got up to go and arrest the old lady's grandson.

Seventeen

After the announcements went out, like most hot local news, Bart and Victoria's upcoming wedding rushed like a tidal wave over home phone lines and into small-talk conversations from the lobbies of post offices to stores and sidewalks. The most common response was 'I thought that girl would never live a normal life.' Those who hadn't seen her for years but knew the tragic history were intrigued. 'What did she look like? How did she behave?'

Natalie and Bea, two of the Yalta Three, naturally fielded questions about Florence Stonefield's reaction to her son's engagement to Victoria Myers. The top question was 'How is she holding up?' Or simply 'What was Florence's reaction?'

Both Natalie and Bea, whose first loyalties lay with Florence, put on as best a front as they could. 'She's fine. Florence can handle most any challenge. She loves her son and supports him as any devoted mother would. Besides,' they added, even though they had little to really go by, 'Victoria Myers is a beautiful, intelligent and quite stable young woman.'

Only someone coming back quickly at them with 'Would you want your son to marry her?' could tighten their lips and get them to change the subject as quickly as they could.

For her part, Florence Stonefield did put on a brave front. After all, she was expert at false faces, hosting charity events and having to be nice to high rollers just to get a donation. She had been a social butterfly who flitted from one event to another and changed to whatever color necessary for as long as she could remember. During the earlier years when she and John were building the car dealerships, she could be as ingratiating and as deceptive as a plantation slave out to please his owner. Even her eyes didn't betray her inner thoughts when she had a mind to wear a mask.

Her biggest challenge came when she met with Helen Myers to discuss the details of the wedding ceremony and reception. Later, she could confess to herself that she had finally met her match in someone who was as adept as she was at turning an argument in her favor, undermining a counterproposal with sharp, swift logic and getting her own way while smiling and behaving as if she had somehow compromised.

No, they wouldn't expand the guest list. It was better to cull mere acquaintances and concentrate on people who really cared about the welfare and happiness of their son and her daughter, wasn't it? Too many weddings are simply another social affair, didn't she think? A wedding, or at least the first one, was one of those once-in-a-lifetime things, too special for just anyone you knew. Didn't she and John, like Helen and Lester Myers, have those special friends, friends who were almost family in fact? When you added mere, casual contacts, it diluted the event, stole from its warmth, didn't she agree?

Oh, how to argue against all that?

Helen Myers was giving her a great lesson in how to be condescending while appearing to care only about what was best for everyone. She didn't wilt, but she left with her minor victories about things that were so trivial that she wouldn't even mention them to John or Natalie and Bea. In fact, when she met with each to discuss the wedding arrangements that she and Helen Myers had created together, she used some of Helen's same logic. It was so much better to plagiarize than appeal for sympathy and look weak.

Nevertheless, she was taking Miltown like candy practically every night and certainly before she had to attend an event or a dinner party where she knew the questions would be coming at her from all directions. To keep her sanity and perspective, she spent an extraordinary amount of time searching for just the right dress to wear to the wedding. Natalie and Bea seized hold of the opportunities to go shopping in New York City. They needed new dresses, too. There was no better way for a woman to get over an emotional or social crisis than to spend money, they decided. Laughter was pushing depression away, sweeping it out of Florence's psyche like wiping cobwebs out of attic corners with an old broom.

On the other hand, Helen and Lester Myers wore their preparations for the upcoming nuptials like battle ribbons, just the way any parents whose child had matured to the stage of setting up his or her own family might. They invited questions and interest. What was there from which to flee? Their child getting a good education, a decent job, marrying, raising children were all proof that they had been successful parents. Yes, personally, they had suffered a major blow along the way, and they weren't blind to the fact that many in the community found a way to place at least some of the blame on them. Every parent, no matter what the circumstances surrounding what their child had done or had done to them, had to live by Harry Truman's desktop saying: *The buck stops here.*

This marriage, this new and promising life for Victoria, would do the most possible to heal her and them. It was undeniable that Dr Thornton, her therapist, helped her survive, but that paled into insignificance in comparison with all this now. They hoped Victoria's husband would become her confidant and therapist, just as she would become for him. That bond of trust and dependence was what made most marriages successful after all, wasn't it?

Their own home would come; their children would come. There would be birthdays and Thanksgivings and Christmases, just like there were for every normal family. The past would weaken. Its strangling grip on their throats would be broken. It would slip away and shatter at their feet like fine china.

No one knew all this better than Victoria. There were moments during the first few weeks when she questioned her own motives. Was she marrying Bart because she loved him more than she could love any other man or because she saw their marriage as her lifeboat? Was marriage merely an escape? Every marriage was an escape in some sense. You were leaving everything – childhood, adolescence and, most of all, dependence on your parents. You would turn them into in-laws and grandparents first, and consider them your parents second. Daddy would always be Daddy, and Mom always Mom, but the first person you would go to now for help and advice was your husband. You were out of their boat. They'd be there to advise and console when needed, just like she would be for her daughter, but the home she had known, the bed she had slept in, the mirrors she had used to ponder herself and the dinner table she had sat at for so many dinners would become someone else's – her parents' and not hers, too. It was sad but wonderful simultaneously.

Bart had felt and sensed all this years ago. Men had more of an obligation to be independent in the 1960s. Other men in his high school class had either graduated college and found good jobs and new lives, or had gone into the armed services and were still enlisted or had left to find work. Many were married; a few like him were involved in a family business, but there weren't many who were living at home and mainly dependent upon their parents even now. Somewhere he had read that the median age for a man to marry in the 1960s was around twenty-three. He was going to celebrate his twenty-fifth birthday in three months. No one could accuse him of waiting too long or marrying too soon. He felt terribly normal, in fact.

Just about every customer who came to have his or her car serviced greeted him with congratulations. Most were genuinely happy for him, but he knew there were many who were also very curious, hoping he would say something more than thank you and perhaps let slip some detail about what it was like to court Victoria Myers, the victim of one of the most famous local sexual assaults. He would simply express his own personal happiness. Sometimes he would add, 'I'm a lucky guy,' deliberately, like a challenge, and wait to see the reaction. No one dared look skeptical. Those who had seen Victoria, in fact, commented on how beautiful she was. They couldn't deny that.

'You two are going to have some gorgeous children,' Margaret Walker, his third-grade teacher told him. She was still teaching and still driving her 1954 Chevy Bel Air, but it had barely twenty thousand miles on it. He was amused at how many used-car buyers were waiting in the wings for that car. It was a standard part of a car salesman's pitch to tell a prospective buyer that it had been owned by a spinster school teacher. 'Don't wait too long to start a family,' Margaret warned. 'I'm not going to teach until my dying day.'

He was buoyed by this Hollywood movie future: a beautiful woman, a new successful business and the start of his own family. The flow of images took him far above the stream of dark doubt that trickled just below his conscience and challenged his motives. It was all going too well now for any defeat or disappointment to challenge them. His mother was resigned to the inevitability of having Victoria Myers as her daughter-in-law, and he was growing closer and closer to Victoria's parents, especially her father, who in his quiet, subtle way had good fatherly advice, especially about business. Bart actually fantasized that when and if Lester Myers got tired of his school business manager position, he would come to work for him in his expanding foreign car dealership.

For many reasons, complicated and not so complicated, his own father offered to do anything Bart needed to help make the wedding and the marriage successful. He was at his side for every detail of planning for the new foreign car dealership and not simply because it was part of what he had created. He was sincerely interested in making it all fruitful for Bart. In the past, he was capable of quickly dismissing a suggestion Bart might make for the business, but now he stepped back to ponder any idea. His worst reaction was 'Well, it's worth a try. Good thinking.'

Bart hadn't needed Victoria to put the idea in his mind that his father was buying off his silence and loyalty. He hated that the suspicion plagued him almost any time his father gave him a compliment or offered something, but it was impossible to get away from it. Someday, he hoped, his father would take him into his confidence and confess, and perhaps even ask his advice. Right now, that was just a fantasy.

But his father raised the suspicion to a new height when he called him into the office soon after the marriage invitations had gone out.

'I have an opportunity to get something,' he began, 'and I think it would make a sensible wedding present for you two. You guys might not like it and you might think it's presumptuous of your mother and me to offer it, but I thought I'd run it past you.'

Bart sat. 'I'm all ears, Dad.'

'Without going into the whys and wherefores, Bill Jackson owes me a few favors.'

'The sheriff?'

'Yeah, he resigned less than a month ago and is moving on. He's remarrying, in fact. You might recall his wife died about a year ago. He hooked up with Nancy Hickman, whose husband died three years ago down in Florida. She sold her house up here and has been living with Bill. They're moving to her place in Boca Raton.'

'OK,' Bart said, still not understanding where his father was going with all this.

'Well, Bill's going to put his house up for sale. It's that sprawling ranch just outside of Monticello on Berne Road. Got nearly three acres with it and it's only five years old. Tip-top shape.'

Bart smiled. He finally sensed where his father was going. 'And?'

'I thought I'd buy it for you guys. If you like it, that is. You can't take that beautiful bride of yours to live in that bachelor pad. Bill's house is move-in ready, but you guys can redo carpets and repaint if you think it's necessary. Every appliance is top of the range. He won't put it on the market if he knows my interest. It's far from a distress sale, but he's damn happy to get it sold ASAP and I can practically steal it. In short, it's a great business decision, but also a great wedding gift, I hope. You can take Victoria over to see it anytime you want, but you might want to do it tomorrow,' he added.

'I don't know what to say, Dad. That's very generous. I know the house, of course. I can't imagine Victoria not being pleased about it. I'll call her and see about tomorrow, late morning.'

His father slapped the desk just the way he always did when he had made a decision about a sale price on a car or a new piece of equipment. Bart used to think he was more like a judge in a courtroom declaring a case closed.

'Let me know and I'll get it going,' he said.

Bart rose. 'Thanks. I will.' He reached out to shake his father's hand. It felt weird, as if he had just bought a car from him. His father shook it but looked away quickly.

Bart was walking on air when he left and went to his office to call Victoria. He assured her that he had no idea why the ex-sheriff would owe his father any favors, but stressed that his father, despite all or any of his faults, had an eagle's eye when it came to a business opportunity.

He could hear the excitement in her voice. 'Our own home? So soon?'

'Without a mortgage,' he added. 'Tell your father that. He might know the house, too.'

'I'm speechless.'

'Just as long as you have the strength to say, "I do,"' he told her.

After they hung up, he buzzed his father and told him to set up the visit. It looked as if nothing could bother him for the rest of this day or the next week – in fact, the next year! There wasn't a work complaint, an unexpected new cost or a dissatisfied customer whom he couldn't placate and satisfy. He was sailing on a sea of happiness and joy like no other sea in the universe.

Until an unexpected call came an hour later.

'Congratulations, Mr Groom Man,' he said. 'Funny thing. I didn't get an invitation.'

'What do you want?' Bart asked.

'I'm closin' at nine,' Marvin Hacker said. 'Meet me in the body shop. Come in the rear entrance. We've got some talkin' to do.'

'I've got nothing to say to you,' he replied. 'I thought you got the idea when you waited for me in my apartment parking lot.'

'It's not what you got to say to me now. I thought you was just havin' a good time. Engaged? Yer a nervy bastard, Stonefield – even worse than yer father. It's what I got to say to you or to your fiancée. We're sort of old friends. I feel I got to speak up.'

Bart didn't respond. His throat seemed to close up.

'Your ass in my place, nine o'clock,' Hacker

256

concluded and hung up before Bart could recuperate enough to speak.

The click was more like a gunshot that sent a bullet right at his heart. When he saddled the phone in the cradle, he trembled as he stood up. He felt as if someone had just struck him across both shins. The surge of sharp fear that traveled up his spine wasn't any less severe. He was actually having trouble breathing and had to close his eyes and suck in air like someone about to go underwater. It didn't stop the trembling. He waited, his hand on his desk. The sound of an air gun loosening tire wheel nuts suddenly turned the pits and lifts out there into a warzone. He hesitated and looked at his watch. Nine o'clock was another eleven hours. How would he get through them?

He fell back on his desk chair. He thought about going straight away, but realized any confrontation in the daytime, in front of witnesses, was not a good idea. The intercom on his phone lit. His father was calling back.

'All set for eleven tomorrow,' he said. 'How are you doing there? I've got Cliff Andersen at the site of the new dealership in an hour with some new thoughts. We can meet him and then go to lunch at O'Heenies. I'm in the mood for one of their fat roast beef sandwiches on rye.'

The very idea of that bloody sandwich nauseated him.

'Sure,' he said. Show one sign of anything wrong and a wall could come tumbling down.

He gathered his strength, concentrated on what was being done at the service center, checked on two things that were left over from the day before, left orders for some cleanup and joined his father in the show area.

As soon as they left for Monticello, his father was more talkative than usual, or else he was talking more because Bart was quieter than normal.

'I'm glad Victoria is excited about the house possibility. Your mother and I have been to parties there. You'll have three bedrooms, so you can set up a nursery pretty quick. Of course, I'm too young to be a grandfather,' he joked. When Bart didn't respond, he quickly added, 'I'm kidding.'

'I know, Dad.'

His father suddenly looked suspicious. 'You know, that was a clever answer Victoria gave your mother when she asked her if she was pregnant, but it wasn't a no.'

'She's not pregnant. I'm not marrying her because I'm forced to,' he said, perhaps a lot more adamantly than he had intended, or maybe he did intend it. It wouldn't be the first time that he had that argument with himself.

'Sure. You'd tell me if she were,' his father said, as if they really were close enough to share the most personal secrets. 'Anyway, I like the picture window in the living room. It's a bay window. Your mother was instantly jealous of that and harangued me day in and day out to redo our living room so we could have a bay window. I kept promising until she gave up. That's a good technique with wives, by the way. Never argue. Pretend you agree and keep finding excuses until the whole thing thins out and disappears. I learned that from your grandfather. It's how he handled my mother. What good are fathers if they don't pass wisdom down to their sons, eh?' he added with a smile as broad as Bart could recall.

Would his getting married ironically result in he and his father becoming closer? It sounded as if he believed Bart would be more sympathetic and understanding to his own situation once he shared some of the same concerns and challenges. *Like father, like son* was not an expression he was fond of, however.

'Victoria's father is a pretty smart guy,' he said, looking for a way to turn the conversation. 'I told him some of my ideas for advertising. You know, it's not easy to sell foreign cars in this market,' he quickly added, 'but he agrees that it's a great idea now.'

'Oh?'

'You know, like I discussed, emphasizing how we're creating jobs for Americans, too, especially Americans here. It will be a higher level of clientele. More expensive foreign cars are something of a status symbol. Our ads will have to subtly suggest that.'

'Right. Smart.' He was quiet a moment. Bart thought he might be upset that his son was complimenting another father, but after another few moments he was to learn otherwise. 'I don't like bringing this up,' he began again. 'Who needs the reminder, especially now?'

'Bringing up what?'

'After what happened to Victoria years ago – about two days after, I think – I had this dinner meeting with the GM people in the Dugout. You

259

remember that place, don't you? Went out about three years ago when Charley Kaplan died. His son wasn't interested in keeping it going.'

'Yeah, I remember it. So?'

'Had this dinner with a couple of executives who were laying down new regulations – suits without any real business sense. They drank too much as is the way with these guys who have expense budgets. After we finished, I was about to walk out when I glanced at the bar and saw Lester Myers by himself. He was eating at a table and looked as if he had downed a few martinis, too. There was something about him that nearly made me cry, so I excused myself, said goodnight to Mr and Mr Horse's Ass, and went over to Lester.

'I felt like I was offering sympathy for someone who died. He was glad to have my company, however. He said his wife was at some education thing. They had both left the hospital, visiting Victoria, and then gone their separate ways. I kept thinking, how do you not stay right beside each other after something like this, but from what I could gather, they both wanted to keep busy, keep their lives as normal as they could in order to keep their strength. Probably right. I mean, what was the alternative? Go home and stare at each other and cry?'

'I don't like hearing about this now, Dad.'

'I know. I just remembered how this sweet Southerner, who was about as Ashley Wilkes from *Gone with the Wind* as any man I ever met from the South, was so lit with rage that he was carrying a thirty-eight in hopes he would somehow stumble upon those animals who had raped and beaten his daughter like that. There was no doubt in my mind he could or would do it – and, you know what, I was hoping he somehow got that opportunity.

'Afterward, whenever he saw me, I think he was embarrassed that I had seen him that way. I tried to assure him that I respected him more because of it, but if there was ever a descendant of Jesus Christ, it's someone like Lester Myers. End of story. I'll never mention anything about it again,' he said, raising his hand to swear.

Bart looked out the window. Inside his chest, his heart felt as if it had twisted around itself.

Eighteen

The most difficult thing was finding a good excuse not to see Victoria and sounding truthful. Was it true that it was more difficult to lie to people you loved? When did his father start lying to his mother? They had to have been in love once, didn't they? Sometime along the way, distrust and an acceptance of deceit grew and settled in their marriage like so much mold on the walls of a damp basement. Could this happen between him and Victoria? Did children truly inherit their parents' sins?

Although it had to be the furthest thing from her mind, he couldn't help but impose and attach suspicious motives around everything Victoria said, every question she asked when he called her to tell her he was going to cancel on their dinner. Was the reverse true about deceit: people who loved someone sensed more easily when he or she was lying? He hoped he wasn't trying too hard to sound innocuous and causing the problem himself.

He had told her he was meeting with some Volkswagen representatives and had to drive to Middletown. It was a half-truth. He would have to meet with them soon, and it would probably be there anyway since they were in the process of establishing a dealership in that vicinity.

'This just happened? They don't give you much notice, do they? You could have had something scheduled that you were unable to cancel. It's not only unfair; it's inconsiderate.'

'We're at their mercy,' he replied, 'especially since we need their full faith and support for the new dealership. They can choose to be choosey.'

'This will be our first night apart since . . .' she started to say and then said, 'I know. After I have dinner with my parents, I'll go to your apartment and wait for you. You can tell me all about your boring dinner,' she added.

A week ago, he had made a copy of his apartment key for her.

'That's a good idea. I'll get home as soon as I can,' he said.

'It's all right, Bart. Don't rush back. Haven't you heard that absence makes the heart grow fonder,' she joked, wanting to make him feel better about it. He knew that's why she was doing it, which only made him feel worse about lying.

262

'Not this heart. It gets weak without you.'

She laughed. How melodic her laugh had become; how light her voice was now. He was sure that it wasn't simply his imagination or wishful thinking. The vulnerable young woman at the beginning of his courting had gradually grown stronger and more self-confident. She had been like a flower struggling in an attic or basement, hungry for a ray of sunshine. He flattered himself by believing he had brought that to her. He was completely the reason she had changed and blossomed. Somehow, that wasn't arrogant of him. He justified it by thinking that it was partly because of the joy he felt in being so significant to her that he was so in love with her now.

But it was not a one-way street. Whatever he invested in her, she returned ten-fold. It was part of her charm to be so dependent upon him. Almost all the women he had dated held on to an escape route. He sensed it. He wouldn't be able to break their hearts by being unfaithful or falling into disinterest. Perhaps it was characteristic of all men to resent that sort of independence in the women they dated. He couldn't help wondering if that was a major part of why his father had drifted.

Above all other things, love meant never being selfish. His parents both shared that unattractive characteristic. If either compromised for the other, it occurred with so heavy an air of regret and such an obvious look of suffering from the self-sacrifice that neither would find any satisfaction in getting his or her way.

'Who'd a thunk Bart Stonefield would be such a romantic?' Victoria kidded. 'Next thing you know, you'll be reading Shakespearean love sonnets to me.'

'I'll ask your mother for the recommended list,' he replied and she laughed. 'I'll call you when I'm finished and on my way back,' he said. He couldn't see how he would be too late. Whatever was going down at nine o'clock wouldn't take long.

'I'll be right beside your phone.'

'Love you,' he said.

'Love you,' she echoed.

After he hung up, he sat for a moment to gather his strength. The best place to go for it was anger, he decided. How dare that bastard insert any threat into his flow of happiness now? He'd cut the legs out from under him as quickly as he could and that would be that.

Forever.

He rose and put out his office lights. No one was left at the dealership. He had told his assistant manager that he would close up. As he moved through the service area, he shut down lights, picked up and placed a forgotten wrench on the proper shelf, and then left, locking up behind him.

The overcast sky felt ominous, not because they might have a downpour any moment, but because every shadow created by a streetlight or passing car's headlights looked darker, deeper, a haven for ghouls. It was the sort of evening lovers of Halloween hoped to have. He chose to take an indirect route. He could have gotten there faster, but right from the start, he didn't want to be seen. He was glad he had a black automobile. It was too generic to attract attention.

There were no streetlights on the side roads anyway. A change of weather was occurring rapidly. Very light mist was thickening into a fog that belonged near the sea and not in the mountains. It draped itself on tree limbs like sheer gray-white silk. His headlight beams sliced through it, but it instantly came back together behind him. It was as though Nature was cooperating and giving him the cover he needed to remain anonymous. These were roads he rarely traveled. People living on them wouldn't be accustomed to seeing him. He had, after all, successfully kept away from the Hacker brothers all these years. It was a friendship he had begun to regret even before that night. Afterward, he immediately found excuses for not joining them no matter what they wanted to do. His retreat hadn't angered them; it amused them. That's how sick they were.

When he arrived, he saw that all the lights were out, except, of course, for the lights in the pale gray clapboard farmhouse-style home with Queen Anne posts and railings next door. The house looked old and deserted, in desperate need of paint, repair and any kind of loving care. The front porch had one small wall lantern beside the door. It was all so peaceful that for a moment he actually wondered if he had imagined the phone call. Perhaps his guilty mind had conceived it. Maybe he had fallen asleep and had dreamed it. It wouldn't have been the first time.

After he slowed and then turned to go around the garage to the pathetic-looking body shop behind it, however, he saw the light seeping out from under the rear door. The building itself was an obvious afterthought.

The main garage was constructed with a dirty-gray stucco finish. The body shop was a wood-framed building with cheap metal siding, some of which had literally fallen off and much had buckled. It had a flat roof and, in the rear, a pipe chimney for a coal- and wood-burning stove that assisted an oil burner that was much too small for the building. He recalled how they and the men they hired worked with coats on during the winter. The floor was still hard-packed dirt and sawdust. The walls were peppered with pictures of nude women from old calendars.

When he was younger, it was a neat clubhouse after hours in which they could drink and smoke. The lack of parental supervision turned the Hacker brothers into R-rated Huckleberry Finns. In those days, they somehow fit the description of heroic because they could drive without licenses and basically do whatever they pleased.

He parked, turned off the engine and sat there for a moment. It was never easy to stand up to either of them. The restraints that kept most boys chained to some variation of the Marquess of Queensberry Rules in a fight were not even a small consideration to them. Headbutting, elbowing, kicking someone in the balls and even biting were not only fair and smart but expected. They were proud of their motto: *Do unto others before they do unto you.* Bart understood they had gotten that from their alcoholic father, which was practically his only attempt to pass down any wisdom he wanted his sons to inherit.

Bart got out of the car, tried to drink from that well of anger he had dipped into earlier, and started for the rear entrance. It was deadly quiet around the body shop, too. The fog had thickened here as well. There was no traffic on the road behind him. It looked as if everything living, even bats and owls, had deserted this part of the world. However, off about an acre or so, a dog was barking hysterically at something. When he reached the door, he heard music from a local radio station. He opened the door and stepped in.

Marvin was sitting in an oversized cushioned chestnut-brown chair, the arms of which were torn and leaked some of the stuffing. He picked a piece of it and rolled it between his large thumb and forefinger as he broke into a smile. He wore coveralls and a faded blue short-sleeve shirt that clearly exposed his large forearms and biceps. He was unshaven, the three- or four-day growth looking like dead moss on his granite cheeks and jawbone.

'Mr Stonefield himself,' he said. His teeth were yellowed with nicotine stains, highlighted in the weak overhead illumination cast by the naked bulb that hung like an icicle dripping light. There was one other light on, a lamp in the rear next to what served as a desk, a crate on concrete blocks with a black folding chair.

Marvin saw how Bart was looking at the body shop. It looked even worse than Bart remembered.

Marvin rose as if he was growing rapidly out of the chair.

'Not as fancy as Stonefield's, huh?'

'What do you want, Marvin? Why did you ask me to come here tonight? I thought we said enough to each other.'

'Yer never usta be in such a hurry ta get outta here, Bart,' he replied, still holding that impish smile. 'Yer spent a lotta time here, fuckin' around. Weren't yer the one who got that pot shit for us to smoke?'

'That was a long time ago.'

'Not that long.'

He crossed over to a shelf and picked up what Bart could see was an old Sullivan County newspaper. It had yellowed with time. Marvin opened it so the front page could be clearly seen. The lead headline and story was about the sexual assault. The picture was of the state investigator, Lieutenant Marcus.

'Remember this bitch?' Marvin asked, folding the paper and holding it up. 'I swear she had balls. She had a mustache. I remember that – fuzz over her lip here,' he said, running his finger over the area above his own upper lip. 'I couldn't take my eyes off it. I remember I asked her why she didn't shave and she looked like she would shoot me right then and there. Would have been good for yer if she had, huh?'

'What's the point, Marvin?'

Marvin lost his smile and put the paper back on the shelf.

'I figured out a way to make me feel better.'

'Feel better? About what?'

'You know what?'

Bart shook his head. 'I don't understand.'

'Yeah. I bet you don't. Anyway, I decided to be smart this time, since you've gone so far with her. You and yer father stole away many of my customers, shithead. I figure yer owe me for that.'

'We didn't steal anyone away. Anyone who came to us came because they wanted to. We don't have to solicit for business.'

'Yeah, I know. What I said was just a – what'dya call it – excuse to make yer more comfortable with what yer goin' to do, asshole.'

'What am I going to do?'

'Get me five thousand dollars. I'll give yer two days. I want to make some improvements here,' he added, smiling. 'So I can compete with Stonefield's.'

'Five thousand dollars!'

'That's cheap. Yer probably goin' ta spend that on all yer preparations for yer weddin'. If she'll marry yer after I talk to her, that is.'

'Talk to her? You couldn't talk to her without confessing and you know where that will get you,' Bart fired back. He had rehearsed the line many times.

'Hey, I know a little bit about broads. She couldn't turn me in without turnin' yer in and that would make for a helluva weddin' afterward.'

'I wasn't there,' Bart said. 'I didn't do anything.'

'You were there. Yer were in the truck, stoned outta yer head, but yer knew it all. Yer told that cop just what we told yer ta tell her – that we all come back here and played cards until two in

269

the mornin'. Yer what they call an accessory, an accessory to the rape of the girl yer goin' ta marry,' he said, widening his smile. 'Which puzzles me anyway. How the hell can yer marry her? Jesus, yer must be desperate or somethin'.'

'I should have turned you in,' Bart said. How many times over the last six years had he told himself that, but he had been very frightened the year it happened. He knew what it would do to his parents and how it could affect his father's business. The more time passed, the harder it became even to consider it.

'Shoulda, coulda – the words of a loser, right? Yer a loser this time, Bart. Be grateful I'm askin' fer only five thousand.'

'That's now,' Bart said. 'You won't stop asking for money.'

Marvin smiled. 'This could get a lot worse, jerk-off. Wi' my brother gone, the second guy coulda been you. Who's ta say otherwise?'

'What would that get you, stupid?' Bart said, his anger returning now. He stepped forward.

'Get me a deal. I know what lawyers can do. I'd turn – what'dya call it – state's evidence, and give them a high-end perp. See? I watch television and learn shit, too.'

'Maybe I'll beat you to it. I have better connections to the district attorney. Now that I'm marrying Victoria, I have realized I have to speak up,' he said. He could see Marvin hadn't considered that logic. He lost his grin and came toward him.

'I'd kill yer the next day,' he said. To reinforce

the threat, he thrust his left hand out and pushed on Bart's chest hard, hard enough for him to feel pain. Bart stepped back. Marvin came forward. 'In fact, maybe I'll find a way ta rape yer fiancée again, only I'd go about it slower this time and enjoy it more. I've been thinkin' about it. Did ya know Lou got his in, too. Thing is she was out of it by then and didn't enjoy it. I think we forgot to tell yer that part. Yer were too stupid stoned to appreciate anythin' anyway.'

Bart instinctively crouched a little and turned his shoulder defensively. Marvin had his hands clenched and each fist looked like the short-handled sledgehammer that was on the shelf to his right.

'You're an animal. You always were. Both of you. I'm glad your brother was killed,' he said defiantly.

'Shut yer mouth, Bart. I'm gettin' pissed and might not offer yer the deal.'

'Take that deal and shove it,' Bart said, regaining his posture.

Marvin's eyes seemed to brighten and sparkle like the wick on a firecracker. He swung his right arm around and caught Bart on the side of his neck. It spun him around and in an instant, driven by an impulse he would debate as good or bad for the rest of his life, Bart scooped up the short-handled sledgehammer and came back at Marvin Hacker with a blow that struck him squarely on the left temple. His eyes seemed to pop and then rise up as if he was looking quickly at the ceiling, and then his large frame sunk into itself, his legs folding up and his arms flying out as if he was trying to fly. He fell on his rear end. Bart would swear later that he turned to look up at him with surprise, but it was probably just the way his head fell back with the rest of him.

He didn't move.

Bart froze, leaning over him, poised to deliver another blow if necessary. He looked as if he had frozen in place, a statue of rage. Gradually, especially when some spittle trickled out of the right corner of Marvin's mouth, Bart began to relax. A shocking realization seemed to rise up his legs, through his torso and into his head as the rage was replaced with fear. Slowly, he knelt down and touched Marvin's cheek. His eyes were already glass. He snapped his hand back as if he had just touched a hot stove.

'Jesus,' he whispered and slowly touched him again, shoving him a bit to see if he would wake. Then he felt his wrist for a pulse, moved quickly to search for it on his neck and, feeling no rhythm, stood up. He looked at the sledgehammer in his hand and then at Marvin's temple. A trauma formed like an ink blot.

He stood there, unable to think for a moment. Then the thoughts followed the silence in his head, rushing in as if each question was being asked by someone else standing with a group of people who could easily be a jury of his peers.

Why did you come here?

What were you talking about that caused you to have such a violent argument?

Why didn't you just turn around and call the police if he was blackmailing you?

He was unable to think of any answers. He put

the short-handled sledgehammer back on the shelf, turned and started to flee, and then stopped. He went back, grabbed the sledgehammer and went to the rear door. He looked at Marvin's body. Maybe he wasn't dead. Maybe he just couldn't feel the pulse because it was so weak, and maybe he would wake up. He'd be very angry, but he couldn't go to the police either. There was a way out of this. If Marvin recovers, I'll tell Victoria everything and he'll be unable to do anything more. He'll just go away, mostly to protect himself.

He opened the door slowly and peered out. It was still dead quiet and the road still looked deserted. He closed the door softly behind him and hurried to his car, the sledgehammer in his hand. He looked at it before he opened the car door. He, too, had seen detective shows and police procedurals on television. He returned to the body shop quickly and re-entered. Marvin had not moved. Practically tiptoeing now, Bart went to the shelf and scooped up the Sullivan County newspaper. He wrapped it firmly around the sledgehammer, glanced at Marvin again and then left.

When he got into his car, he placed the wrapped sledgehammer carefully on the floor and started the engine. He didn't put on his headlights until he was out on the road. He checked to make sure there was no one nearby watching him leave and then he sped up, turning on his headlights just before the bend in the road.

In moments, he was driving rapidly away. He realized he was speeding and slowed down. Being pulled over by a traffic cop would be dangerous. He was still too close to the scene of the crime. It wasn't a crime, he told himself. It was self-defense and, ordinarily, he could have success-fully argued that, but how could he do it without bringing up the subject or creating all sorts of suspicions?

Instinctively, he knew where to go and what to do. In fact, the idea came so quickly that he was surprised at his own scheming. He didn't know he had it in him to be so devious. If he had such a dark strand of thought alive inside him, who didn't? Maybe, deep down, we were all as bad as Marvin. The rest of us were simply better at keeping it under lock and key. Well, tonight it had to have its way.

Less than an hour later, he pulled into his parking spot by the dock at Echo Lake. He took his boat keys from the glove compartment and then carefully picked up the sledgehammer wrapped in the newspaper. When he got out, he paused and looked around. It was as deadly quiet here as it had been at Marvin's garage, but here the fog was even thicker.

He quickly went down to his boat, put the sledgehammer, still tightly wrapped, on the driv-er's seat and completed removing the boat cover. After he untied the rope used to keep it secure in its docking slot, he got in, started the engines and headed out slowly, slipping into the fog like someone trying to avoid being detected while escaping Nazi-occupied France. He could see the tree line on the right side of the lake and felt he was far enough out. He took the sledgehammer and tossed it overboard beside the boat. It sank, but the water-soaked newspaper unwrapped itself and floated to the surface. He cursed, scooped it up and crushed it into a ball. He didn't throw it back in the water. He could imagine it coming up again and floating about until it was caught on some bush on the shore where it dried in the sun and was eventually discovered. Innocuous enough, but it was still a lead.

He headed back to the dock. He thought he saw someone about a thousand yards to his right. The fog had thinned, but it was still too thick to be sure. He worked as quickly as he could to tie up the boat and cover it again, and then dropped the balled newspaper pages in the garbage can. For a moment, he stood there looking out at the lake. It would never be the same place to him now, he thought, but it was a sacrifice worth making. He walked back to his car, feeling exhausted now, not so much from the physical effort as from the emotional rollercoaster. He took a deep breath, started the car and drove away slowly, sliding through the night.

Shit, he thought when he was more than halfway home, *I never called Victoria to tell her I was on my way.*

When he entered the apartment, he found her dozing on the sofa beside the telephone. He was very quiet, first going to the bathroom to check what he looked like. He was still quite flushed and there was a slight redness on his neck where Marvin had struck him. He washed his face and his hands and brushed his hair. Then he walked softly back to the living room, took a breath and sat beside her. He leaned over and kissed her. She opened her eyes slowly.

'I thought you were going to call,' she said, sitting up.

'I was, but then I thought that would waste five minutes, five minutes I could use getting here.'

She smiled. 'How did it go?'

'Exactly as you described – boring – but we're fine. Now, we're fine forever,' he added.

Her smile deepened. He filled his eyes with desire and she widened hers with delight.

Then he took her hand and stood. She followed.

Neither said a word.

They spoke instead with their lips, their eyes and their hands.

He made love to her as though it was for the last time.

And he saw how much that pleased her.

'I hope it's always like this,' she said.

'How could it be otherwise?' he replied.

Nineteen

Rob Luden stepped back like someone who wanted another view of the body, a view from a different angle. He actually tilted his head a bit as he studied the corpse and put on a pair of plastic examination gloves.

Ralph Baldwin, who had been on the town police force for nearly ten years, looked at him

276

oddly, almost angrily. There was a general under-standing that detectives were better at handling and solving crimes. They had actually gone to school for it. Still, Ralph resented being thought to have limited capabilities. He had come out of the military, where he had experience as an MP, which was, in his opinion, unfairly assumed to be all about rounding up unruly soldiers on liberty. There were robberies and assaults and even two murders during his term.

Because he was a local, born and raised in the township, he had inside information on the first job opportunity in the police department and he was proud of his resume. It should have brought him more respect.

Ralph was thirty-six, married with two children now, a son of eight and a daughter of seven. His wife, Dorothy, whom he met after he left the service, had a good job at the Universal National Bank. She had recently been promoted to loan officer and was close to making more money than he did, which both pleased and annoyed him. One could safely say he had a surly manner about him. He always began anything new with a cynical attitude. He even had a banner over his workshop in the basement that read *Prove It To Me*. He had yet to grant this relatively new town detective a modicum of respect, but Rob Luden seemed oblivious to that, which only reinforced Ralph's opinion of him.

'He look better to you from that angle or some-thing?' Ralph quipped. He glanced at Tony Gibson, who stood off to the side, still in some-thing of a state of shock. Marvin's one steady assistant was the one who had discovered his body this morning when he appeared for work. He was a lean, six-feet-one-inch man with a body that looked as if it had been stretched to reach that height. His friends called him Plastic Man, after the comic book character. His thin narrow face was habitually mournful because of the way the sides of his mouth dipped. Despite his twenty-two years, he looked like someone who could count his lifelong smiles on one hand.

Rob didn't respond immediately. He continued studying Marvin's body, looked at the shelves on the right and then at the floor around the sprawled corpse.

'Anybody touch him?' he asked without looking at Ralph.

Ralph looked at Tony.

'I shook him and I felt how cold he was and that was it. Then I called you guys.'

'Who put the sheet over his body?' Rob asked.

'It's not a sheet. It's what we use to put over a car when we're workin' on the engine some-times, so we don't scratch it or somethin',' Tony said. 'I did. I thought I should. I put it over him. Ralph here uncovered him somewhat,' he added in an accusatory tone.

Rob looked at him.

'Confirming he was deceased,' Ralph said. 'He's deceased. He's good and deceased. I've seen plenty of dead bodies,' he added, like someone listing his qualifications.

Rob carefully knelt beside Marvin's corpse and looked at the head trauma without touching the body.

278

'Doc Lewis is on his way,' he said, referring to the medical examiner. 'When did you last see him alive?' he asked Tony when he stood.

'About eight last night. We were workin' on that truck over there,' he added, nodding at a 1960 Ford pickup that was getting a new paint job after some body repairs. 'I'd a' stayed later, but he called it quits. We ate that pizza,' he added for no apparent reason and nodded at a pizza box on the makeshift desk. There were empty beer bottles beside it.

'Do you know if he was expecting anyone?' Rob asked.

'Not that I knew, no. His mother called over because she thought he was coming to dinner and he told her no. I remember that.'

'Did you speak with her yet?' Rob asked Ralph.

'No. I thought I'd leave that pleasure for you.'

Rob squinted.

'I haven't seen that woman for years,' Ralph continued. 'The two times I did were not very pleasant. One minute with her and you'll know how someone like Marvin and his brother Louis was spawned.'

Rob nodded and looked at Tony. 'Any other relatives nearby who could be with his mother after she gets the news?'

'There's a cousin, Arron Cook, lives in Woodbourne, but they don't talk. He didn't like his uncles much. None live in New York. I don't know what the fight with his cousin was over. Just know they don't like each other. There's nobody else I know offhand. His twin brother Louis was killed in Vietnam this year.'

Rob turned to Ralph.

'February,' he said.

'Twin brother, huh?'

'Not enough brain power between the two of them to light a cigarette,' Ralph muttered. He glared at Tony to see if he would say something in Marvin's defense. He looked down quickly.

'You and Marvin get along all right?' Rob asked him.

Tony looked up quickly. 'Sure. We know each other since high school. I was in the class behind him and Lou. I've been workin' for him ever since I graduated high school.' He looked mournfully at the body. 'Guess I'm goin' to need to look for another job.'

'As you can see, he's all broke up about it,' Ralph said.

Rob looked at the body again. 'I don't need the medical examiner to tell me he was hit with a blunt instrument.' He looked around. 'Where are the sledgehammers you guys use?'

'There's one short-handle in my tool kit there. There's a long-handle against the wall,' he added, nodding at it.

Rob walked over to it and, without touching it, examined the head. Then he reached into his pocket and took out a plastic bag. He put it carefully over the head of the sledgehammer.

'Let's see yours,' he told Tony, who quickly opened his tool kit and took it out.

Rob looked at it and then placed another evidence bag over it and placed it on the floor. He looked at Tony, whose eyes were wide with surprise.

'I wouldn't a' done that,' he said. 'I didn't like everythin' he said or did, but I wouldn't a' killed him. Shit.'

'Where did you go after you left about eight?' Rob asked.

'Home.'

'Anyone see you? Anyone there?'

'No, not until I went out about ten.'

'Any other sledgehammers?' Rob asked, ignoring him.

'Well, there's another usually on that shelf,' he said, pointing to the wall shelf near Marvin's body. 'It ain't there.'

'Where is it?'

Tony looked around the shop and shook his head. 'Don't see it,' he said.

Rob looked at Ralph. 'Possible murder weapon might be gone,' he said. 'Let's check here carefully and then we'll need to check around the property and the sides of the road leading in both directions just in case it was tossed.'

'We'll get some of the volunteer police officers to help with that. I'll give the place a good going over,' Ralph said. Despite his attitude, he was beginning to respect Rob Luden. His slow, careful manner spoke of self-confidence and efficiency as well as experience.

'You have any ideas about who he might have had a fight with? Any particular enemies?' he asked Tony.

He shrugged. 'He had some arguments with customers lately. He threw one guy out of here – Chuck Porter, who accused him of putting used spark plugs in his car. That happened last week.'

'Physically threw him out?'

'Grabbed him by his neck and shoved him out the door. Chuck said he was going to call the cops.'

Rob looked at Ralph.

'No complaint filed as far as I know, but you're probably going to run into a list as long as your arm when it comes to people who weren't particularly fond of Marvin Hacker. I personally had to see to a few commotions between him and some other men in Whiskey Joe's this year.'

'Murder on the Orient Express,' Rob muttered.

'Pardon?'

'Agatha Christie detective story about a murder on the train. Practically everyone else on the train had a motive for killing the victim.'

'Yeah, well, you're on that train,' Ralph said. They both looked at Marvin's body.

Rob looked up when the door opened and Dr Lewis entered. He was a short, stout sixty-four-year-old man with a dark brown goatee showing encroaching gray strands and a balding head with age spots that looked like coffee stains. Rob knew him from a half-dozen unattended deaths that were determined to be heart attacks and strokes.

He paused and looked at Ralph and Tony first.

'What do we have?' he asked, like someone hoping all his work had been done for him.

'You tell us, Doc,' Ralph said. 'Detective Luden believes he was murdered with a blow to his skull.'

Dr Lewis nodded and approached Marvin's body. He contemplated it for a moment. Then he pulled back the sheet Tony and Marvin used to protect a car's surface while they worked on it. He knelt beside the body and examined the head trauma.

'Feels like some of the skull was fractured. Hard blow, all right. Nothing sharp – a blunt tool perhaps,' he added.

Ralph looked at Rob Luden with even more appreciation.

Dr Lewis turned the head. 'No other trauma visible.' He looked at Marvin's hands. 'Didn't draw blood from anyone else with a punch or anything. Rigor set in.'

'Tony saw him last about eight last night,' Rob offered.

The medical examiner nodded. 'At least that,' he said. 'I'll get it more exact.'

He turned Marvin's body so he was flat on his back and then opened his bag.

'Hold it,' Rob said. He stared down at Marvin.

Dr Lewis looked up. 'What?'

It leaped out at him. A garage smell of gasoline.

'That – on his belt . . . ring of keys,' Rob said.

'I'd say you hit it on the head as good as whoever did this,' Dr Lewis replied. 'Yes, that is a ring of keys,' he added and looked at Ralph, who smiled broadly.

'Ingenious,' Ralph said, smiling. 'The case is solved.'

'Might just be,' Rob countered. He turned to Tony. 'When you knew him in high school, did he carry a ring of keys on his belt like this?'

Tony shrugged. 'Yeah, I guess. They had keys to cars they were workin' on sometimes and took them for rides. I remember that. And there's all sorts of stuff locked up in the garage. I think that made Marvin feel like a big deal.'

'A ring of keys?' Ralph said.

Tony shrugged again. 'I guess you look like you're in charge or somethin'.'

'See what I mean?' Ralph asked Rob. 'Not enough brain power to light a cigarette.'

'OK. I'll go speak to Mrs Hacker,' Rob said.

They all watched him leave.

'Ring of keys. Dick Tracy has arrived,' Ralph said.

Even Tony found he could laugh.

When Rob stepped up on the porch, he saw the two boxes lying smack in front of the door. He slid them out of the way and pushed the door buzzer, but realized quickly that it didn't work so he knocked. He looked back when he heard a second and then a third patrol car arrive, one of them being the state police. *Probably more excitement than they've had around here for some time*, he thought.

He knocked again, harder this time. He waited, put his ear to the door and then tried the door knob. It opened, so he stepped in and called, 'Hello? Mrs Hacker?'

The house had a moldy, stale odor. There was brown wallpaper with small white circles on the entryway walls and the hall. It had peeled in some places. The floor was laid with a coffee-colored linoleum and looked as if it had been last washed on D-Day. He walked farther in and gazed into the living room on his right. The floor was a dull, battered hardwood with a single light brown area rug that was threadbare. An oval cherrywood table, which had on it some magazines, an ashtray with the remnants of cigarettes filling it to the brim, and two empty glasses beside a half-empty bottle of beer, was the best piece of furniture in the room. The light green sofa on the right had torn arms and the bottom visibly leaking a spring or two.

He turned slowly to his right and stepped back when he saw the scrawny woman in a faded blue robe sitting in the oversized cushioned chair. Her thin gray hair revealed some balding. The strands looked as if they had been left to do what they wanted for years, some of them lying over her forehead and some down the sides of her head like broken, thin wires. She had a head that looked too big for her nearly emaciated body, with arms that were nothing more than bones with skin, ending in boney, high-knuckled hands with spidery thin fingers slightly curled.

For a moment, he thought she was dead too and wondered if whoever had killed Marvin had decided to kill what was left of the family as well.

'Mrs Hacker?' he said and then repeated it much louder.

Her eyes opened as if the lids had to be prized apart the way you might open a clam shell. Nothing else in her face moved. In fact, her face looked like a Halloween mask with its thin, long nose and curled, thin, pale lips. She blinked, but she didn't sit up.

'He ain't here,' she said. 'Go look in the garage.'

She closed her eyes again.

'I'm not looking for your son, ma'am,' he said.

She opened her eyes again. 'When you see him, you tell him I told him that if any of them niggas bring his parts and stuff, I warned him I wouldn't touch nothin' or sign nothin'. They should be bringin' that stuff to the garage. His father never let no blacks bring stuff to the house neither.'

Rob simply stared at her. 'There's been some trouble,' he began. 'Your son was either in a fight or attacked last night. I'm sorry to say he's dead, ma'am.'

Normally, he eased into such a revelation, but the bitterness of this woman and her prejudice stripped away any decency in him.

'Louis is dead. Marvin's not,' she replied. 'I told him not to join the army, but he was as stubborn as his father.'

'I'm sorry, but we're talking about your son Marvin, ma'am.'

She stared. 'What about him?'

'He's been killed either in a fight or in a premeditated murder.'

She closed and opened her eyes. 'He was in a fight? Well, who's going to make my coffee?' she asked.

He had a litany of questions to ask, hoping that she would be able to tell him something that would serve as a lead, but he swallowed them all back. She either didn't understand or refused to. In either case, she was not much good to anybody or anything, he thought.

'Is there anyone you would like me to call for you?' he asked, hoping that would emphasize the seriousness of what he was saying.

'Call my butler,' she said. She didn't laugh at her own joke so much as choke on it, coughing and then spitting into what looked like a well-soaked yellowed handkerchief. 'Can you make some coffee?'

'I'll get someone to help,' he promised and left quickly, suddenly needing to get into the fresh air.

Ralph Baldwin came walking up from the garage.

'I've got a few volunteers on their way. We'll search the area for that sledgehammer or whatever. So far, no others in there. How's the old lady taking it?'

'She's heartbroken,' he said. 'I never realized you had rednecks living here.'

'We don't call them that. We call them stump jumpers. So she impressed you?'

'She's not all there. We'll have to call in social services and an exterminator.'

'Exterminator?'

'I'm exaggerating, but maybe not as much as even I think. Get on the horn. I'll start on what we have after I speak with Doctor Lewis. I think we should bring Tony in for some more questioning.'

'You think he did it?'

'I don't know. None of the rules that govern the behavior of civilized people seem to apply here,' Rob added.

Ralph laughed. He didn't expect it, but he was starting to like this guy, like him a lot.

When Rob returned to the station after arranging for the two sledgehammers to go to forensics to be examined closely for fingerprints and evidence of blood or tissue, he filled in Chief Skyler on what he knew. It was easy to see the man was overwhelmed. Rob then went into his own office.

He went straight to the file cabinet that contained the cold cases and pulled out the Victoria Myers rape and assault case. He looked at that note he had discovered, the one that referred to repressed memories. Then he thumbed through the attached stack of interviews and found Lieutenant Marcus's interview of the Hacker brothers. From the length and the detail of it, he sensed that they ranked high in her list of possibles. What threw her off or prevented her from closing? He noted the name at the bottom of the report, which led to another interview, the purpose of which was to verify statements made by the Hacker twins.

He paused and thought about them. He could feel his eyes widen with the realization that came bursting into his mind like fireworks on the Fourth of July.

Wasn't this the name of the young man who was now engaged to Victoria Myers?

It didn't make any sense . . . Then again, maybe it did. Maybe he wasn't kidding at all when he told Tony and Ralph in the body shop that the keys were going to lead him to the killer.

He rose and went into the examination room where Ralph had brought Tony Gibson. Tony was sipping a soda and eating from a bag of potato chips as if he had been brought in to watch a baseball game on television. He looked relaxed, too relaxed to be their killer, Rob thought.

He sat across from Gibson and opened a folder. That always spooked suspects because they thought you had some sort of evidence at your fingertips.

'Were you very friendly with Marvin and Louis in high school?' he asked.

'I wasn't best friends or anything like that. Unless you paid for gas or somethin', they weren't too interested in you.'

'So they liked to hang with richer kids?'

Tony shrugged. That was obvious.

'What does the name Victoria Myers mean to you?'

'Mean? I know who she is,' he said.

'You know more than just who she is, Tony,' he said, leaning toward him.

'Yeah. Who doesn't?'

'Did you know Bart Stonefield?'

'Yeah, I knew him.'

'How friendly was he with the Hacker twins?'

'I told you, they liked to hang with rich kids who paid for everythin' when he drove them around because they weren't old enough to drive. Bart was one, so they were good friends once.'

'Why did they stop being good friends?'

'I don't know. As I said, he's a rich kid and probably decided not to hang out with them because they were milkin' him like a cow.'

'Where were you the night Victoria Myers was attacked?'

'Where was I? I was at this girl's house. Lois Zalsky. We were kinda goin' together.'

'So you weren't at the lake?'

'No. What's that got to do with anything?' he asked.

Rob sat back. 'What did Marvin tell you about that night? And don't bullshit me,' he added quickly. 'You were with him for years. He talked.'

Tony's face went through a small contortion as he moved from quiet confidence into a gray area that was full of booby traps.

'He bragged a bit, didn't he?' Rob said. 'He's dead now, so what's the difference to you? I'm not looking to get you into trouble. I just want you to tell me the truth.'

Tony took a gulp on his soda.

'You're not my number-one suspect for killing Marvin Hacker either,' Rob offered. 'But you don't want too much more of me sniffing around your life.'

Tony nodded. 'Yeah, he bragged,' he admitted.

'Recently, right?'

Tony's eyes moved from one side of the room to the other. Rob could almost hear his thoughts. *How did he know it was recent?* 'Yeah,' he said.

'Because the news is out about her getting married, right?'

'Right.'

'And Marvin was bragging because she's marrying Bart Stonefield, right? Tell me why that struck him as funny, Tony,' he said, leaning forward again. 'I want to hear you say it.'

Tony hesitated, but he was quite impressed. *This guy's going to know a lot*, he thought.

'Because he was there,' he said. It just seemed to roll off his tongue.

'Where?'

'He was in their truck, stoned. He smoked a lot of pot in those days. Maybe he still does. I don't know.'

'Did Marvin ever tell you how much he knew?'

'No. He just said . . .'

'What?'

'That he knew.'

Twenty

Victoria ran her right hand over the smooth black marble countertop in the Jackson house kitchen. Whether the ex-sheriff had his house spick and span because she and Bart were coming over to consider it or not, everything gleamed as if it was all just recently installed and constructed. She knew her mother wanted this rich-looking floor tile in her kitchen, too, and constantly talked about having it installed. She'd love the gas range oven/griddle/rotisserie combo and this side-by-side refrigerator, Victoria thought.

'Anything you guys want that's here in the way of furniture is yours,' Bill Jackson said. 'Consider it my wedding gift.'

'Thank you,' Bart said.

'Yes, thank you,' Victoria said, her voice filled with amazement.

The burly ex-sheriff, with a full head of thick, salt-and-pepper hair, stood behind them like a proud father. 'I had a decorator do this house. There was a picture of it in one of those fancy

New York magazines. I got it somewhere, buried in a closet.'

'It's beautiful,' Bart said. 'Looks very comfortable, too.'

'Cozy is what they called it because of the warm color schemes and the furnishings. I regret not spending enough time here, but I had one of those twenty-four-hour on-call jobs.'

Bart leaned in to bring his lips close to Victoria's ear. 'Looks hardly lived in.'

She nodded.

Neither Bill Jackson nor his prospective new bride, Nancy Hickman, had any pets, nor were there any children living with them. There was little evidence of a normal daily life. No dishes or glasses were left out, magazines were neatly placed in the magazine rack, all beds were made, the pillows fluffed, and towels were folded over the towel rails. It looked more like a model home. Every little thing was chosen to coordinate.

Victoria was almost too excited to speak. The house was quite a bit larger than her parents' home, and with all the upgrades in fixtures, new carpets, tiled bathrooms and walk-in closets in the master bedroom that were almost as large as her bedroom, it was truly overwhelming.

'You can have the television and stereo system, too,' Bill added. 'It plays the new tape cassettes. I got speakers in all the rooms. Teddy Kolansky set it all up. You know Teddy?' he asked Bart.

'Yes. We sold him a van recently. He's a whiz with television repairs.'

'Yeah. He put up that amazing antenna that brings in the best picture in the county.'

They continued to explore the house and then looked at the two-car garage. There was a good-size box freezer in it. Bill opened it to show them it was stocked.

'Saves running out for stuff,' he said, smiling. He was still quite a good-looking man with practically no deep lines to suggest his age. 'We have town water and sewer out here, you know,' he added.

Bill Jackson was doing such a good job of selling his home that Bart wondered if his father was being honest about catching a bargain. He suspected he had offered him an amount well above the possible listing price.

They walked back to go through the rear entrance and look at the land. The closest neighbor was at least an acre away. Much of the rear, even beyond what was part of the property, was untouched woods.

'You're close to everything, but you've got your privacy,' Bill added. 'Of course, the house has an up-to-date alarm system. No worries about that stuff. It's as safe as the maternity ward in the hospital. I can't deny being the sheriff's had something to do with it,' he added. 'Not that we've had much in the way of burglaries.'

They walked back through the house, looked at the guest bedrooms, the views from all the windows, and then stopped again in the living room with its step-down floor and big fieldstone fireplace and mantle. There was that bay window Bart's father said his mother coveted. The whole room was to be coveted. Unlike most upstate New York homes, it had high ceilings, which made the living room look larger than it was.

'I can't thank you enough for letting us come over at such short notice,' Bart said.

'No problem.'

'I'll tell my father to speak with you,' he continued, feeling certain Victoria would agree.

'Good. And best of luck to you both. I'm about to become a new groom, too.'

'We heard. We wish you both health and happiness,' Victoria told him.

'Why is this guy so lucky?' Bill Jackson replied, nodding at Bart.

'We both feel lucky,' Victoria told him as she took Bart's hand.

'Oh, to be young again,' Bill Jackson said as he walked them out.

'You're not doing so bad,' Bart said and Jackson laughed.

Bart and Victoria said goodbye and got into Bart's car. For a moment, they both just looked at the house.

'It's a real home,' Bart said. 'Of our own,' he added. They waved again to Bill Jackson, who waved back.

He stood there watching them drive off.

'Pinch me so I know I'm not dreaming,' Victoria said as they continued to town where they would have lunch before Bart returned to work.

'We should celebrate tonight,' Bart said. 'I'll make a reservation at Spenser's in Liberty for eight. I feel like splurging. And later, let's talk about our honeymoon.'

'I feel as if I'm already on it,' Victoria said. She cuddled up beside him.

They seemed to be floating into their future

with nary a cloud or a drop of rain to spoil the bright world into which they were heading.

Victoria's mother was home first. She had little more than a half-day. Almost as soon as she entered the house, Victoria went into a full detailed description of the Jackson house. Helen Myers sat there in the kitchen listening, a small smile on her lips. It had been so long since she had seen her daughter so excited, so vibrant and alive.

The air of exhilaration lingered and was still heavy when her father returned from work. She took off from the beginning of the description of the Jackson house again, this time sitting in the living room. He kept shaking his head and looking to Helen. He, too, was elated about Victoria's resurrected *joie de vivre*.

'We're going to dinner tonight at Spenser's to celebrate,' she told them after she had exhausted every detail about the house that she could recall. 'And later plan our honeymoon.'

'That's great, Vick. You deserve every second of happiness,' her father said and hugged her. Her mother stood by, smiling, and as soon as her father released her, she held out her arms to hug her, too.

When she went to her bedroom to get ready for her date, she got a new idea. She scooped up what she was going to wear, the dress she wore on their first date, along with the shoes, some sexy new panties and bra, as well as the pearl necklace Bart had bought her to celebrate their first week together. He made it seem as if it had been more of an accomplishment for him than her. She put it all in a travel bag along with some makeup and her hairbrush.

If she went there to dress, he wouldn't have to come here and practically double-back to go to the restaurant in Liberty. Besides, she liked the idea of showering and dressing for a date at his place. It would give her the feeling of what it was going to be like very soon. They had spent evenings together right into the early-morning hours, but she had always come home. Tonight, she might not.

Her parents looked up when she came out with her things.

'It's easier to leave from Bart's place,' she said before either could ask why she had her clothes in a carry bag.

'You have all you need there?' her mother asked, smiling with amusement.

'Just about,' she replied. She turned to leave and then looked back. 'Oh, don't wait up,' she added. 'I might not come home tonight.'

Neither spoke. Neither had the heart to utter a single syllable that might diminish her joy. It wasn't the Victorian age. Even men and women who were not officially engaged were living together with the promise of marriage on the horizon. However, there would still be a number of particularly jealous women to stir up gossip around that nowadays, Helen Myers thought, especially because it involved Victoria. She almost welcomed the opportunity to smother whoever dared.

She looked at Lester to see what he was thinking. He just shook his head and smiled.

Victoria was out the door and in her car driving off before they could say much about it to each other anyway. She thought it would be fun to surprise Bart, and when she arrived at his apartment, she parked her car off to the side just so he wouldn't see it and know immediately that she was there. Then she went into his apartment, set her things down on his bed and thought about how she would wear her hair.

Back at the town police station, Rob Luden went through his notes. He had been working this cold case all day, confident he would solve two at once. Forensics had told him that there was no evidence on either of the sledgehammers taken from the Hacker body shop, and the volunteers with the available patrolman had not come up with a discarded one on the property or along the road. Whoever had struck Marvin Hacker did not want to come forward with a claim of self-defense. However, since the killer hadn't brought the sledgehammer, Rob was certain it was something impulsive, perhaps indeed in self-defense. He could have been someone simply afraid of what had happened, shocked and terrified he wouldn't be able to explain it and avoid a charge of manslaughter, at minimum. Or he could have been someone who didn't want to be connected in any way to Marvin Hacker.

Rob thought he had the reason for that in his hands, his own notes after two follow-up interviews. Before he let Tony Gibson go, he had him list the names of some other boys who were friendly with the Hacker twins. Three had left the area, but two were still here, one working for the telephone company and the other working for town sanitation. When Lieutenant Marcus had interviewed them because they were seen at Sandburg Lake that night, their explanations of how long they had stayed, which was quite a bit past the assault on Victoria Myers, were substantiated. He didn't follow up with them to challenge that. He was more interested in having two witnesses to confirm that Bart Stonefield was with the Hacker twins when they had left the lake. Both of these men confirmed it.

He looked at his watch. It was time to confront Bart Stonefield. He called home to tell Becky he would be late for dinner.

'I'm finishing up something important,' was all he would tell her. She never pursued him about his work, which was something he really admired about her. He would have told her things if she asked, but she was cautious about his bringing what she once had called 'the toilet bowl view of humanity' into their home and lives. Sometimes she made him feel as if he was a CIA agent or something. When friends asked how she handled his stories, Rob piped up first and, smiling, said, 'I could tell her, but I'd have to kill her soon after if I did.'

He started out and paused at Lillian Brooke's desk. She had just hung up from listening to a complaint and was shaking her head and mumbling to herself. She saw him standing there and pulled herself up into her habitual stiff posture.

'They call here to complain about their water

pressure,' she said. 'Too lazy to look up the telephone number for the water department.'

'We were talking about the Victoria Myers case the other day and how she has rebounded and is getting married.'

'Yes. I'm sure it will be quite a beautiful wedding.'

'Do you know when?'

'I wasn't invited,' she replied and then relaxed, 'but I know people who were. It's soon after Labor Day – the following weekend at the Olympic. Maybe you should read the social column in the local paper every week,' she added. 'Get to know the community better.'

'You're probably right. Thanks,' he said and left quickly.

He drove directly to the Stonefield dealership and went to the service department. It was a little after six. He could see they were closing down, one mechanic putting tools back into a kit, another washing up. The first mechanic turned to him as he walked farther into the bay areas.

'Bart Stonefield?' he said.

'Just missed him,' the mechanic replied. 'Must have a hot date tonight. He skedaddled outta here like a man in love. Nearly bumped into the wall.'

The other mechanic laughed.

'Thanks,' Rob said and returned to his car. *A man in love*, he thought. And then rethought his theory of Marvin's death. *Perhaps Bart Stonefield purposely had gone there to kill him after all. Perhaps now that he was in love with Victoria*

Myers and marrying her, he wanted revenge or thought he was dispensing justice long overdue.

That was premeditated.

That was first-degree murder, no matter what the motive.

He drove faster.

He pulled up beside Bart just as he had parked and turned off his engine. Bart knew who Rob Luden was even though they had never met. He had seen his picture in the paper and had seen him at public events. He got out slowly, feeling fear bring a numbness into his arms and legs.

Luden stepped out of his car. 'Mr Stonefield,' he said.

'Yes?'

'I'd like to talk to you,' Rob Luden said, coming around Bart's car. He had his identification out. Bart looked at it and nodded.

'Sure. I was just coming home. Shall we go inside?' he said. His mind was spinning. What had he done wrong? Had someone seen him at Marvin's shop? Was there someone in the house looking out the window when he drove in or drove away, someone who would recognize him in that fog? He couldn't recall anyone on the road. There was that figure he saw at a distance at the lake, someone who probably saw him as well, but he wasn't doing anything anyone could see that would tie him to Marvin Hacker.

'Great,' Rob said and followed him to the door. Rob nodded at him after he opened it, and then stepped back to let him in first.

'Why don't we sit in the living room,' Bart said

and led the way. 'So, what's this about?' he asked, nodding at the sofa.

Rob sat and Bart sat in the chair across from the sofa.

'You know Marvin Hacker?' Rob began. It was like building a house, laying the foundation. Good interrogations were designed so the person questioned was eventually led to the obvious conclusion, that way diminishing his or her resistance. They would see the futility of lying and either confess or, by demanding an attorney, reveal they had reason to worry.

Bart felt the blood rising up his neck and into his face. He fought it back down. *Whatever you do*, he thought, *don't look guilty*.

'Sure. He was in my high school class. He and his brother Louis were friends of mine for a while. Louis was killed in Vietnam,' he continued. 'I don't really see Marvin much.' He forced a nice smile. 'We don't hang about in the same circles these days. What about him?'

'He's dead. Someone hit him pretty damn hard with a short-handled sledgehammer – killed him in his body shop. We know that was probably the weapon because it's missing, according to his assistant, Tony Gibson.'

Bart's mind spun again. *Had Tony been there, somewhere unseen?*

'When did this happen?'

'Last night,' Rob said.

'I see.'

'I have good reason to believe that Marvin Hacker and his twin brother Louis assaulted and raped your fiancée, Victoria Myers, that summer

301

night six years ago,' Rob continued. He waited. Bart did not speak. He looked like someone waiting for the second shoe to drop, so Rob decided to drop it. 'But I think that's something you've always known.'

'Why would you say that?'

'You were with them that night. You didn't participate in the assault,' Rob added, 'but you were in their vehicle.'

'And you know this how?'

'Witnesses who saw you with them when you were at the lake, when you and the Hacker twins left, which fits the time frame, and what Marvin Hacker eventually told Tony Gibson about that night.'

'I was stoned out of my mind,' Bart confessed. 'I never even knew they had left the truck and gone into the woods.'

'But you knew what they had done.'

'Eventually.'

'Why didn't you tell the policewoman investigating at the time or anyone else for that matter?'

'I was afraid.'

'Afraid that the Hacker brothers would say you were there?'

'That and being stoned. People took that sort of thing more seriously back then. It would have devastated my parents, especially my mother.'

Rob nodded. 'Did you kill Marvin Hacker last night?' he asked.

'He couldn't have,' Victoria said, stepping out of the bedroom. She was wearing Bart's robe. 'He and I were together here all last night,' she said.

Her sudden appearance and comment knocked the legs out from beneath Rob Luden's body of confidence. He was on the verge of solving the two crimes. The sight of her, the victim – the one person who should have come screaming out of that room – literally took his breath away for a moment. He felt his jaw drop.

Bart stood. 'I didn't know you were here,' he said. 'I didn't see your car.'

'I thought I'd surprise you.' She went to him, hugged him and turned to Rob Luden. 'We're celebrating a bit tonight. We saw our wedding present from Bart's parents earlier today. They're buying us a house – ex-sheriff's Jackson's house. He's moving to Florida,' she continued. She drew Bart closer.

Rob just stared at her.

'It's an extravagant gift,' she continued, 'but parents do extravagant things for their children. We're just a lucky couple,' she said, glancing at Rob and then at Bart, her smile soft and full of joy.

'Did you hear what I said about the Hacker brothers?' Rob asked.

'Yes. Frankly, I always suspected them. It's not an easy thing for me to talk about even now, but I can't help feeling . . . relief. I think that's the word. Maybe it's not always the good who die young after all, Detective. Fate saved us all a lot more grief, don't you think?'

Rob stood. 'I don't depend on Fate to solve crimes or punish the wicked,' he said. He felt foolish, sounding frustrated or angry in the flow of the victim's obvious delight. 'I might have more questions for you, Mr Stonefield.'

'Whatever I can do to help now,' Bart said. 'I was a dumb kid back then. I'd like to do whatever I can to make up for it.'

Rob nodded. He felt as if he was standing in a pool of confusion. Or maybe the young woman was reacting from shock.

'I'll see myself out,' he said and left Stonefield's apartment. For a long moment, he stood by his car, thinking. What was the right course of action to take now?

Maybe, just maybe, he might confide in Becky and break their unspoken rule.

Victoria went to the window and looked down at Rob Luden. She watched him until he got into his car and backed out to drive away. Bart had not moved. He looked terrified of turning in either direction. The silence was flooding the room. He thought he wasn't even breathing. He was terrified of her first question, her first comment, but what she asked shocked him because it was something he had asked himself a few times. She didn't turn to him. She was still looking out the window when she spoke.

'Did you start this romance because of real affection for me or guilt, Bart?'

'For a long time, I avoided you because of guilt. The first time I saw you after you had begun college, I still felt it,' he continued. She turned around. 'Then something began to happen. I began to see you as you had matured into this soft, shy, almost angelic person. I remember feeling regret after we had danced that time and I didn't follow up with anything. I convinced myself you were going to find someone soon because you were so beautiful now and so sweet. I saw you a few times before you came into the garage that day, but I didn't approach you. I asked about you and was surprised and then happy to hear you weren't seeing anyone at school, and then, when you came in that day, I found the courage to ask you out. I kept thinking you wouldn't go with me, that somehow you resented me. When you were interested, whatever other motive that had once showed its face disappeared. I fell deeper and deeper in love with you. I know that's the truth,' he said.

She didn't smile. 'You didn't meet with any car executives last night, did you?'

'No.'

'You killed him?'

'He called me. He wanted to blackmail me. He was going to tell you I was in their truck that night and I knew what they had done. We got into an argument. One thing quickly led to another. He struck me pretty hard, and I reached for the small sledgehammer and hit him. He was a pretty big guy. I wouldn't have had a chance otherwise. But I didn't expect to kill him. I was just trying to keep him off me.'

'What did you do after that?'

'I took the sledgehammer, drove to Echo Lake, got into my boat and dropped it somewhere in the middle of the lake. Then I came home and found you asleep on the sofa. I washed up and—'

'Made love to me to forget it all?'

'It didn't hurt,' he said, trying to lighten the moment. She didn't smile. 'I'm so sorry I was such a coward years ago. My father—'

She put up her hand. 'Don't explain it, Bart. Let me get it all digested,' she said.

'That detective might still charge me with withholding evidence concerning what the Hacker brothers did.'

'You think?'

'I don't know. He could. It would . . .'

'Destroy my parents,' she said.

'I imagine it would,' he admitted. He sat and stared at the floor.

'I think it's better if I just go home tonight,' she said. 'We both need to be alone to think.'

He nodded.

'I'll tell my parents something came up business-wise.'

'Whatever you think is best, Victoria.'

'It's best. For now,' she said. She went into his bedroom to get dressed.

He was still sitting there when she came out to leave.

'I'll call you,' she said. She didn't kiss him.

'I love you, Victoria. I swear,' he said when she opened the door.

She stood there silently, her head down, and then she walked out and closed the door softly behind her.

To Bart, it could just as well have been the lid on his coffin.

Twenty-One

She was afraid her mother would see right through her the moment she walked in the door. Victoria thought she could cloud her shock in a look of disappointment. She rehearsed her little speech on the way home. Something critically important had come up involving the new dealership and Bart had to attend to it. He was sorry and felt bad, but it couldn't be helped. It sounded feasible, but she was never good at hiding anything from her mother. Her father either accepted what she said or pretended he did to avoid conflict. Even when she was a little girl trying to get her way, she was reluctant to be conniving. In fact, she was fascinated by how easily her girlfriends could put on a phony act or distort the truth when it came to manipulating their parents.

Tonight she felt she had to do it to survive the rest of the evening. Bart was right about her parents, too. They would be devastated when they learned the truth about what Bart knew and had kept secret. He would be destroyed forever in their eyes. That might happen anyway, but at least for now, at least until she caught her breath, she was hoping to delay the emotional storm that would inevitably come.

She sprinkled some anger and what her mother would surely label being spoiled by behaving petulantly about Bart's canceling their evening. She actually whined.

'I was so set on having a great evening and this happens,' she added after giving them the excuse quickly. 'We almost had our first fight.'

'You'll have thousands of nights to take its place, darlin',' her father said, hoping to comfort her.

'That's just what he said. You men think alike. Don't they?' she asked her mother. Oh, it was such a conniving thing to do, form a fake alliance.

Her mother studied her a moment. Victoria held her breath. Would she pass the scrutiny?

'They have similar defense mechanisms,' she replied and gave her father a look that said *Let it go.* 'I can warm up what we had,' she offered.

'Oh, I'll come out later and get myself something. Right now, I feel like soaking in a bath.'

She marched to her room, feeling both elated that she had gotten away with it and sad that she had had to try. She did run a bath, however, even though she had taken a shower at Bart's. Baths had an additional purpose. She often soaked in a tub and thought, meditated or just relaxed.

After a few hours, she anticipated him calling. She hoped he wouldn't. His voice on the phone now was going to be too distant. If it was ever important to look at one another when they spoke, this was the time. She did get herself something to eat, not because she was hungry, but because she knew if she didn't, her mother would get suspicious. A tantrum could last only so long and it usually didn't kill an appetite anywhere nearly as much as a shocking revelation.

It wasn't good to avoid them completely either, so after she made herself a sandwich, she went into the living room to see what they were watching on television. Her father was watching *Bonanza*, but her mother was reading. She had the ability to do both and from time to time make a comment about something on the show.

'You know you might think of getting involved in the business,' her father suggested. 'That way, you might better understand and appreciate what Bart's problems are.'

'Worse thing she could do,' her mother countered. 'It's enough to get along with a home and a family. You'd never leave work at work either. My suggestion is to think about teaching again,' she offered. 'Until you're going to start a family.'

'I might,' Victoria replied.

'Start a family?' her father asked quickly.

'No. I might look into teaching,' she said.

Her mother nodded and returned to her book. After a few more minutes, Victoria said she was going to bed to read, too. She kissed them both goodnight and retreated. She had gotten through tonight, but what would be tomorrow?

It was almost impossible to sleep. She tried fighting back the images and memories of that horrible night. They poked at her, and when they could, they came pouring through her defenses, walls it had taken years to construct through her therapy and her effort to develop a new persona for herself. Those college years, her work ethic and the distance between the two worlds – one the bustling, exciting city of New York that had no tolerance for private problems, and the quiet, sometimes almost deserted country hamlets and slow-moving daily activities during which people actually looked at each other – had all helped to harden her. She no longer constantly imagined the whispering behind her back. She didn't always think people were staring at her when she crossed a street. What had happened and who she had been slowly faded. She was almost home to a new life.

Now it was to come roaring back. She had fought every image, every fear to what she believed was at least a draw. The world she and Bart were about to create for themselves here would so overshadow the past that people would willingly forget it. It would truly be like something that had happened to someone else. What hope, what promise, what dreams had come true, all swiped off the surface of her life like precious words erased from a blackboard. The letters were dust.

She tossed and turned, moaned and pressed her face in the pillow to smother her tears. She went from disappointment to rage to self-pity. She could see herself crying softly in front of the Jackson house, their soon-to-be magical home going up in flames, the smoke rising so high and so thickly that it blocked out the sun. Gloom and darkness fell around her.

Before the morning light penetrated her sheer curtains, she returned to images from that dreadful year. She searched her memory for the sight of

Bart in the school hallways that fall. Was he looking her way? Did he deliberately ignore her, avoid her? Could she recall any of that? It never occurred to her to be suspicious of him. And those times he referred to when she returned from college and they had met, did she now see the guilty look in his eyes, the regret? Was she so vulnerable that she looked only for affection and love, blinding herself to anything else? Were there any hints, clues she had ignored, missed?

She thought about that day at Top's Diner where they had gone for sandwiches for their picnic on the lake. She had noted how Marvin Hacker was watching them and she remembered the look on his face when she saw him in the window as they left. Bart's explanation seemed so logical, but was she gullible? And what about how hard he avoided any references to the Incident? She had thought he was just being sympathetic and kind. He was helping her recuperate and find a future. Now was she to think that it was all deception, too? Was concern for her ever any part of it or was it always him protecting himself?

What was she to believe?

Even if she wanted to give him the benefit of all this doubt, how could she without betraying herself?

Exhausted, she fell asleep for a half-hour, but her mother woke her. She knocked on her door and peered in.

'We're leaving for work,' she said. 'I just wanted to see how you were. You usually don't sleep so late.'

'I'm OK,' she said quickly and sat up. She

brushed her hair back and pushed a smile to the surface.

'Did you take a pill?'

'No.'

'Maybe you should have,' she said. 'Don't work yourself up so much about this, Victoria. Your father is right. There'll be so many more days of happiness to come.'

She held the smile, but she felt as if she was on a balance beam. She was tottering.

'I have an administrative meeting after classes today. If you go out, leave a note,' she said.

'Will do.'

Her mother nodded and closed the door softly. She fell back on her pillow and stared up at the ceiling.

This could easily be the first or last day of my life, she thought.

She rose, showered and put on a pair of jeans and a light-yellow peasant blouse. Then she slipped on some sneakers without any socks and went out to make some coffee and have some toast and jam. It was all she thought she could eat. As she worked up her meager breakfast and then sat nibbling almost in a daze, she vaguely anticipated the ringing of the phone.

What would she say? How would she sound? But there was no call before she had finished and cleaned up. She looked out the window and saw it was a perfect summer day. She stepped out and gazed at the small fluffy clouds that were sliding slowly over the Wedgwood-blue sky. The light breeze toyed with strands of her hair. She started walking, her head down most of the time.

312

For some reason, she was thinking of herself only as a young girl, maybe a year or so before everything had all happened so quickly to change her life.

When she was alone because her parents were working, she would often take walks in the spring, summer and fall. Unlike her girlfriends, she could tolerate solitude and even welcomed it. She liked thinking about poems she had read or a line or two she had created about Nature, her immediate surroundings and her feelings. When someone like Jena or Mindy asked where she was because she hadn't answered the phone, and she told them, they always shook their heads or looked at her askance.

'How boring,' Mindy might say.

'Weird,' Jena might offer.

Then they would start to talk about some new record or a phone conversation with someone else to explain how sensible they were when they were alone. *Am I different?* she would wonder. *Will it be more difficult for me to make friends, to be popular, to have boyfriends, to go to parties and someday marry and have children of my own?*

Am I Emily Dickinson or someone similar, withdrawn and lost in her own imagination?

These memories didn't trouble her. She smiled to herself as she thought about them now. She would, in fact, trade anything and everything to be thrown back to that time when innocence was so fresh and beautiful, when it had connected her in a magical way to everything around her – the song of a bird, the sight of one sailing through

313

trees, the quick movements of curious rabbits and squirrels who, although not coming too close, apparently had no fear of her. Perhaps they felt she was like them, born to wear the wind and the rain, the clouds and the sunlight and never think of being naked and vulnerable, but blessed instead.

As usual, the walk was like some gently healing balm. She didn't feel stronger so much as a little more content and capable of facing the day, no matter what it was destined to bring. She found herself walking in the direction of the bungalow colony again. She could hear someone making an announcement over the loudspeaker about the arrival of the costume jewelry man. Vendors who sold ice cream, clothes, bakery goods and jewelry traveled from one bungalow colony to another to sell their discounted wares. That announcement was followed by another about the day camp counselors taking the children to a movie matinee.

When she was close to the entrance, she was delighted to see the same elderly lady emerging from the woods with two bowls of blueberries under her arms. She smiled at her and Victoria paused to wait for her to step on to the road.

'You keep catching me,' she said. 'Enough for a new pie and some muffins,' she declared proudly.

Victoria laughed at how something so small could bring such joy. 'I might come back for a piece.'

'You'll be most welcome. I'm in bungalow eleven with my husband, David.'

'Do you have children, too?'

314

'We have a daughter – Ethel. She's named after my husband's mother. I got married soon after I arrived in America,' she explained. 'We met at that place, Ellis Island.'

'Oh, right. Did they make you change your name?'

'No. It was Nussbaum. My husband made me change my name,' she added, smiling. 'I'm Dora Malisoff.'

'I'm Victoria Myers.'

'So? Since I saw you last, did some young man find you?'

'Yes,' she said.

'I knew it couldn't be much longer.'

Victoria tried to hold her smile, but couldn't. She nodded at the numbers again. 'I don't want to ask you what it was like. I understand why you need to forget.'

'Need, yes. Every day it's a battle, but it's less and less difficult.'

'You lost a lot of friends?'

'In the camps and out,' she said. 'I left many behind.'

'They weren't taken?'

'They weren't Jewish,' she said, 'but they were neighbors. In those days, you knew your neighbors. We got along until the Nazis came.'

'Did those friends try to help you?'

'Like an Anne Frank in that diary? No, there was no one who would hide us.'

'Do you hate them now?'

'No,' she said. She smiled. 'They were frightened, too. They had to think of their own families. You can't hate them for that. In a real way, they suffered because of their silence and blind eyes. We all have our own nightmares. But why should you think of these things? You live in a beautiful place. Fall in love, have a life. You need someone to eat your berry pie,' she added with a smile. 'Come for a piece.'

Victoria watched her walk off. The woman had been deeply wounded, but she still had hope and joy.

Dora Malisoff's words rolled around in her mind as she walked on toward the turn in the road that would take her home.

Miles away, Rob Luden entered District Attorney Steve Farmer's office. The six-feet-four-inch fifty-four-year-old prosecutor remained seated behind his large, dark walnut desk which was so covered with files and stack of briefs that anyone coming in to ask for a favor or complain about his workload would instantly feel insecure.

Farmer was one of the sharpest politicians in the county. He had been elected and re-elected district attorney for the last twenty-two years. His opponents were usually names sacrificed so the opposing party wouldn't look totally insignificant. There was talk now of his running for Congress. That was going to be a mere stepping stone for an eventual run for the Senate.

Rob knew all this before he came to Farmer's office. He had met him before, of course, and was always impressed by how prepared Farmer was and how quick to get to the bottom line. He looked like a man who believed with William Penn that time was what we want most, but what we use worst. No one had to warn Rob that Farmer was impatient and intolerant of anyone wasting a minute of his attention.

'Have a seat, Rob,' he said. Rob's report was in front of him. He tapped it with his pen. 'So you want to prosecute a dead man?'

'No, sir,' Rob said, smiling.

'You haven't located the murder weapon?'

'No.'

Farmer sat forward. 'So, let me understand this. Bart Stonefield withheld evidence six years ago concerning a sexual assault on the woman he is now going to marry, and this woman is providing him with an alibi for the night of Marvin Hacker's murder. There are no witnesses to contradict that and there is no forensic evidence to place him at the scene of the crime. Is that right?'

'Nothing now.'

'Furthermore, from what you tell me, she was aware of her fiancé's not revealing what he knew at the time. Am I leaving anything out?'

'No, sir.'

'And so not being able to prosecute him for murder, you propose that I charge Bart Stonefield with obstruction of justice and bring him before a jury of his peers who will see the chief defense witness, his fiancée, testify that she knows this and still wants to marry him?'

'It fits the definition, so I thought I'd bring it all to you.'

Farmer nodded and then looked out his window.

'This office and just about every one like it in every state and every federal district survives because of how it handles its priorities, Rob. Like

317

everyone else, we have just so much manpower, money and energy. We'd love to have a perfect world where none of this matters and we're concerned with only the letter of the law. Ever read John Stuart Mill on justice?'

'No, I don't recall doing that.'

'Mill argued that justice is what is right and what has the best consequences. What, in your opinion, would be the best consequences here?'

Rob was silent.

'The men who did this terrible thing are dead. Even their own mother doesn't seem to mind that they're dead from what you've described. The girl who was violated has recuperated to the point where she can have a normal life. The man she's marrying is from a very successful family who contribute to the economy of the area. Any suggestions about the best consequences?'

'I talked about it with my wife,' Rob confessed.

Farmer smiled. 'That's something I do from time to time. Someone who loves you and whom you love is the best person to trust, as corny as that might sound. So? Share her opinion.'

'She said lose it.'

'Lose it?'

'That file,' Rob said, nodding.

Farmer smiled. 'What's your wife's name?'

'Becky.'

'Tell Becky she has a great political future if she ever so chooses to try.'

Rob laughed.

'Go pursue the killer of this Marvin Hacker if you like, but remember what I said about priorities.'

'I've already put it in a file,' Rob said.

'What file?'

'Cold cases. Actually, it's under a new title. *Frozen cases*,' he added.

Farmer nodded. 'I'm going to keep my eye on your career, Rob. I'm anticipating some very good things.'

Rob Luden rose when Farmer did. He extended his hand. They shook and he walked out.

Technically, he was agreeing to let someone get away with a crime, but oddly, or maybe not so oddly, he felt better about it than he had when he had gotten criminals convicted.

Epilogue

Mrs Wilson, the receptionist at Stonefield's, told her that Bart was home sick. She was surprised that Victoria did not know, and then, to help her feel better about it and not feel guilty herself about telling his fiancée something she should have known, she added, 'He probably doesn't want you to worry.'

Victoria went right to the worst possible scenario.

She had the experience that would have brought her there, too, if she had let it.

During a few early sessions especially, Dr Thornton got her to confess that she was so depressed that she had contemplated suicide.

It was both ironic and painful for her to feel

guilty about this, but she recognized that the guilt was a stepchild of the love she still had for Bart. Just as he couldn't live with what he had done or not done, she knew she would suffer such permanent damage emotionally and psychologically that she might as well make it a Romeo and Juliet ending.

She rushed out of the house, got into her car and drove as fast as she could to Bart's apartment. When she arrived, she didn't even shut the car door after she got out. She charged up the steps, shoved the key into the lock and stepped into the apartment. It was deadly quiet, a stillness that triggered a surge of chills up her spine and then, in cold fingers, seized her neck.

'Bart?' she called. Timidly, she walked through the living room and into the bedroom.

He wasn't there, but the sight of her black dress with the mess shoulders carefully laid out on his bed took her breath away. In her haste to leave the night before, she had left it hanging in the closet. His leaving it there was the act of someone captured by the deepest melancholy, suffering now from the intensity of his love, something that was supposed to bring him great joy. It was summed up quickly in her mind by Dante Gabriel Rossetti's famous line. *Beauty without the beloved is like a sword through the heart.*

She swallowed back her small cry of fear and turned to rush out of the apartment. She hadn't even noticed on arrival that Bart's car wasn't there. Where would he have gone? Where had they enjoyed some of their happiest moments together? Where did their love mature and take so firm a hold of each of them? She thought she knew, but she also knew that she might be wrong, that she might waste whatever time was left, or that, worst of all, she'd be right but too late.

Less than an hour later, she arrived at Echo Lake and walked to the dock where Bart's boat was moored. As she feared, it wasn't there. She looked out and thought she saw it somewhere in the middle. She was moving on fumes now, her legs feeling numb as she walked about looking for someone to help. She paused when a boat came from the right and slowed as it approached the dock. A man wearing a captain's hat, sun glasses, a New York Yankees T-shirt and a pair of white shorts drew closer. She thought he looked about sixty.

When she waved to him, he looked at her, obviously wondering who she was. Nevertheless, he politely waved back. She hurried to meet him at his mooring place on the dock. He kept a puzzled smile on his face as she hurried to get closer.

'I need your help,' she shouted over the sound of his engine. He cut the engine down to an idle and put his hand around his ear.

'What?'

'I need your help. I think my boyfriend is in trouble out there. I'll pay you whatever it costs.'

He brought the boat closer and then shut the engine and drifted to his place.

'I don't get you,' he said. 'Who's in trouble? Where?'

'My boyfriend, Bart Stonefield. I think that's his boat in the middle of the lake.'

'Stonefield?' He turned and looked in the direction she indicated. 'Yeah, I know Bart Stonefield.' He put his hands above his eyes to shade them and looked. 'That could be his boat. What's his problem? Engine trouble?'

'I think he's very sick,' she said. 'He shouldn't have gone out today.'

'Sick?' He looked again.

'Please, can you take me to him? Whatever it costs . . .'

'Doesn't cost that much, lady. Hop in,' he said. 'I'm George Samuels,' he said.

'Victoria, Victoria Myers,' she told him as he helped her into the boat.

'Well, let's go see what's what,' he said. He started his engine and put the boat in reverse until he could turn it and go forward. It was not as fast as Bart's but she was just relieved to find someone to help. 'I don't see him,' he said as they drew closer.

Her heart felt as if it had turned to stone.

'It looks anchored,' he added.

'Can we get right up to it?'

'Close as I can,' he said. He circled it. They didn't see Bart. He slowed down and put the engine on idle as they drifted alongside. She stood up. When she was able to, she reached out and grabbed the side of the boat. 'Careful,' he said as she turned and threw her leg over the side of Bart's boat. 'He's not in there.'

She didn't respond. She had to get into the boat anyway. She did it awkwardly, practically falling on her rear end. She managed to get into the boat and stood, hoping perhaps he was lying down. He was not there.

'He's not swimming,' George Samuels said, shading his eyes and looking farther out. 'I don't see him. Think he fell out or something?'

'I don't know,' she said, the tears forming.

'Maybe I'd better get some help,' he offered. 'You want to go back.'

'No. I'll wait here,' she said.

He nodded. 'I'll be back as soon as I can,' he said and accelerated, turning and heading back toward the dock.

She sat and stared at the steering wheel and controls. Then she buried her face in her hands and began to sob softly. Suddenly, she heard a loud thud and looked down at a short-handled sledgehammer.

Bart, wearing a mask and an oxygen tank, pulled himself up on the side of the boat and then started to get in. When he saw her, he froze.

She didn't say a word.

He got into the boat and sat on the floor, pulling the mask off and unloading the oxygen tank.

'Am I dreaming?' he asked her.

'No. I had someone bring me out here . . . George Samuels. He went back for help.'

'Help?'

'We thought . . . you might have drowned.'

'Oh.'

'I called your office and Mrs Wilson told me you called in sick, so I went to your apartment.'

He got up and sat on the cushioned bench. 'You thought . . . .'

'Yes.'

He nodded. 'I considered it.'

'What did you do, Bart?'

'I brought up that sledgehammer to bring to the police. If I wasn't going to have you, it didn't make a difference anymore.'

She nodded. 'Well, it does,' she said. 'You *are* going to have me.'

The blue in his eyes was as electric as it had been that first night when he came to pick her up and had brought the corsage. She couldn't hold back another moment. She moved forward and embraced him. They kissed and he looked at her.

'Are you sure?'

There was no other way to make him believe. She let go of him, picked up the short-handled sledgehammer and tossed it back into the lake.

He smiled.

'Just think,' she said, 'how good I will feel every time I waterski on this lake.'

His smile was a promise she knew they would both keep. There was one other thing she really wanted them to do.

'Now get us back quickly,' she said. 'I need you to go somewhere with me.'

'Where?'

'To a bungalow at the colony near my house.'

'Bungalow? Why?'

'For a special, very special piece of blueberry pie,' she said.

Author's Note

Andrew Neiderman is the author of 115 published titles, under his own name and as V.C. Andrews. With national and international media now revealing and interviewing Neiderman, he is – arguably the most successful ghostwriter in American publishing. Having brought V.C. Andrews from seven novels at just under thirty million books sold worldwide to more than seventy-five titles over one-hundred and six million sold worldwide, he has reached new heights of fame and accomplishment. During this remarkable side of his career, he has kept the V.C. Andrews franchise alive and it is now the longest-running in American publishing with consistent titles for more than thirty-five years. Recently, he has promoted and helped sell five of the titles to Lifetime; *Flowers in the Attic* broke their viewing record. Warner Bros. has now contracted to develop another series written by Neiderman as V.C. Andrews, the first title of which is *Ruby* for cable television.

Under Neiderman, he has published more than forty-five novels, the most famous being *The Devil's Advocate*, a major feature film produced by Warner Bros. and starring Al Pacino, Keanu Reeves and Charlize Theron. He is developing this with his co-librettist in London as a stage musical and will, this coming year, be presenting

it to major theatrical production entities interna-
tionally. In addition, the stage play version opened
in the Netherlands November 18, 2015 and will
tour there and in Belgium. Finally, the television
series based on his novel is being considered by
Warner Bros. for development.